BEYOND
THE
HEADLINES

BEYOND THE HEADLINES

A CLARE CARLSON MYSTERY

R.G. BELSKY

OCEANVIEW PUBLISHING
SARASOTA, FLORIDA

ISBN 978-1-60809-503-2

Published in the United States of America by Oceanview Publishing

Sarasota, Florida

www.oceanviewpub.com

10 9 8 7 6 5 4 3 2

PRINTED IN THE UNITED STATES OF AMERICA

For Laura Morgan

"*The truth is inconvertible. Malice may attack it, ignorance may deride it, but in the end, there it is.*"

—WINSTON CHURCHILL

"*I could announce one morning that the world was blowing up in three hours and people would be calling in about my hair.*"

—KATIE COURIC

BEYOND
THE
HEADLINES

PROLOGUE

A black-pajama-clad figure crouched alongside the sandbags piled up to protect the building in Saigon—a building filled with U.S. soldiers.

Putting an explosive charge between the sandbags powerful enough to blow up the building and everyone inside.

He was a Vietnamese youth, with dark hair and dark eyes, his face covered with sweat.

He had laid his weapon—a Chinese-made AK-47—down on the ground as he worked on planting the explosives.

When he was spotted at the last minute by a U.S. soldier, he lunged for the rifle.

He managed to get off one shot.

But it was too late.

A bullet hit him in the head and killed him instantly.

Vietnam.

January, 1973.

Just before the war ended and U.S. troops went home for good.

So long ago, and yet it seemed like yesterday.

OPENING CREDITS

THE RULES ACCORDING TO CLARE

DEATH IS A funny business sometimes.

Especially in big-city newsrooms, where I've worked for most of my life.

I remember one of them where we all loved to play a game called Somebody Famous Died. The idea was to fantasize about celebrities dying and try to come up with the ones that would be the biggest stories to put on the air or on the front page.

Like say Kim Kardashian. In bed. While making a sex tape. With a man who was not Kanye West.

Or Justin Bieber—who had sixty-four tattoos at last count—dying from an infected needle while getting a tattoo of Selena Gomez removed for a new one of Hailey Baldwin.

Or Oprah Winfrey—this was back when she was the biggest thing on TV, both figuratively and literally—choking to death on a ham sandwich. "Just like Mama Cass!" said the guy who came up with that one. I think he won the game in our newsroom that day.

It's impossible to work in a newsroom and not hear a lot of gallows humor about death.

My favorite story is from a long time ago when New York City newspapers actually had dedicated people who did nothing but write obituaries. Legend has it that one of them was known for yelling in a loud voice to a copyboy whenever anyone newsworthy died: "Boy, get me the clips on so-and-so." Until one night, he had a heart attack and died at his desk. Someone in the newsroom stood up and yelled: "Boy, get me the clips on . . ." I have no idea if this story is true or not, but I've heard a million stories like that in newsrooms.

I had a firsthand encounter with this kind of morbid newsroom humor not long ago when I covered a story where a man was shot to death right in front of me, then I rushed back to the office to get the story on air.

"No video?" my boss at the TV station complained to me. I pointed out that trying to shoot a video in that dangerous situation might have cost me my life. "Well, at least it would have been good video," he said.

I guess we joke about death because we have to deal with so much of it as journalists—murder, plane crashes, sickness, and all the other things that make up the TV newscasts and newspapers and news websites every day.

Laughing about it helps us put a distance between ourselves and the reality of the deaths or deaths we're covering.

Most of the time it works, but not always.

Take the O.J. Simpson story, for instance. O.J. is a punchline now. A national laughingstock. Comedians still make jokes about the whole circus the O.J. story became—Kato Kaelin, Johnny Cochran, O.J. on the golf course after his acquittal vowing to catch Nicole's real killer and all the rest. Funny stuff, right?

Except one day, a long time after the O.J. story was over, I spent some time in Los Angeles. I decided to visit the crime scene—the house in Brentwood where Nicole Brown Simpson and Ron Goldman had been murdered.

I was stunned when I got there. Not because of anything spectacular that I observed. Just because it all seemed so . . . well, ordinary. For months and months, we'd seen that house on TV and in the papers. The condo where Nicole lived; the street and neighborhood outside; the front yard where the bloodied bodies of Nicole and Goldman were found.

But, standing there in person now on a sunny Southern California afternoon, I could have been on any block in America.

I suddenly felt for the first time the terror Nicole and Goldman must have felt on that night when a killer came at them out of the darkness. They would have had no reason to be afraid until the end. They probably had only a few seconds to realize the terrible thing that was happening to them before it was all over. They had no idea that their murders would turn them into the most famous victims in tabloid and TV history.

Even all these years later, I still remember looking at that seemingly normal house and yard and street where two people were butchered on a hot summer night in 1994. Nicole Brown Simpson and Ron Goldman died a horrible death, and sometimes we forget about that. Me, I don't make O.J. jokes anymore.

Death remains the biggest mystery for all of us—no one really understands it.

And so we do our best to avoid taking it seriously for much of our lives until one day it comes knocking at our own door.

And then it's no laughing matter . . .

PART 1

LAURIE

CHAPTER 1

"Do you know who Laurie Bateman is?" my friend Janet Wood asked me.

"I do," I said. "I also know who Lady Gaga is. And Angelina Jolie. And Ivanka Trump. I'm in the media, remember? That's what we do in the media, we cover famous people. It's a dirty job, but somebody's gotta do it."

"Laurie Bateman hired me."

"As an attorney?"

"Yes, as an attorney. That's what I do, Clare."

We were sitting in my office at Channel 10 News, the TV station in New York City where I work as news director. I should have known something was going on as soon as Janet showed up there. We usually met at Janet's law office, which is big, with panoramic views of Midtown Manhattan, and a lot nicer than mine.

Janet never comes to see me at Channel 10 unless she has a reason.

I figured I was about to find out that reason.

It was early December and outside it was snowing, the first real storm of the winter. The snow started falling during the night, and by now it was covering the city with a powdery white blanket. Pretty soon the car exhausts and trucks would turn it into brown slush, but for now it was gorgeous. From the window next to my desk, the city had an eerie, almost unreal quality. Like something from a Norman Rockwell painting.

My outfit for the day was perfect for the snowy weather, too. I'd walked in wearing a turtleneck sweater, heavy corduroy slacks, a blue down jacket with a parka hood and white earmuffs, scarf and mittens. The ski bunny look. I felt like I should have a cup of hot chocolate in my hand.

"Why does Laurie Bateman need you as an attorney?" I asked Janet.

She hesitated for what seemed to be an inordinately long amount of time before answering.

"Are we talking off the record here?"

"Whatever you want, Janet."

"I need your word on that."

"C'mon, it's me. Clare Carlson, your best friend in the world."

She nodded.

"Laurie Bateman wants me to represent her in divorce proceedings."

"Wow!"

"I thought you'd like that."

"Is it too late to take back my 'best friend in the world/ off-the-record' promise?"

Janet smiled. Sort of.

"How much do you know about Laurie Bateman?" she asked me now.

I knew as much as the rest of the world, I suppose. Laurie Bateman seemed to have the American Dream going for her. Since coming to the U.S. as a baby with her family after the fall of Saigon in 1975, the pretty Vietnamese girl had grown up to become a top model, then a successful actress, and finally, the wife of one of the country's top corporate deal makers. She had a fancy Manhattan townhouse, a limousine at her beck and call, and her face had graced the covers of magazines like *Vogue* and *People*.

Her husband was Charles Hollister, who had become incredibly wealthy back in the '70s as one of the pioneers of the burgeoning computer age. He was a kind of Steve Jobs of those early days, and he later expanded into all sorts of other industries— from media to pharmaceuticals to oil drilling and a lot more. He was listed as one of the ten wealthiest businessmen in America.

When Hollister married Laurie Bateman a few years ago, there were a lot of jokes about the big difference in age between the two—she was so much younger and so beautiful. Like the jokes people made about Rupert Murdoch with Wendy Deng and then Jerry Hall, his last two wives. People always assume that a younger and pretty woman like that is marrying for the money. But Laurie Bateman and Charles Hollister insisted they were in love, and they had consistently projected the public persona of a happily married couple in the media since their wedding.

Except it now appeared they weren't so happily married.

"Is she trying to divorce him to get her hands on his money?" I asked.

"Actually, he's trying to divorce her and stop her from getting her hands on any of his money."

"So the bottom line here is this divorce is about money."

"Always is."

"Isn't there a prenuptial agreement that would settle all this?"

"Yes and no."

"Spoken like a true lawyer."

"Yes, there is a prenup. But we don't think it applies here. That's because other factors in the marriage took place, which could invalidate the terms of the prenup they agreed to and signed."

"Okay."

I waited.

"Such as?" I asked finally.

"For one thing, Charles Hollister has a mistress. A younger woman he's been seeing."

"Younger than Laurie Bateman?"

"Much younger. In her twenties."

"Jeez! Hollister's such an old man I have trouble imagining him being able to have sex with his wife, much less getting it up for a second woman on the side."

"Her discovery that he was cheating on her, along with a lot of other reasons, have turned Laurie Bateman's life into a nightmare—a living hell—behind the walls of the beautiful homes they live in. She's kept quiet about it so far, protecting the happy couple image they've put on for the media. But now she wants to let the world know the truth. That's where you come in, Clare."

Aha, I thought to myself.

Now we're getting down to it.

I was about to find out the real reason Janet was here.

"Laurie Bateman wants to go public with all this," Janet said. "She wants to tell her story in the media. The true story of her marriage to Charles Hollister. We know Hollister is going to use his clout to try and smear her and make her look bad, so that's why we want to get her version out quickly. What I'm talking about here is an exclusive interview with Laurie Bateman about all of this. Her talking about the divorce, the cheating—everything. And she wants you to do the interview with her."

"Why me?"

"What do you mean?"

"Why not Gayle King? Or Savannah Guthrie? Or Barbara Walters or Katie Couric or Diane Sawyer or another big media name? I'm just the news director of a local TV station here."

"She wants you, Clare. In fact, I think that's the reason she hired me for her lawyer. She found out you and I were friends—and she's hoping I can deliver you to her to do this interview on air with her."

"I still don't know why she wouldn't want to go with someone really famous . . ."

"You're famous, too, Clare. You know that as well as I do. And that's why she wants you. You're as famous as any woman on the air right now."

Janet was right about that.

I was famous.

It could have gone either way—I could have wound up being either famous or infamous because of what I did—but in the end I'd wound up as a media superstar all over again.

Just like I'd been when I won a Pulitzer Prize nearly twenty years ago for telling the story of legendary missing child Lucy Devlin—even though I didn't tell the whole story then.

"Laurie Bateman's life with Charles Hollister is a big lie," Janet said to me. "Now she wants to tell the truth on air about all those lies she's been hiding behind. Like you did when you finally told the truth on air about you and Lucy Devlin. That's why she wants you to be the one who interviews her."

I still wasn't sure how I felt about all this newfound fame I'd gotten from my Lucy Devlin story, but there was no question that if it got me this Laurie Bateman story . . . well, that would be a huge exclusive for me and the station.

"When can I meet her?" I asked Janet.

CHAPTER 2

I WENT TO the Channel 10 morning news meeting after Janet left. I like news meetings. We talk about the big stories of the day, how to cover them, and which reporters to assign. Much of my time as news director is spent dealing with budgets, ratings, and advertising demographics. The news meeting gives me a chance to do a little real journalism. Well, most of the time it did. But not today.

There were several personnel crises I had to deal with this morning. Starting with our anchor team of Brett Wolff and Dani Blaine.

"I'm planning on taking paternity leave," Brett announced at the beginning of the meeting.

"Okay," I said.

We'd recently instituted a new policy where fathers could be granted paid leave—the same as mothers.

"Well, I'm not planning on taking maternity leave," said Dani.

Now this should be interesting, I thought to myself. That's because Brett and Dani were married to each other now. After a lengthy off-and-on-again office romance, they'd tied the knot a year ago—and were expecting their first baby soon. Dani had been noticeably pregnant on air for a few months. Women TV journalists these days often work almost up until their due date. So I was fine with that. I wasn't expecting this wrinkle though.

"I plan to keep working after the baby," Dani said. "I'll take a few weeks vacation, then be right back at the anchor desk. I don't need any maternity leave."

"Let me get this straight," I said. "You're going to keep working on air after the baby, while Brett isn't?"

"Yes."

"I'm confused."

It turned out Brett was confused, too.

"Wait a minute," Brett said. "You didn't tell me about this, Dani. Who's going to take care of the baby?"

"You can do it. You'll be home on paternity leave. You just said so."

"Well, I'm not going on paternity leave if you're not taking maternity leave."

"Someone has to do it."

"Well, somebody has to do the news, too."

"I'll do the news, and you can stay home with the baby."

"Now wait a minute, Dani . . ."

"I want to do the news, Brett. And that's what I'm going to do. With or without you."

Brett and Dani had spent much of their time fighting before when they were having an affair while Brett was married to his ex-wife. Now that they were together, I'd figured the open warfare between them would calm down. But I was clearly wrong. They were still fighting, only now they were doing it as man and wife.

"How about we let the baby do the news and you two can stay home together and watch?" I finally said before telling them we'd figure out the logistics for the anchor desk later.

The next problem was Steve Stratton, our sportscaster. I'd sent Stratton a memo a few days earlier telling him he needed to do more coverage of soccer and women's sports—neither of which he covered very much on our broadcast. Stratton was an old-time sports guy who only followed baseball, football, basketball, and hockey.

"No one cares about soccer or women's sports results," he said to me now.

"I do."

"You're a woman."

"Jack Faron does."

"He's the executive producer. He's only bowing to pressure from politically correct activists who hate real sports."

"Brendan Kaiser cares, too."

Kaiser was the owner of the station. And he'd been the catalyst for my memo. His daughter had gotten a soccer scholarship to Cornell. And his wife was the new part owner of a pro team in the women's basketball league.

"It all started with that Title IX crap," Stratton said now, shaking his head in frustration. "First, we had to start giving scholarships to women for soccer and lacrosse and all that nonsense. Then women started demanding to play sports the men played. Basketball, baseball—hell, there's even women trying out for football teams now. Sports news today is filled with all this politics and protests and diversity stuff instead of box scores and football stats like it should be."

"Welcome to the twenty-first century, Steve," I told him

Then there was Wendy Jeffers, our weather person. Wendy was mad at me because I'd made her stop doing her weather reports outside while standing in the middle of a snowstorm or a downpour or high winds. Instead, I told her to give the weather to our viewers from the studio, like the rest of the Channel 10 news team.

"Being outside lends authenticity to my reports," she said now.

"You really think you need to be holding an umbrella to tell people that it's raining?"

"It helps for them to actually see the rain."

"They could just look out their window," I pointed out.

"C'mon, Clare, every other weather reporter in this town does the weather while standing outside in the weather."

"If every other weather reporter in town decided to jump off the George Washington Bridge, would you do that?"

Okay, it was a childish response. But weather forecasters who stood outside in pouring rain or snow—to tell the viewers that it was pouring rain or snowing—were one of my pet peeves about TV news. It wasn't journalism, it was cheap theater. And I wanted to change that. Even if Wendy didn't.

I finally decided to offer her a compromise. She could report from outside if a snowstorm went over six inches, the winds were over fifty mph or the rain was falling at more than an inch an hour.

"That way we can still watch you getting drenched or covered in snow or blown away in hurricane-force winds," I said. "But otherwise you do the weather safe and dry and warm from inside the studio."

"I can live with that," Wendy said.

Ah, Carlson, you clever devil.

Problem?

I've always got a solution.

"Anyone else have a complaint?" I asked everyone in the meeting room.

"I do," said Maggie Lang, my assignment editor and top deputy at Channel 10. Maggie was super intense and dedicated to her job.

"Go ahead, Maggie. Take your best shot. What's your problem?"

"My problem is we still don't know what news we're going to put on the air tonight."

She was right. So we spent the next forty-five minutes going over all the big stories of the day. A looming taxi driver strike. Questions about voting irregularities in the last City Council election. Lots of crime, including a woman who had miraculously survived after being stabbed more than a dozen times by her ex-boyfriend on the Upper East Side. A protest over a homeless shelter the city wanted to build on the same block as a school. Plenty of news to fill up the Channel 10 news broadcast later.

"What do you think?" I said to Maggie after we'd gone through it all.

"We could still use a big story."

"We could always use a big story."

"No, I mean something unique for us—an exclusive."

"I might have a story like that very soon."

"What is it?" one of the other editors at the meeting asked.

"I can't tell you yet, but I'm working on it."

CHAPTER 3

"Laurie Bateman's life with Charles Hollister is a big lie,"
Janet had said to me in my office. "Now she wants to tell the truth
about all those lies she's been hiding behind. Just like you did."

Yep, I sure had told the truth about myself. The truth, the whole
truth, and nothing but the truth. It took me long enough to do it
though. Almost twenty years.

But I'd finally gone on the air and revealed the whole story, including all the secrets I'd been hiding about the biggest news story
of my career.

The disappearance of eleven-year-old Lucy Devlin on her way
to school in New York City a long time ago.

I won a Pulitzer Prize as a young newspaper reporter covering
the Lucy Devlin story. But there was a lot I didn't reveal then: how
I'd been sleeping with Lucy's adoptive father at the time of her
disappearance; how she'd really been taken by a self-styled vigi-
lante trying to protect Lucy from her abusive adoptive mother;
and, most important of all, how I was Lucy's biological mother
who had given her up for adoption at birth.

Fifteen years after Lucy Devlin's legendary disappearance, I'd
finally tracked her down—alive, all grown-up and with a daughter

of her own—and eventually decided to go on air with the real story about me and Lucy Devlin.

Even though I knew by doing so, I could destroy my credibility as a journalist and possibly even end my career.

But sometimes you have to go with your gut instincts about what's right and not worry about the consequences.

In this instance, my instincts turned out to be dead-on accurate.

Oh, it probably wouldn't have been that way ten or fifteen years ago. Maybe even five years ago. A journalist who screwed up—who played loose with the facts—never could recover from that. Janet Cooke, Jayson Blair, Stephen Glass—the past is filled with media scandals that ruined careers.

But it's different now in this instant gratification age of social media where things go viral quickly and public opinion is formed instantly about a controversial topic.

In my case, I was forgiven for my judgment lapses and hailed for my courage in coming forward and talking about my secret search to find my daughter no matter what I had to do and no matter what rules I had to break.

Everyone wanted a piece of me after that.

I was interviewed on the *Today Show*. I went on *60 Minutes*. I got big play on all the cable news channels. There were articles about me and my long, emotional search for my daughter in the *New York Times*, *USA Today*, the *Wall Street Journal*, and other papers. I got an offer to write a book about it all, a potential movie deal was in the works, and I even received a handful of marriage proposals from men who said they would help me ease my pain over everything that I had endured with Lucy.

So I didn't ruin my career at all by coming clean with everything I did. Instead, I became a media superstar all over again.

Even bigger than I had been the first time for winning a Pulitzer for a story that wasn't totally true. Go figure.

I have a picture of my daughter on my desk that I look at a lot during my workday. Her name is Linda Nesbitt now, but I still call her Lucy. She'll always be Lucy to me. She lives in Virginia with her nine-year-old daughter, Audrey, and her husband, Gregory Nesbitt. There's a picture of my granddaughter, Audrey, on my desk, too.

I see them as often as I can. We've been talking about spending Christmas together, if I can get away from work to go down there. It would be our first Christmas together as a family. It's nice to have their pictures here with me in my office all the time now. It's nice to be a part of a family.

Of course, we're not your normal everyday family. Not after everything it took to get us to this point. It makes me think of the old gag line: "Hey, they're just as normal as the next family. As long as the next family is the Manson family!"

Well, we're not the Manson family. Far from it. More like the Addams family. Strange, different, and a bit odd—but still lovable.

I thought about all that now—and also about Laurie Bateman.

Laurie Bateman was a celebrity superstar. A lot bigger than me. And she'd be an even bigger celebrity superstar once she went public with all the dirty laundry about her marriage to Charles Hollister and told her story of whatever she'd gone through while being married to one of the world's richest men.

No question about it, this interview would put Laurie Bateman in the public spotlight even more than ever before. She would ride this interview to even bigger fame and fortune. And me, well, I'd go along on that ride with her.

It's a funny thing about fame though. Sure, it was Andy Warhol who made the classic "everybody will be famous for fifteen minutes" statement. But I always preferred a quote from Marilyn Monroe: "Fame doesn't fulfill you. It warms you a bit, but that warmth is temporary." And then there was Alanis Morissette who once said: "Fame is hollow. It amplifies what is there. If there is any self-doubt, or hatred, or lack of ability to connect with people, fame will magnify it."

Nope, fame isn't always as great a thing as it's made out to be.

I'd found that out the hard way.

Maybe Laurie Bateman had, too.

CHAPTER 4

THE LAURIE BATEMAN story was a pretty damn interesting one, even before all the divorce stuff.

I sat in my office, going through background material I'd pulled together about Laurie Bateman—and Charles Hollister—to get ready to interview her.

She was only six months old when she first arrived in America along with her mother, who had fled Vietnam in the last days of the war as North Vietnamese and Viet Cong forces captured Saigon.

Laurie's father had died while she was a baby. It wasn't exactly clear how he died, but I remembered seeing pictures and film from then of Vietnamese people hanging on to U.S. helicopters in a desperate effort to flee before the Communists arrived in Saigon. I could only imagine the nightmare that must have been for Laurie Bateman's family.

Her name wasn't Laurie Bateman then. It was Pham Van Kieu. The name Kieu means "pretty" in Vietnamese lore. So it seemed like the perfect choice for her. Her family name of Pham was one of the most common surnames in Vietnam—sort of like Jones or Smith here. In another time and another place, she might have grown up and gone on living her life as Pham Van Kieu.

But her mother changed her first name to Laurie after they arrived in Southern California, trying to help the little girl fit in as they learned to adapt to life in their new country. Not long after that, the mother met and married a man named Marvin Bateman, a prominent and highly successful Hollywood producer.

It seemed like an unusual pairing to me at first—Bateman and the refugee woman from South Vietnam. But then I saw pictures of the mother. She was beautiful, like her daughter would grow up to be. Well, that certainly explained how she captured Marvin Bateman's attention. And, once they were married, Bateman formally adopted Laurie as his daughter.

So Pham Van Kieu became Laurie Bateman.

Laurie's mother quickly became a Hollywood stage mom, sending her daughter out as early as three years old on modeling and acting auditions. Little Laurie wound up starring in a series of TV commercials as a little girl—helping to sell everything from cars, to appliances, to clothing lines. She was cute, adorable, and precocious. No doubt Marvin Bateman's connections in Hollywood helped open a lot of doors for her. But, one way or another, Laurie was a child superstar.

Then, as she blossomed into a real beauty as a teenager, she switched to modeling and became one of the biggest names in the modeling world.

There were magazine covers, more TV appearances, and lucrative celebrity endorsement deals for the teenaged Laurie. There was even a brand of jeans named after her. She was the same kind of modeling celebrity that people like Brooke Shields were back then, but maybe even bigger.

I looked at pictures of a young Laurie Bateman, modeling for newspapers, magazines, and billboards—as well as TV commercials—and I was stunned by her breathtaking beauty. Sleek figure, dark black hair, high cheekbones, and classic model face—she looked perfect. No wonder American consumers fell in love with Laurie Bateman and all the products she endorsed.

Thus, it was no surprise that she became a Hollywood star after that, with appearances in numerous TV shows and movies beginning when she was in her twenties. She wasn't a great actress—she never won an Oscar or Golden Globe or any other major award—but she worked a lot. Many of the roles she was in were forgettable, but she wasn't. Everyone knew who Laurie Bateman was.

And that popularity and name recognition from the public exploded into super-celebrity stardom once she married Charles Hollister.

Hollister—like Bill Gates or Warren Buffett or Rupert Murdoch—had been a modern-day legend for the billions of dollars he was worth and the power and influence he wielded both in the U.S. and internationally.

There were oil wells; pharmaceutical firms; media holdings in TV, movies, and publishing; and vast holdings in tech industries. He had been on the scene for a long time. Ever since he got rich back in the '70s by developing a new kind of chip that revolutionized the computer industry and was the pioneer for all that went into our computer-dominated world today of smartphones, iPads, Echo, and all the rest.

But it was his marriage to Laurie Bateman—thirty years younger than he—that had truly cemented his place on TMZ, Page Six, and all the other entertainment/gossip websites that Americans seem addicted to these days.

The age difference between the two of them drew a lot of attention and disapproval from the public—as well as plenty of jokes. "They had a great honeymoon except Charles can't remember much—he napped through most of it." There were all sorts of memes and GIFs posted online depicting him as a doddering old man and her as a scheming gold digger. And a Las Vegas bookie even offered a betting line on how long the marriage would last—the popular over/under number was six months.

And yet, despite all the ridicule and skepticism and overall negativity about the validity of the relationship, Laurie Bateman and Charles Hollister seemed to be happy together in the marriage. Even though their lives played out on the pages of every newspaper and website and on every gossip show—like watching episodes of *Keeping Up with the Kardashians* or the *Real Housewives*. There were pictures of them attending art and theater openings in New York City; summering on his boat at Nantucket or the Riviera; and skiing in the winter at Aspen or in Switzerland.

In every recorded moment of their public life, they were smiling and affectionate and apparently deeply in love in this April-December marriage of theirs.

Except now . . . well, I knew that wasn't true.

According to my friend Janet—who I had no reason not to believe either as a friend or a lawyer—there had been serious problems going on behind the scenes for quite some time. Serious enough to have led now to a divorce.

It was hard to believe that it had all turned out so ugly.

But it was a great story.

And, even better than that, it was going to be my story.

Everything was falling into place for me here on Laurie Bateman—this was going to be an easy exclusive for me to pull off.

Really, really easy.

Maybe too easy.

CHAPTER 5

My boss at Channel 10 was Jack Faron, the executive producer. There are all kinds of bosses. Good bosses. Bad bosses. Lazy bosses. But the best kind of boss is the kind you can go to with a problem. A boss who will work with you calmly and rationally—until you come up with a solution for the problem. When you've got that kind of boss, it sure makes your job a lot easier. Unfortunately, Jack Faron was not that boss.

Faron hated problems. He only wanted to hear good news from me. Bad news or problems made him mad—at me. It was definitely a "shoot the messenger" situation when I went to his office with anything he didn't want to hear. We'd had a long conversation about this recently. He accused me of being too negative. Too cynical. He said I needed to bring a more positive, upbeat approach to my job.

So I went to his office now to tell him the good news about my upcoming interview with Laurie Bateman.

"That's terrific," Faron said.

"I thought you'd like it."

"This Laurie Bateman interview story will get us a lot of attention."

"True."

"And we should draw big ratings for it."

"Also true."

I didn't say anything else.

"Problem?" he asked.

"No problem."

"You look like you have a problem."

"Me? No way."

"Good to hear."

He opened up a bag with his lunch in it. Faron had put on a few pounds—well, more than a few—over the past year and he'd been eating at his desk recently instead of going out for fancy lunches. He unwrapped something from the bag. It was a container of cottage cheese and a variety of fruits. He made a face.

"How's the diet going?" I asked him.

"Okay."

"How many pounds have you lost so far?"

"You can't judge a diet by weighing yourself every day to see if you've lost a pound or two. The key to a good diet is the long haul."

"You haven't lost any weight, have you?"

"Actually," he admitted, "I've gained five pounds."

"Jesus! How did that happen?"

"Beats me."

"You been cheating on the diet?"

"Well . . ."

"C'mon, Jack."

"Okay, I've been so damn hungry from starving myself all day that I go home at night and kind of lose control. Last night, I wound up at both a McDonald's and a Baskin-Robbins."

"Aha!"

"What does that mean?"

"Much like Hercule Poirot, I think I've solved the mystery of the added weight."

Faron stared down at his cottage cheese. "Don't worry about my weight. Just worry about this Laurie Bateman interview. When can we do it?"

"I'll let you know as soon as I find out more from my friend Janet who set this up."

"The sooner the better. This could be a huge ratings-grabber for us, Clare. Just what we needed. It's perfect."

"Almost too perfect, huh?"

Faron stared at me across the desk.

"What do you mean?"

"Nothing."

"Something *is* bothering you. What?"

"I'm not sure, Jack. Something seems wrong about it all to me. Laurie Bateman lives this fairy-tale life, always seems happy, and now she suddenly wants to tell the world this tale of woe. It seems off, like there's a missing piece to the story that we don't know about yet."

"So go interview Laurie Bateman and find out what it is."

"Sounds like a plan to me."

Faron and I talked for a while about the logistics for the interview. I told him Janet was going to get back to me later with a time and place for a preliminary meeting with Laurie Bateman. Then I'd go back with a video crew to actually shoot what we were going to put on the air. We discussed what video people I should use. The kinds of questions I should ask her. And the best place to conduct the interview.

I told him I'd prefer to do it outside—in a park maybe—rather than inside her fancy apartment. I said that would add more of an authentic New York feel to it. Make it seem more like a real-life conversation for our viewers rather than sitting in an expensive townhouse. I'd done outside interviews like this before, and they had been very effective.

"What if it rains?" Faron asked.

"It won't rain."

"How can you be sure?"

"It's always sunny for us at Channel 10."

He smiled.

"You're taking that positive thinking lecture I gave you pretty seriously, huh?"

"I'm just a glass-half-filled kind of gal."

*　*　*

That night turned out to be a slow one on my social calendar. Bradley Cooper didn't call. Leonardo DiCaprio kept playing hard to get. And Tom Brady was still trying to make me jealous with Gisele Bündchen. So I had dinner with an old friend. Fellow named Stouffers. He makes a damn tasty macaroni and cheese, that Stouffers. Efficient too. All you do is pop it into the microwave and presto—instant gourmet delight.

Afterward, I watched TV, switching around between the various news channels. All the TV people on them seemed to be happy, seemed to be having fun. None of them ever sat home eating Stouffers TV dinners by themselves, I bet. I wondered if I should get a roommate. Or a dog.

My phone rang a little after eight. It was Janet.

"I figured you might be out," she said when I picked up on the first ring. "You're home?"

"Hard to believe, huh?"

"No date tonight?"

"I've quit dating."

"Again?"

I ignored that.

"Clare, you need to find someone. A man who is good and decent that you like. A man that you might want to spend the rest of your life with. There are men out there like that."

"I know, Janet. In fact, I had a date with a guy not long ago who told me he thought marriage was a wonderful institution. He said he wants to stay with one woman for the rest of his life."

"That sounds promising."

"Yeah, except that woman is his wife. He's already married."

"Sorry."

"Don't be. Feel sorry for her."

Janet sighed. "You still need to think about settling down. Getting your life in order. How old are you now?"

"I'm forty-seven."

"Well, move fast. You're not getting any younger."

"Thanks," I told her. "I really needed to hear that."

She told me that Laurie Bateman wanted to meet me the next day at her apartment here in the city. She said we could figure out then the best time and place to do the on-air interview. Laurie Bateman's apartment. I assumed that was the one she lived in with Charles Hollister. I wondered if he'd be there. That could be uncomfortable. But I didn't say anything. I didn't want to complicate things in any way that might delay my sit-down with Laurie Bateman.

"Where's the apartment?" I asked.

"Right off of Central Park. On Fifth Avenue."

"Where else?" I said.

* * *

It was the middle of rush hour when I headed up there the next morning, and not a cab to be found. There'd also been a subway derailment near my apartment in Union Square so I knew the trains were all delayed. I trudged to a bus stop. That wasn't much better. It took twenty minutes before the first bus came, and then there were three others right behind it—bunched together in a pack.

"What's the matter?" I asked the driver as I got on. "You afraid to travel around the city by yourself?"

He looked me over from head to toe and scowled. "That's what I like about this job," he grunted. "You meet such interesting people. You got any other complaints, lady?"

I used my Metro card to pay the fare.

"How about the air-conditioning on this bus?" I asked.

"How about it? It's working, isn't it?"

"Yes."

"So what's the problem?"

"The problem is it's December."

The driver shook his head and chuckled. "Yeah, that's something, isn't it? All summer long we sweltered because it was broken, and now the damn thing won't shut off. New York— ain't it grand?"

By the time we got near Laurie Bateman's Fifth Avenue townhouse, I was freezing and shivery and contemplating a lawsuit against the Transit Authority.

What I needed was a cup of coffee. I hadn't had time to get any before I left my place. I figured I'd find a Starbucks or other coffee place before I went upstairs to talk to Laurie Bateman.

But that all changed when I got off the bus, walked to her address, and saw what was there outside.

The police.

Squad cars with flashing red lights lined up in front of Laurie Bateman's building.

Other cars carrying detectives.

And an EMS vehicle parked by the door.

I raced toward the building. When I got closer, I recognized one of the detectives standing outside. It was Sam Markham, who also happened to be one of my ex-husbands. Sam was a homicide cop. He only showed up if someone was dead.

"What are you doing here, Clare?" Sam said with surprise when he saw me. "No one else from the press knows about this homicide yet."

"I was supposed to talk to Laurie Bateman this morning."

"Well, you can't talk to her now."

Oh, my God, I thought to myself. Had the behind-the-scenes marriage battles between her and Hollister turned violent? Deadly violent. She'd wanted to tell the world her story with me, Janet had said—but maybe she didn't go public in time.

"Is Laurie Bateman dead?" I asked him.

"No, she's very much alive."

"Who's dead then?"

"Charles Hollister."

"What about Laurie Bateman?"

"She's under arrest for her husband's murder."

CHAPTER 6

BREAKING INTO OUR regular daytime TV programming for a news story is not something we do a lot at Channel 10. The station makes big advertising money from the daytime talk shows; courtroom and other reality stuff; plus, reruns of popular sitcoms from the past. Hey, there's a reason you see *Friends* and *The Big Bang Theory* on TV dozens of times a day. It takes a really big news story to interrupt that juggernaut of a viewing lineup.

The murder of Charles Hollister was that big of a news story.

I called it into the office as soon as I found out from Sam. I was still in a state of shock, but that didn't stop me from doing what I had to do. I was a reporter at heart. Always have been, always will be. And, no matter what the circumstances were, my adrenaline always kicked in on a big story.

I got Maggie first and then Faron on the line. Faron decided to put my voice on the air immediately over my cell phone. He said I should just tell the viewers whatever I knew. Which wasn't much, I'll admit. But enough for us to get the story out first before anyone in the news media even knew anything about it.

And so Channel 10 viewers suddenly saw a black screen with the letters: "Alert: Breaking News." Then a crawl along the bottom of the screen said: "On the phone is Channel 10's Clare Carlson."

I then said on air:

> Charles Hollister, the billionaire businessman, has been
> found murdered at his home in Manhattan. And, even more
> shocking, his wife, Laurie Bateman, is in custody as the chief
> suspect. Police and medical personnel arrived this morning
> to find Hollister dead inside his spacious townhouse on
> Fifth Avenue.

I stretched it out as long as I could with any more details from
the scene I could see at the moment.

By the time I'd run out of things to say, our Channel 10 anchors, Brett Wolff and Dani Blaine, were in place and reporting
more on the story from the studio. They showed B-footage of
Hollister and Laurie Bateman in happier days. They also reprised
the story of the marriage—beset with controversy about the age
difference—as well as a capsule history of Hollister's incredible
success in the business world.

Meanwhile, Faron had dispatched a video team. Once they arrived, we were ready to do a live report from the scene.

When an on-air story is hurriedly put together without time
for the reporter to go over the script beforehand, we call it a "rip
and read." There's no preparation, the reporter just reads what's on
a teleprompter in front of him. But this time, Brett and Dani
couldn't even do that. They had to report it all live, as it was happening. Just like I was doing right now at the scene. I was winging
this whole thing off the top of my head.

But this was where my experience as a reporter on the streets in
the past saved time. I knew how to do a breaking news story like
this, something a lot of young TV reporters couldn't handle. I just
did what I used to do as a reporter at a fire or a police shooting or

other big breaking news story. Told the story I had with whatever details were available.

> This is the building near Central Park where Charles Hollister was found murdered today. Details remain sketchy, but Hollister's wife, Laurie Bateman, is still upstairs being questioned by police. A police source told me that she is the leading suspect in this murder.

I managed to get a few people to talk on camera with me. Several cops. Medical personnel. Curious onlookers and neighbors. None of them knew anything significant, but that didn't matter. This was a big news event, and every bit of color from the street outside the crime scene helped me to tell our viewers the story.

Other media were starting to show up now, alerted by my own broadcast. Local TV stations. Newspaper reporters and photographers. And even big trucks belonging to the networks and cable news channels. This was going to be a big story. It had everything. Money. Celebrity. Just like Jodi Arias or Casey Anthony and all the rest of the big crime stories that have dominated the news in the past. And I was the one who broke this one.

The biggest moment, the most dramatic scene that would lead every newscast in New York and around the country later, was about to happen next.

The police brought Laurie Bateman down from where she and Hollister lived to the street, then to a waiting patrol car where she'd be taken to the station house for further questioning—and likely formally charged later with the murder.

It was a media circus.

Laurie Bateman wasn't handcuffed, but there was a cop holding each of her arms as they walked her through the gauntlets of press and cameras and onlookers desperately trying to see it all. She looked straight ahead, a grim look on her face. Like this was a bad dream she would suddenly wake up from. She sure didn't look like the glamorous celebrity I'd seen on the screen so many times in the past.

It all seemed under control until she was almost at the police car that was supposed to take her away. At that moment, she broke free from the two officers holding her, whirled to the TV cameras and the rest of the media, and began to say in a pleading, sobbing voice:

> I didn't do it! I didn't kill him! Oh, my God, I can't believe they think I murdered him! I'm innocent . . . you have to believe me . . . you all have to believe me that I didn't kill my husband!

The two cops grabbed her at that point, dragged her away from us in the media, and put her into the police car, which drove away.

But wow!

That was awesome!

And very convincing. I mean, I knew she used to be an actress, so maybe she was just playing the part of an innocent wife wrongfully accused of her husband's murder. But she played it damn well.

I looked at my watch. I'd been there two hours already, but there was a lot more to come. Waiting outside at the precinct while they finished questioning her. Then most likely a formal charge, followed by an arraignment and—no doubt—a high-priced lawyer arguing for her to be freed on bail.

"C'mon, let's go, Clare," one of the Channel 10 video people yelled at me from our van. "Get in. We've got to get down there in a hurry to get a good spot for the perp walk and at the courthouse."

"Do I have time—?"

"No time for anything. Let's go."

Damn.

It was going to be a long day.

I sure wished now I'd had time to stop off and get that coffee.

CHAPTER 7

IT TOOK MOST of the rest of the day to put together the details about the Charles Hollister murder.

They turned out to be pretty sensational.

When the Hollisters' maid—a woman named Carmen Ortega—arrived for work at nine a.m. that morning, she found Hollister dead on the living room floor, his head bashed in with a lamp. She said Laurie Bateman was attempting to flee the apartment leaving the body behind her—but that Bateman stopped running once she saw the maid.

Ortega was the one who called police.

When they got to the scene, the cops discovered that Hollister had also been shot. Three times—two in the chest and once in the head. It wasn't clear what came first: the blows from the lamp or the gunshots. But the assumption was the killer first attacked him with the lamp and then fired three shots into his body to make sure he was dead.

There were pieces of the broken lamp scattered around the living room. The base of the lamp was on the floor a few feet away from the body. Police found a gun in another part of the house. It had been stuffed into a drawer underneath a stack of clothes. The gun was registered to Laurie Bateman. The gun had been fired three times—there were three spent shells in the cylinder. It would take a while longer to make a ballistics check comparing the bullets from the gun with the bullets in Hollister's body. But police had little doubt that this was the murder weapon.

In another part of the sprawling apartment, they found more explosive evidence. A series of pictures spread out on a desktop. The pictures showed Charles Hollister having sex with a woman. The woman in the pictures was not Laurie Bateman. She was a stunningly beautiful blond, based on what could be seen of her in the passionate sex shots of her in bed with Hollister. This must be the Hollister mistress Janet had told me about. According to caption information on the back of the pictures, they had been taken—with a hidden camera in the bedroom, no doubt—by a private investigator named Victor Endicott.

Detectives tracked Hollister's movements from the night before. He'd attended a series of business meetings at his office in Midtown Manhattan until about five p.m. His corporate CEO, a man named Bert Stovall, said Hollister seemed fine at that point, and he had no hint of any kind of danger or concerns on Hollister's part.

Later, Hollister took his wife, Laurie Bateman, to a big charity event at an art gallery on Central Park West. The event had been scheduled for some time, and they had committed to it back then. But it appeared they didn't want to be there together that night. Witnesses said they had an argument in front of people, which was surprising because they normally put on such a "happily married and in love" front for the public. No one was sure what the argument was about, but they appeared to be extremely agitated with each other.

Maybe it was about the pictures of Charles Hollister in the sack with another woman, I thought to myself. Yep, that will generally spark a martial fight pretty quickly.

The last time Charles Hollister was heard from was early the next morning. He called his office to leave a message for his secretary that he wouldn't be in at his usual time because he was going to stop first at the *New York Chronicle*, a newspaper he had recently bought, to deal with a problem there.

The secretary wasn't in the office yet, but police listened to the message from Hollister on her phone. It said: "I'm heading directly over to the *Chronicle* this morning to meet with that goddamned editor there as soon as he gets in. He screwed up the front-page story today. I had to order them to rewrite the front-page headline. I want to deal with him right away this morning. I'll see you after that."

The time of the message was 6:38 a.m., a little more than two hours before the maid arrived at the Fifth Avenue townhouse and found Laurie Bateman trying to leave with Hollister's body in the living room.

Detectives talked later to Victor Endicott, the private investigator who had secretly taken the sexy pictures of Hollister in bed with the other woman. Endicott told them he'd been hired by Laurie Bateman to find out if her husband was cheating on her. He said he'd given the documented proof—the pictures in the bedroom—to Laurie Bateman earlier that day. Asked what her reaction was, Endicott said she was "very angry." Hence, the argument at the charity event between the two of them later in the evening.

Laurie Bateman admitted hiring the private investigator to spy on her husband, admitted to fighting with him the night before, and admitted to owning the gun that was found at the crime scene. But she said she had not spent the night there. She told police she had instead gone to another apartment after the argument they had.

She and Hollister had numerous homes around the country and the world—but she also still had her own place. A condo in Greenwich Village where she had lived before marrying Hollister. She said she sometimes went there for quiet space from the public turbulence that constantly surrounded them and because of the growing tensions in their marriage.

On that night, Bateman said, she had a lot to drink when she got to the Greenwich Village place and eventually passed out into a deep sleep. When she woke up in the morning, she remembered that she was supposed to meet with me about the interview in the Fifth Avenue place. She went back there, intending to tell me we should probably do it somewhere else given all the unpleasantness that had gone on the night before between her and Charles. But when she got home and found her husband's body, she said she panicked. That she was in a daze and didn't know what to do or if the killer might still be in the apartment. All she could think of was getting out of there—that's why she didn't call the police right away. But then the maid walked in, saw Hollister dead on the floor, and began screaming—and the police arrived soon afterward. She insisted she was not the person who killed her husband.

That was Laurie Bateman's story. It wasn't much of a story. And it was all quite damaging to her. There was no doorman at the building. Instead there was an elaborate security system and electronic gate you had to pass through to enter the townhouse. A check of the security records showed two people entering the Hollister townhouse after 6:38 a.m., when Charles Hollister had made what was presumably his last phone call. They were Laurie Bateman, then the maid. No one else was there.

Based on the overwhelming evidence, it was pretty hard for anyone to believe her story.

Not the police.

Not the Manhattan District Attorney.

Not the judge who she found herself standing before in Criminal Court for her arraignment.

Laurie Bateman was formally charged with first-degree murder, and she gave an O.J.-like "I'm 100 percent not guilty" plea. The judge then remanded her to Rikers Island without bail until the next court hearing.

CHAPTER 8

AT NINE A.M. the next morning, I was back at my desk in the Channel 10 newsroom.

I'd only gotten a few hours of sleep. The actual courtroom appearance had lasted for only a few minutes. But there had been hours of waiting before it happened in late afternoon. After that, I kept reporting the story as best I could. Then I had to do both the 6 p.m. and 11 p.m. newscasts to report everything on air that I had been talking about on the breaking news bulletins, website podcasts, and everything else we'd done all day to cover the story.

Sure, it was exhausting. But it was also exhilarating for me to be a real reporter again—even for a little while—instead of dealing with ratings numbers, ad sales, and demographic charts like I usually did in my job as news director at Channel 10.

I sat at my desk, looking out the window of my office and thinking about Laurie Bateman.

It was snowing again.

All this snow was starting to give me the Christmas spirit too. Chestnuts roasting on an open fire. Jack Frost nipping at your nose. Who was this Jack Frost guy anyway? If you ask me, he's got a bit of a nose fetish. Sounds like a good topic for Dr. Phil. I wondered if I should belt out a few Christmas carols in the Channel

10 newsroom. Probably not a good idea. Jack Faron wouldn't like it. He's such a stickler for decorum.

Almost Christmas again. Where did the time fly? I thought about Laurie Bateman sitting in a jail cell at Rikers Island. She was a long way right now from her apartment on Fifth Avenue, her Long Island beach house, chartered plane, yacht, and all the rest. Whatever happened, it sure wasn't going to be a joyous holiday season for Laurie Bateman.

Meanwhile, I had a dilemma. An ethical dilemma, which is the worst kind. I knew something about Laurie Bateman and Charles Hollister's marriage that the rest of the world didn't. Maybe even not the authorities. Bateman and Hollister were about to be getting divorced. A messy divorce. Which would involve lots of money and lawyers and the rest.

Janet had told me there was a prenuptial agreement they were trying to break. If they couldn't, Laurie Bateman would only get a small amount of money from Hollister. But, if he was dead, she presumably might stand to inherit a huge chunk of his fortune. That was a helluva story. And a helluva motive for Laurie Bateman to murder her husband.

Except Janet had told me about this off the record, and I'd given her my word as her best friend—and, even more importantly, as a journalist—that I wouldn't reveal it publicly.

Hence, my ethical dilemma.

I didn't deal with it yesterday because the breaking news of the murder and Laurie Bateman's arrest was the big story. But we'd need a big follow-up for the next day. And the fact that Laurie Bateman and Hollister were making plans for a messy divorce would be another blockbuster story for me and for Channel 10. Yep, I'd scoop everyone else in the media again. Except for that damn ethics issue. I couldn't compromise myself as a journalist no

matter how good a story it was. Every worse, I couldn't compromise my friendship with Janet. Unless I could get her to agree to
let me reverse my "off-the-record" promise to her. I knew the police would find out about it sooner or later, if they hadn't already.
And, when they went public with that information, everyone
would get it at the same time and I would lose my exclusive.

I called Janet and laid it all out for her. I pointed out to her that
circumstances had changed dramatically since I promised her
that the Hollister-Bateman divorce she'd told me about would re-
main off the record. I said I felt I had a responsibility as a journalist to reveal it to the public now. I said she had a responsibility
as a lawyer to make this information available in the interests of
justice. I talked about our long friendship and how that meant the
world to me. I promised her I would never ask for another favor
from her for the rest of my life, if she did this one for me. And I
even promised her I'd pick up the check the next time we went
out to dinner.

"Go for it," Janet said when I was finished.

"Huh?"

"You can go with the divorce stuff on air, Clare."

"Just like that?"

"Isn't that what you wanted me to say?"

"Yes, but I didn't think it would be that easy."

"Look, it's going to come out sooner or later now. Probably
sooner. If it's going to be splashed all over the media, I'd rather
you were the one doing the splashing—instead of having anyone
else break it."

"Then I definitely can go with what you told me about the
divorce?"

"It's not off the record anymore."

So much for the ethical dilemma.

*   *   *

A short time later, I was running the Channel 10 news meeting. Maggie brought us up to date with the latest details on the investigation.

"It all looks pretty cut and dried," she said, relating a lot of the details from my story last night and adding a few new ones that had been updated since then. "The DA thinks they've got an air-tight case against Laurie Bateman. First-degree murder."

"Is that the highest charge there is?" asked Cassie O'Neal, one of our on-air reporters. Cassie's long suit is looking good on camera. But she's definitely not the brightest bulb in the room. Yet she's tremendously popular with our viewers and makes a big salary. Bigger even than me. Welcome to the wonderful world of TV news.

"Yes, Cassie, it's a degree higher than second-degree murder." I sighed.

Jeez.

"What else do we have on the story?" I asked Maggie.

"Okay. We've put together an updated profile on Hollister and Bateman. We talked to a lot of people who knew or had come into contact with them. A lot of it is pretty colorful. Hollister was a damn ruthless businessman, willing to do anything to anyone to make money. Bateman was supposed to be difficult to deal with too—flaunting her wealth and her celebrity status at every opportunity. She wasn't exactly the adorable little girl anymore that people remembered. A long way from being America's sweetheart. Bottom line is neither of them were very popular with those around them."

"Nice people, huh?" Maggie muttered.

"Money corrupts," I said. "It's the root of all evil."

Someone laughed. "I wouldn't know, I work for Channel 10 News."

I waited until the end to reveal my news. About the Hollister and Bateman divorce that had been in the works when he was killed. I said I would report that part of the story myself on the news that night.

"Wow, that's big!" Brett Wolff said. "A motive for murder like that sounds like the final nail in the coffin for Laurie Bateman's conviction."

"Yeah, how did you find out about that?" Dani Blaine asked.

"Carlson's my name, exclusives are my game," I said brightly.

CHAPTER 9

"So what's Laurie Bateman's defense strategy?" I asked Janet.

"I have no idea at all."

"That's a helluva thing for her lawyer to admit."

"I'm not her lawyer."

"You were her lawyer."

"For the divorce. But that all changed once Hollister died. She's got a criminal lawyer now. If she gets convicted for his murder, she can't get any of his money. If the lawyer helps her beat the murder rap, then she'll need an estate lawyer to represent her as the legal heir to whatever share of her inheritance that's spelled out in Hollister's will. I don't do criminal or estate work. I was only there for the divorce. That means I'm out of the picture now."

"How do you feel about that?"

"Fine."

"Really?"

"Sure, I don't enjoy being involved in a big high-profile case like this."

"That's the difference between you and me," I said. "I love high-profile cases."

"There's a lot of differences between us, Clare."

We were eating dinner at Friend of the Farmer, a restaurant on Irving Place just south of Gramercy Park. I liked the place because it had a fireplace. A real fireplace, not one of those gas flame things you turn off and on. Nothing better than sitting in front of a roaring fire on a cold winter night. I always wanted to have a fireplace in my house. Only thing is I don't have a house, just an apartment. First things first.

Janet was eating a salad, which she usually did. I never knew exactly what kind of salad she ordered when we went out. I just referred to them as "that green stuff you're eating," which generally elicited a roll of the eyes from her. Me, I was in a mood for comfort food because of the cold and blustery weather outside. I had the meat loaf with mushroom gravy on top, and buttery mashed potatoes on the side. Okay, it pretty much used up most of my calorie count for the day. But I'd skipped lunch, so I figured the daily calorie thing should work out about even. Of course, I wasn't sure I could resist sampling the pastry tray later. But I'd worry about that when it happened.

"Who's the criminal lawyer for Laurie Bateman?" I asked between bites of my meat loaf.

"Donna Grieco."

"Good choice."

"Do you know her?"

"No."

"Then why . . . ?"

"I just figured Laurie Bateman would hire the best when it came to a defense attorney. I mean she hired you for her divorce, right?"

Janet smiled. She picked up a small piece of lettuce along with a plum tomato on her fork. Janet ate very neatly. She did everything very neatly. Me, I had already spilled mushroom gravy on my sleeve and made a mess on my plate with the buttery mashed potatoes.

"Can you get me in to see this Grieco woman?" I asked her. "Maybe I could still get a Laurie Bateman interview. She owes me an interview, remember?"

"Bateman's in jail."

"What if she gets out on bail?".

"They don't usually grant bail in a murder case."

"Okay, then I could do a jailhouse interview with her. It would be a great story. I could use this interview to prove that Laurie Bateman is innocent of murdering her husband."

"And if you can't do that?"

"Then maybe I can get her to admit she did kill him. Either way, that's a big story for me."

Janet shook her head.

"I think you have a better chance of the second option—a Laurie Bateman confession—than the first one."

"You think she's guilty?"

"Based on the evidence, I don't see any other possibility."

"Jeez, and you're her lawyer."

"Was her lawyer."

"Still . . ."

I'd finished my meat loaf and potatoes. Janet was only halfway through her salad. I didn't want her to feel awkward about eating without me, so I perused the pastry options. There was an apple pie a la mode—with vanilla ice cream and whipped cream on top. A real calorie buster if I ever saw one. I told myself I needed to show restraint. I thought about doing this for thirty seconds or so. Then I ordered the pie and the ice cream—but without the whipped cream. I figured that was a nice compromise.

"Between you and me, Clare, there was another motive Laurie Bateman had to want her husband dead," Janet said. "Even more of a motive than the divorce or the prenup or the other woman. I'm pretty sure the authorities know about it by now, and I'm betting this will be the biggest part of the case they build against her."

The apple pie with vanilla ice cream was really, really good—and it was going to take something damned big for me to stop eating it.

But what Janet just said qualified as damned big.

I put down my fork.

"Okay, I'm listening," I said.

"At one point early in their marriage, when things were good between them—and he was apparently head over heels in love with her—Hollister rewrote his will. He previously had left pretty much everything to his family, especially his son Charles Jr. But under the current will he left the bulk of his money and, maybe even more importantly, controlling interest in the Hollister business empire, to his wife, Laurie. But recently, when things had begun to fall apart in the marriage, Hollister had notified her that he was in the process of rewriting the will again to cut her out of it because of the looming divorce. He died before he could do that. So his will giving everything to her is still the one in effect."

"Jesus! That is a pretty damning motive."

"Like I said, all the evidence looks to be stacked against her."

The apple pie and ice cream were still sitting there in front of me. They didn't look so good anymore. But I wasn't ready to give up yet. On the apple pie and ice cream. Or on Laurie Bateman. I dug my fork in, took a big bite, and thought for a few minutes about everything Janet had told me.

"Sure, all the evidence makes it look like Laurie Bateman killed him," I said finally. "But that's only the evidence we know about. Maybe there's more evidence out there. Evidence we don't know about yet. And that evidence could point the finger at someone else as Charles Hollister's murderer."

"And you're the one who's going to find that evidence?"

"I have before on other stories."

"Yes, you have."

"So will you ask Donna Grieco about getting me an interview with Bateman?"

"I'll see what I can do," Janet said.

CHAPTER 10

EVERYONE THOUGHT LAURIE Bateman was guilty. The police. The DA's office. Even Janet, who had been her attorney, assumed she did it. All of the media had already pretty much convicted her, too. The *New York Post* polled readers on Twitter and found that more than 75 percent of them believed she had murdered Charles Hollister. Most of the others said they weren't sure. Hardly any of them said she was innocent.

The police had—and were continuing to add to—a pretty impressive collection of evidence that she was the one who killed her husband. There was motive—actually a couple of possible motives: money and jealousy; means, she owned the gun he was shot with; and opportunity, she was the only person at the apartment with the body and the broken lamp which had been used to deliver a deadly blow to his head when the maid arrived—and saw her trying to flee the crime scene. Yep, Laurie Bateman was obviously guilty as hell. Hardly even worth wasting time on a murder trial. Let's lock her up now and throw away the key.

Unless you looked at it all from a different perspective.

You see, I had seen seemingly airtight cases like this—even stronger cases than the one they had against Laurie Bateman—fall apart in the past. Once the police zeroed in on a prime suspect, they did their best to collect any and all evidence to prove that person did the crime. And, if they do come across any evidence that doesn't support their "guilty" scenario, they ignore it. There wasn't anything corrupt or illegal or negligent on their part; that was simply the way a police investigation worked. They want to convict the bad guy—or woman—they've got in their sights. So that's the case they build, and anything that doesn't fit into that neat little package is pushed aside.

Just for the hell of it, I decided to do the opposite.

Ignore the obvious suspect, Laurie Bateman.

And look at who else might have murdered Charles Hollister.

* * *

Maggie brought me an updated file she'd pulled together about Hollister—and we sat in my office going through it.

"The bottom line is—and I found examples of this over and over again—Charles Hollister had made a lot of enemies," Maggie told me. "He screwed all kinds of people over the years, both in bed and in the business world. If Laurie Bateman wasn't caught red-handed at the scene, there'd be a long list of potential suspects. Charles Hollister was not a nice man."

"How *not nice* was he?"

Maggie ran through a list of questionable, often barely legal, business transactions Hollister had been involved with over the years. He'd made a great deal of money from them. But he'd also left a lot of anger, heartbreak, and tragedy in his wake from people whose lives he had destroyed in his quest for profit.

"It wasn't only the big-money deals," Maggie said. "He could be unbelievably cruel and heartless in other ways.

"One story people who worked for him tell is about his long-time secretary who asked for a day off to attend her granddaughter's first piano recital. She was told no. She called in sick and went anyway. Hollister hired a private detective to track down people who saw the woman at the recital. Then he summoned her to his office and personally fired her after years of dedicated service."

"It wasn't so much the day off," Hollister explained later, "but the fact that she lied to me about it. She was disloyal. I won't tolerate disloyalty from anyone."

Then there was a prominent business rival, a man named Max Gunther, whose company lost a big city contract to Hollister. Gunther accused Hollister of dirty tricks and unscrupulous tactics and even making payoffs to city officials to get his way. Gunther vowed that one day he would get back at Hollister; he declared he would get his revenge in one way or another.

Also, there was supposed to be a federal investigation into Hollister's dealings—by the SEC and maybe the tax people, too—because of questionable investments, missing pension funds, and a suspicious money trail that even led to secret bank accounts around the world. Nothing had been proved yet, but it certainly sounded like he was under federal scrutiny at the time of his death.

There was plenty of dirt, too, about Charles Hollister's personal life. Including the woman he was having the affair with when he was killed

"Her name is Melissa Hunt," Maggie said. "She's a model/actress, like Laurie Bateman. Except much younger. In her twenties. Charlie Hollister seemed to like young girls."

"I wonder at his age if he could . . ."

"Still get it up?"

"It does seem like that could be an issue for a man his age."

"Whether he could or not," Maggie said with a laugh, "I'm not sure it mattered much to Melissa Hunt. All she probably cared about was how much he was worth."

"What else do we know about her?"

"She's a real looker. Surprise, surprise. She's married, or at least she still was when I checked. Her husband was in the process of filing for divorce against her. He claimed in the divorce papers she'd been unfaithful with another man. And that man was none other than Charles Hollister."

"Melissa Hunt's estranged—and presumably enraged—husband could be a suspect in the Hollister murder," I pointed out. "Jealousy is always a good motive for murder."

"But Laurie Bateman could have killed him out of the same jealousy. And she had another motive Melissa Hunt's husband didn't have. Money."

I'd reported on the air the previous night the news I'd gotten from Janet about Hollister planning to rewrite his will to cut off Laurie Bateman from inheriting his fortune and control of the Hollister businesses.

"You're still left with this one basic fact, Clare: if Hollister divorced Bateman, she would only get a small amount of money under the terms of the prenuptial agreement she signed before the marriage and the new will he was preparing. But if he was dead, she'd inherit pretty much all of it as his wife. Sorry, but Laurie Bateman is still the best suspect out there for the murder."

Maggie went through a lot more material I'd asked for about Hollister's background and life history.

Charles Hollister had been married twice before Laurie Bateman. Three times, technically. But the first one didn't actually count.

"Her name was Janice Novak, and he'd met her in California in the seventies right after he'd been discharged from the Army after spending a year in Vietnam," Maggie explained, reading from her notes. "Apparently celebrated by getting drunk and high on smoking pot with this Novak women. At some point, they decided it was a good idea to drive off into the desert and get married at a wedding chapel in Las Vegas. Which is exactly what they did. Then the next day, after they sobered up, they went back to the wedding chapel and got the marriage annulled."

"Wow, talk about a wild one-night stand, huh?" I said.

"Wife #2—or his first real wife—was a woman named Susan Daily. This one lasted nine years, but it ended badly. She had psychological problems that got worse as the marriage went on. Eventually, he had her committed to a psychiatric hospital before finally divorcing her. From what I found out, she was in such bad shape no one ever knew if she even realized the divorce had happened.

"His next marriage to Karen Sykora was the one that lasted the longest. Although the people who knew him said he played around a lot with other women during the marriage. Hollister clearly had an eye for the ladies. But they stayed together as man and wife until Laurie Bateman came along. He divorced Karen Sykora, married Bateman, and . . . well, the rest is history."

Maggie also had detailed notes about how Charles Hollister had acquired his fortune. It happened at an early age, not long after he'd left the Army. He came up with an idea for a new microchip concept that revolutionized the computer industry. It was the seventies when most people didn't have computers in their homes or businesses yet. That all changed when Hollister launched his computer company, which made him a fortune. From that he expanded into all sorts of other fields—media, book publishing, pharmaceuticals, real estate, a chain of fast-food restaurants around the country, and he'd recently even bought a New York City newspaper, the *New York Chronicle*. That was what he'd been talking about in that phone message he left just before he died. The idea was he planned to use this newspaper to build himself up

into a formidable media political force—as well as a business force—the way Rupert Murdoch had done with the *New York Post*, *Wall Street Journal* and Fox News.

The one constant in all this had been his longtime business partner, a man named Bert Stovall. Stovall was the CEO of the Hollister corporation. People who knew him said he was the exact opposite of Hollister. While Hollister loved being in the celebrity limelight with all his fame and wealth and success, Stovall kept a low profile behind the scenes. But everyone agreed he was very good at his job. "Bert's the guy who makes the trains run on time for Charles Hollister," was the way one longtime business analyst described it.

Hollister had two children, a son and a daughter—both with his previous wife Karen.

The daughter, whose name was Elaine, had disappeared from Hollister's life many years ago, people said. Moved out of the country and lived abroad. No one knew much more about Elaine Hollister.

His son was a different story. Charles Blaine Hollister Jr. worked for his father's business as an executive vice president. He had always been presumed to be the heir apparent when Hollister died or got old enough that he decided to step aside. Although, from what I now knew about his father leaving the largest part of his business empire to Laurie Bateman in his will from a few years earlier, Hollister must have had second thoughts about that.

"I wouldn't be surprised," Maggie said when I brought that up. "Charles Jr. is supposed to be a real piece of work. Arrogant, not particularly bright, and living pretty much off of his family name. The word is that people in the Hollister companies call him 'Chuckie' instead of 'Charlie.' Because of the 'Chuckie' horror movies. About the maniacal doll. You couldn't get rid of him, no matter how hard you tried. He was always there. Making your life a nightmare. Well, that's how they feel about 'Chuckie'—or Charles."

"Hard to get rid of someone when their father owns the business."

"Yep. It sounds like Hollister protected the kid more than a few times over the years even outside the business."

"What do you mean?"

"A while back, Charles Hollister Jr. was arrested for drunken driving in a hit-and-run case. He ran over a guy crossing the street, then sped away without stopping. A witness got the license number and the cops picked up Charles an hour later. Even with the extra hour, he still blew 2.0 on the DUI test.

"The victim lingered in a coma for a few days, before finally dying. Charles was then charged with vehicular manslaughter. But a funny thing happened. First, the DUI test was thrown out by a judge who said the cops didn't read him his rights clearly before they administered it. Then the witness who said he'd gotten a clear look at the car's license plate wasn't sure about that anymore. Charles said he didn't remember hitting anyone. And, even if he did, it was a tragic accident. In the end, he made a deal and got off with probation and a fine."

"You think Hollister paid off the witness and used his influence on the judge to get the charges dropped?" I asked Maggie.

"Duh, what do you think?"

I nodded. This was all interesting. I wasn't exactly sure how, but Charles Blaine Hollister Jr. might be the best possible alternative to Laurie Bateman as Hollister's killer. I played that around in my head for a while, and then tried to talk it through with Maggie.

"Charles Jr. always thought he'd be the heir apparent to his father's financial empire," I said. "But then the father wrote a will that left the bulk of everything to his current wife, Bateman. Hollister was likely planning to change his will again because of the pending divorce to Bateman, but when?

"From what we know, the previous will—the one so generous to Laurie Bateman at the expense of his son—was still in effect. Maybe the kid didn't know about the divorce or his father's plans to rewrite the will again to leave Bateman out of it. So he decided to take things in his own hands. To claim the inheritance he thought was rightly his. He murders his father.

"But he makes it look like Laurie Bateman did it. That's the key to the murder for him. He needs her to be convicted of Hollister's murder. That way she can't claim any of the fortune because a criminal isn't allowed to profit from their crime. Once she'd been convicted, the estate would presumably go back to Hollister's next closest heir. Which would be Charles Jr." I smiled triumphantly. "Makes sense, right?"

Maggie shook her head no.

"You're forgetting about one big flaw in that theory of yours, Clare. The one that has the kid as the murderer and Laurie Bateman just an innocent victim who's been wrongly accused."

"What's the flaw?"

"The flaw is that Laurie Bateman was the one found standing over Hollister's body at the crime scene."

"Right . . ."

* * *

I made a list of the people I wanted to talk to after Maggie left my office. It was a pretty long list.

Bert Stovall, Hollister's right-hand man.

Victor Endicott, the private investigator who took the secret pictures of Hollister with his young girlfriend.

Melissa Hunt, the girlfriend.

Melissa Hunt's jealous husband.

Max Gunther, a disgruntled business rival.

Susan Daily, Hollister's first wife.

The two Hollister children, Charles Jr. and Elaine, who apparently had seen a large portion of their inheritance go to Laurie Bateman in the current installment of his will.

Plus, a lot of other people Hollister had done business with in recent years and were unhappy with him.

I originally planned to talk to Karen Sykora, Hollister's previous wife—but I found out she'd died a few years after their divorce.

Still, I had a pretty impressive list of people—and potential suspects maybe in Charles Hollister's murder—to deal with here.

I could feel the excitement and the adrenaline rising in me, the way it always did when my instincts told me I was on the trail of a big news story.

Sure, my exclusive on Laurie Bateman being arrested for the murder of her husband—and the fact that they were in the process of divorcing when that happened—had been a great get for me.

But what if Laurie Bateman was innocent?

And I could find the real killer?

Now that would be an even better story!

CHAPTER 11

BERT STOVALL HAD lost more than a lifelong business partner when Charles Hollister was murdered. He'd lost a lifelong friend. Stovall told me that when I went to see him in his office at the building at Lexington Avenue and 53rd Street called Hollister Tower, where most of Hollister's businesses were headquartered.

"That's one of the toughest things about getting old, you lose a lot of friends," Stovall—who looked to be about the same age as Hollister, in his seventies—said to me. "A lot of it you expect. Cancer. Heart attacks. I've said too many goodbyes to people I cared about in recent years. But nothing like this.

"Charlie was my oldest friend in the world. We were in our early twenties when we met. Can you believe that? And we stayed close all these years. In business. And as friends. But now . . . he's gone. Just like that. And his death all seems so senseless; that's the hardest part of all for me to accept. It shouldn't have happened."

Stovall had agreed to meet me, but insisted he wanted to do the interview off camera. Which didn't surprise me much once I'd heard from Maggie how he was low key, always behind the scenes of Hollister's business dealings. The public didn't know much about Stovall, but he'd been at Hollister's side for all the years and all the deal making and all the building of the vast worldwide

Hollister empire. Which was why I wanted to talk with him. I figured he could give me a close-up view of what Hollister the man was like—and maybe even provide a clue about the events that led to his death.

"I've known Laurie for a long time," he said when I asked him about Laurie Bateman. "I was there on the night Charlie met her. It was at a celebrity charity event in Los Angeles. Charlie was being honored for a big donation he'd made to fight breast cancer or a similar cause. She was one of the celebrity guests. There were plenty of big names there, actors and actresses who were bigger than she was.

"But Charlie only had eyes for her. He spent the entire evening staring at her and then talking to her. Later, they went out together for a drink. Charlie had his yacht there, and he invited her aboard it for a cruise that weekend. She accepted and . . . well, the rest you know. Everyone made fun of them. Said Charlie was a dirty old man and she was only interested in his money. But he and Laurie didn't care. Charlie loved her, and she loved him too. Or at least I thought she did.

"Listen, I was aware they'd been having problems recently. I knew it wasn't all happiness and love and fun between them like they portrayed their marriage in the media. But I never expected anything like this. Who would? Charlie murdered, and Laurie in jail for it. My God! I want to believe she didn't do it. I want to believe it was someone else. It would make it easier to accept."

I suddenly realized that he called Hollister "Charlie."

"Everyone else always called him Charles," he said. "But to me he was Charlie. That was the guy I had known all my life. Charlie Hollister, just another kid like me back at the beginning trying to figure out what to do with our lives. So even after all this time and all that has changed, he was still 'Charlie' to me."

I asked him about any enemies—business or otherwise—who might have wanted Charles Hollister dead. I included Max Gunther, the business rival I'd read about earlier who was involved in a nasty legal feud with Hollister.

"There were a lot of people who didn't like Charlie." He shrugged. "At times for a good reason, I guess. Charlie could be a tough businessman. You have to be, otherwise people will take advantage of you. But it wasn't just people he dealt with in the business world who had a gripe against Charlie. Other people did, too.

"When you're rich like he was, people are jealous. Like Bill Gates. Or Warren Buffett. There's plenty of people who don't like billionaires out there these days. Blame them for everything wrong in society, want them to pay unreasonably high taxes and all that sort of thing.

"No billionaire is a perfect person, but few others are either. The Charlie I knew was a lot like everyone else. He had good points and bad points. But he was my friend. I knew the real Charlie Hollister. I knew the man pretty much all my life. He was a good man and a good friend."

I noticed a picture that was positioned in a prominent place on his desk. There were two men in the picture. Young men, in Army uniforms. Sitting on sandbags in front of a bunker in South Vietnam. They looked a lot different now, but I realized one of them was a young Bert Stovall. The other man in the picture was Charles Hollister. I asked Stovall about the picture.

"That's when we met," he said to me.

"In Vietnam?"

"In 1972. Before the final pullout of U.S. troops, a year later. We were there at the end of that war. Both of us had gotten drafted, so we had no choice. It was a crazy time."

Stovall stared at the long-ago picture, seemingly lost for a few seconds in his own thoughts and memories of that time. Then he turned back toward me.

"Did you know Charlie was a hero over there? He got a medal for bravery."

"What did he do?"

"Shot a Viet Cong soldier who was trying to put a live explosive charge into a building filled with U.S. soldiers. The blast would have killed a lot of us. But Charlie saw the Viet Cong doing it, confronted him, and ordered him to drop the bomb. When he didn't, Charlie shot him to death. The explosive was never detonated. Yep, he saved a lot of lives. Not many people know about that story. But I do because I was there. I was one of the people whose life Charlie saved that day."

At one point in our conversation, I brought up Hollister's son. I was interested in finding out more about him.

"Charles Blaine Hollister." Stovall sighed. "Charles Jr. The prodigal son."

"What is your relationship with him like?"

"In a word: difficult."

"Why is that?"

"Charles is a troubled person. Always has been. All the way back to when he was growing up. And he never got much better as he grew older."

I remembered the story Maggie had told me about the traffic accident where his father had helped him beat the charges—and I wondered if there were more legal issues like that in the Hollister son's past.

But instead, Stovall told me another story, a relatively minor incident involving Charles Jr. that had happened many years ago.

He told me it kind of summed up what kind of a person Hollister's son had always been, even at an early age.

"He was probably only about eight or nine when this happened. His sister, Elaine, was a few years younger, and she had this little doll that she loved. Carried it with her everywhere. Anyway, we were at a party at Charlie's house, and everyone talked about how cute she was with her little doll. Charlie thought so too. He picked his daughter up in his arms and kissed her, saying: 'My favorite little girl.' Well, I was watching Charles Jr. while Charlie picked up Elaine and her little doll. Everyone around them laughed and clapped. But not Charles Jr. He just glared at them. He looked furious.

"Later, Elaine came running to her father and mother in tears. She still had the doll. But the head was missing. It had been ripped off and the doll was destroyed. I never found out the real story. But my assumption was that Charles had done it. Because he was jealous and envious at the attention Elaine had gotten from Charlie and the others with her doll. So he lashed out at her by destroying the possession that was the most important thing to her in the world."

Stovall shook his head sadly. "Charlie knew his son had a lot of problems, but he kept talking about how one day the kid would grow up and turn out okay. It was like he thought by doing that he could keep up this pretense that Charles Jr. was the heir to the Hollister empire he always wanted, even though everyone knew he wasn't."

I asked Stovall when was the last time he had met with Charles Hollister.

"Oh, I saw him every day," he told me.

"Including that last day?"

"Of course."

"Tell me about that."

"Well, we talked about a lot of business matters. There was always a lot of stuff going on, decisions that had to made. Then Charlie told me about the other thing he was dealing with at the moment. The stuff with Laurie. The divorce and his will and everything else."

"The way I understand it, the will leaving most of everything to Laurie—which he'd done when he was head over heels in love with her in the early years of their marriage—was still in effect."

"That's right. Charlie was going to rewrite the will, cutting her out of it—but he never got a chance to do it before his death."

"She still inherits all that?"

"The current will in effect is very clear. She gets the bulk of his fortune and a controlling interest in Hollister Enterprises."

"Unless she's convicted for murder," I pointed out.

"Yes. If that happens, it nullifies her claim to Charlie's estate. And the estate would go to the next beneficiaries, his two children."

I thought about what he'd told me.

"One thing I don't understand. If Hollister went to all the trouble to set up this rigid prenup before he married Laurie Bateman to protect his money, why did he change his will after they were married to give her so much wealth and power to inherit?"

Stovall shook his head sadly. "Because he was in love with her. He was in love with her at the beginning of the marriage, and—as hard as this might seem to believe—I believe he was still in love with her at the end."

"Then why did he have a mistress?" I asked.

"You're talking about Melissa Hunt."

"Why would he cheat on Laurie Bateman if he was in love with her? I'm told he cheated on his ex-wives with other women during their marriages. He didn't seem to be in love with anyone. He wanted to bed as many women as he could. Which I guess is easy when you're as rich as Charlies Hollister was, huh?"

Stovall looked over at the picture on his desk again of the two of them in Vietnam a long time ago when they were both young and had no idea what was ahead for them.

"Did you ever see the movie *Citizen Kane*?" he asked me.

"Sure."

"Well, there's a scene in there in which an old man talks about seeing a pretty young woman in white when he was a young man. He only saw her for a fleeting few seconds, and then she disappeared before he could talk to her. But he said he still thought about that woman practically every day of his life since then. And always wondered what would have happened if he could have met her that long-ago day.

"It was the same thing for Charlie. We were in a restaurant in Saigon one night, and he saw a beautiful Vietnamese woman sitting there. Charlie fell in love with her at first sight. He wanted to introduce himself to her but—by the time he got up the courage to go over to where she was—she had left. Soon after that, the last U.S. forces pulled out, and we got sent home. He never saw that Vietnamese woman again. But he never forgot her for the rest of his life. He told me that once. How there wasn't a day that went by when he didn't think of that beautiful young woman in the Saigon restaurant and wonder about what happened to her."

"Laurie Bateman was Vietnamese," I pointed out. "Do you think that was what attracted him to her? Because she looked like this woman did?'"

"I've thought about that. That he saw in Laurie the woman of his dreams. That she was the woman in white for him. Or at least as close to her as he would ever get. That he could live happily ever after with the woman he was always meant to love."

"Except it didn't work out that way."

"No, Charlie's dream never came true."

CHAPTER 12

MELISSA HUNT LIVED in a three-bedroom apartment on the East Side along the waterfront, overlooking the East River and with panoramic views from an impressive balcony outside that stretched the length of her place. The building had doormen, a concierge, and valet parking. Since Melissa Hunt was ostensibly a struggling young actress, I assumed someone else paid the rent for her to live here. And my guess about the identity of that generous benefactor was Charles Hollister. Hey, I'm an investigative journalist. I get paid to figure out tricky stuff like that.

Melissa Hunt herself looked like something straight out of a casting call for a sexy young movie star. Blond, beautiful, statuesque figure, and a sultry voice. I thought about how incongruous a couple she must have made with Charles Hollister. But then I remembered how rich he was. Apparently having a lot of money can get you an attractive woman like Melissa Hunt. Who knew?

I'd had a bit of trouble getting in to see her when I first called. She claimed she didn't even know a Charles Hollister. I pointed out to her that I'd checked the building records and found that the apartment she lived in was paid for by Hollister. I also said that the police had told me she was having a romantic relationship with Hollister. And I added that with Hollister dead, the publicity about their relationship could only help her career at this point. I think that was the thing that convinced her. In the end, she agreed to meet me and gave the okay to the doormen and the concierge and all the other building personnel to let me up to her place.

So there I was, sitting in her living room on the thirty-sixth floor and talking about her and Charles Hollister.

"The police have already been here," she said.

"I figured they would."

"They asked all sorts of questions."

"What kind of questions?"

"Mostly about the relationship Charles had had with his wife, Laurie Bateman."

"What did you tell them?"

"Not much to tell. Charles hardly ever talked about her with me."

"Did he seem happily married?"

"What do you mean?"

"Well, happily married men don't usually carry on an affair with a woman like you on the side as his mistress."

She smiled slightly at first when I said it. But then she got defensive. About my reference to an affair and describing her as Hollister's mistress.

"It wasn't like that with Charles and me. I wasn't just another fling in the sack for him."

"What were you then?"

"He was going to marry me."

"That's what he told you?"

"Yes, many times. He loved me. I don't care whether you believe me about that or not. I know it was true. Is there anything else you want to ask me? To be honest, I'm not sure exactly why you came here and what you think you'll get from me."

"I'm trying to find out who killed Charles Hollister," I said.

"His wife. The police have already arrested her for it."

"They did. But I'm not convinced she's the killer. I'm looking for someone else who might have wanted him dead."

Melissa Hunt looked shocked when I said that.

"Wait a minute . . . you can't suspect me!"

I didn't say anything.

"I've got absolutely nothing to gain from Charles' death. His wife, Laurie Bateman—if she isn't convicted—will inherit the biggest chunk of his estate. I'm the *other woman*. I'm left out in the cold. I'm not even going to be able to stay in this apartment once the rent checks are due. What possible reason could I have for killing Charles Hollister?"

"How about your husband?"

"Wayne? He's my ex-husband. We got divorced."

"Okay, your ex-husband. I heard he was furious at Hollister for taking you away from him. Do you think he might have been furious enough to have murdered Hollister over that, Melissa?"

"No, Wayne's all talk and no action." She smiled. "He's a loser. I would have left him even if I hadn't met Charles. I can do better than Wayne. And I did. I did a lot better with Charles Hollister. Except now it's over."

"Do you know if the police questioned your ex-husband about Hollister's death?"

"Why would they want to talk to him?"

"As a suspect in Hollister's murder."

"They've already got the person who did it: Laurie Bateman."

I sighed. She was right. This wasn't particularly helping me in advancing the story. But I pressed on in the hopes of getting any kind of useful information out of her.

"You spent a good deal of time with Charles Hollister. Can you think of anything different or unusual that happened in the time you spent with him at the end?"

"Well, Charles was very preoccupied."

"Preoccupied how?"

"He was talking all the time about that newspaper he bought."

"The *New York Chronicle*?"

"That's right. It was all he had on his mind, even when he was with me. He was almost obsessed with everything about the newspaper business. I think he fancied himself as becoming a media baron or something. He'd accomplished so much else in the business world, I guess that was his next goal. Even when we were in bed, he would get up to talk to people at the paper. He was determined to learn everything about the newspaper business. I remember one night I heard him telling someone on the phone he wanted to change 'the wood.' I asked him afterward if he was talking about a fireplace, and he laughed. He said 'the wood' was a newspaper term for the Page One headline. Can you believe that?"

I smiled. That brought back a lot of memories for me of my own newspaper days before I got into TV news.

"It's called that because in the old days of Linotype machines the Page One headline actually was hammered out of wood," I said. "But they still refer to it in the newsroom as 'the wood.' Or sometimes, it's called 'the splash' as well. But hardly anyone says the Page One headline. Not at a paper like the *Chronicle*."

"Another time he talked about the 'lobster.' It took me a while to realize that wasn't about . . ."

"A seafood dinner? No, that's what they call the overnight shift at a newspaper. From midnight to early morning."

"Anyway, he learned all those newspaper terms and used them all the time. He prided himself on knowing all the jargon. He said he wanted to be a real newspaperman, not just a guy who owned a newspaper."

A real newspaperman? Maybe Charles Hollister hadn't been a totally bad guy after all. I wondered what would have happened if he'd lived to turn the *Chronicle* into the kind of political and editorial voice he was hoping to make it.

"What does any of this have to do with his death anyway?" she asked. "His wife murdered him. Listen, you said you were going to shoot some video of me for TV news. Let's go on air and I'll tell you whatever you want to know about my relationship with Charles Hollister. Like you said, the publicity will be good for me. It will probably get picked up by TMZ and a lot of other places. Bring in your video people and let's do this."

CHAPTER 13

MENTION THE TERM *private investigator* and most people—including myself—think about an image of Sam Spade or Philip Marlowe or someone else out of an old movie or a Mickey Spillane crime novel. Wearing a crumpled old raincoat, a fedora pulled down at the brim, working out of a cramped little office in a run-down building—and carrying a gat.

Victor Endicott—the private investigator who took the pictures of Hollister in bed with Melissa Hunt, then gave them to Laurie Bateman before Hollister's murder—wasn't like that at all.

When I went to see him, I was surprised to find out his office was a corporate suite in a high-rise building on Park Avenue South, near Madison Square Park.

I was greeted there by a pleasant-looking red-haired woman in the reception area. She asked me to sit down for a minute on the couch while she alerted Endicott I was here. The couch was long, with big cushions and covered in plush velvet. It looked like something out of *Home Beautiful*. I sank into it and looked around the rest of the place. There were expensive-looking paintings on the walls; a stack of publications like *Forbes* and *The New York Times* and *Wall Street Journal* spread out on a coffee table in front of me; and soft classical music playing through a stereo system. Not at all what I expected. More like an office for a financial company or a high-priced realty firm than a private investigator.

The receptionist returned and told me to follow her. She led me down a long hall of offices until we came to a large conference room. There was a big round table in the center of the room, surrounded by leather chairs. I sat down in one of the chairs and waited for Victor Endicott.

Endicott himself turned out to be a lot different than I expected, too.

He was wearing a three-piece pin-striped navy-blue suit, a red tie, and a pale blue shirt with fancy cuff links. He gave me a big smile as he came into the room. The kind of smile that he no doubt put on for all his prospective clients. Endicott had almost no hair on top of his head, either because he had lost it or it had been shaved. But he had a lot of hair on his face in the form of a bushy goatee that covered his chin. The weird juxtaposition made him look like a colorful character, but also a bit scary. I wondered if his other prospective clients felt the same way the first time they saw him.

Yes, I was a prospective client.

At least as far as he was concerned at the moment.

I had told his office when I called that I wanted to hire him as a private investigator.

I figured that was the easiest way to get a meeting with him.

Now I had to figure out how long I wanted to keep going with this phony story before I got to the real reason I was there.

"How can I be of service to you?" Endicott asked.

"I think I need to hire a private investigator."

"Well, lucky you came here. By a strange coincidence, that's what I do for a living."

He smiled when he said it. Like it was a joke he'd used countless times before to ease the fears of his clients. It was a clever move.

Endicott was clearly a clever guy. Based on what I'd found out about him, I didn't like Victor Endicott or what he did. But I did have a feeling he was good at his job.

"Now you said on the phone when you called the office before that you wanted me to look into someone for you. Tell me more details about what it is you're looking for."

I didn't have any more details.

I didn't have much more of a phony story.

"I lied about that," I said. "I made that all up so I could have an excuse to get in here and talk with you. You see, I'm actually . . ."

"A reporter," Endicott said.

His smile was even wider now.

"How did you know that?"

"I've seen you on TV. Your name is Clare Carlson. You're quite famous these days, you know. If you're going to try to pull off an undercover operation like this, it's important that the other person hasn't already seen you in another situation. Like all over the TV screen. Just a little investigative tip for you, Ms. Carlson."

He didn't seem mad at my attempt at subterfuge though, more like he was simply amused by me.

"What I really want to do is talk about the pictures of Charles Hollister in bed with another woman that you took for Laurie Bateman."

"I'm sorry, but the ethics of my profession don't allow me to discuss the details of any case or client I handle."

I rolled my eyes.

"Mr. Endicott, your PI license has been suspended three times for questionable activities. Ethics don't seem to rank very high on your list of priorities."

He shrugged. "Okay, I'll tell you what I know, but only under one condition."

"That I don't use your name?"

"No, that you do use my name. Just don't say the information came from me. I don't want clients to think I'll reveal stuff about them publicly. But what the hell, this could be good publicity for me. So you just say you got the information from someone else, not me. Is that a deal?"

Like Melissa Hunt, Endicott wanted to score good publicity over his involvement in the Laurie Bateman story.

Well, no matter how I felt about it, that's the business I was in.

Giving people publicity on the air.

I told Endicott we had a deal.

"Yes, Laurie Bateman hired me to find out if her husband was cheating on her," he told me then.

"How did Bateman wind up hiring you?"

"She knew me. I'd done things for her husband."

"You worked for Charles Hollister?"

"Yeah, a lot of times. Big corporate stuff—investigations of business rivals, surveillance, background checks."

"And then you took his wife's money to investigate him?"

He smiled. "Hey, I've got to pay the rent on this place. All this space, all this furniture—it doesn't come cheap."

We talked for a while more. He told me about a few of the big celebrity crime cases he'd been involved with over the years. How he'd once been hired to reexamine the death of Natalie Wood who drowned on a boat trip while she was with her husband Robert Wagner and film costar Christopher Walken. He'd also been involved in the JonBenét Ramsey investigation, he said. And even done work for a client on the O.J. Simpson case.

"Do you want to know what really happened to Nicole Brown Simpson that night?" Endicott asked.

"You know?"

"I have a pretty good idea who did it. And it's not who you think."

"I think it was O.J. Just like the rest of the world does."

"For the right price, I could give you an O.J. exclusive that would blow the lid off everything people believe. I'm telling you, this..."

"Sorry," I said, "but I only work one high-profile murder story at a time."

I had one other question for Victor Endicott.

"What happened when you showed those pictures of Charles Hollister in bed to Laurie Bateman?"

"She got mad."

"How mad?"

"How mad would you be if you saw your husband carrying on with another woman like that?"

"Do you remember exactly what Laurie Bateman said?"

"Sure, I do. And that's what I told the police when they asked me the same question. She said, 'I'll kill the lousy two-timer.'"

CHAPTER 14

"Is this Clare Carlson?" a voice said to me at the other end of the phone.

"Uh, possibly," I said sleepily.

"You don't know if you are Clare Carlson or not?"

I looked over at the alarm clock next to my bed. The digital display informed me it was a little before seven a.m. My alarm wasn't supposed to go off until eight. I cut it close when it comes to waking up in the morning and then making it to work on time. Let's just say I'm not exactly a morning person.

"Not at this hour. Who are you?"

"My name is Mitchell Lansburg, and I'm a vice president for talent at West Coast Media."

"Well, that wouldn't have been my first guess."

"I'm sorry if I woke you up. But I wanted to make sure and catch you before you left your house for work."

"Congratulations, you did it."

I sat up in bed. My head was clearing now, at least enough for me to ask this guy the most obvious question.

"Why are you calling me?"

"I have something important I'd like to discuss with you, and I think it would be worth your while to listen . . ."

"How in the hell did you get my home number anyway?"

"You're listed in the book."

"Oh, right."

"Ms. Carlson, are you free to meet me today for lunch?"

"I don't eat lunch."

"Ever?"

"Yes, I do eat lunch. But I don't go out for lunch much. Most of the time I grab a sandwich at my desk."

"So make an exception today."

"Mr. Langton . . ."

"Lansburg. Mitchell Lansburg."

"Okay. Mr. Lansburg, why does someone from West Coast Media, whatever that is—a vice president for talent no less—want to take me out to lunch anyway? Is this about a story I'm doing or what?"

"It's about you, Ms. Carlson."

"Why do you care about me?"

"We care about your future."

*   *   *

It turned out to be a job offer. Or at least the promise of one. Which is how I wound up sitting in the 21 Club, the legendary Midtown restaurant where politicians, celebrities, board chairmen, and media movers hung out, having lunch with Mitchell Lansburg later that day.

Lansburg was barely thirty—everyone seemed to be getting younger and younger, even media vice presidents—and he talked like a guy who was in a hurry to rise even higher. Rapid-fire delivery, short-clipped sentences—there was no wasted time with this guy.

He had blond curly hair, cut short and neatly trimmed, and he was wearing a blue pin-striped suit, sky blue paisley tie, and a pink shirt. I put him at about an eight or a nine on my sex appeal meter. But he was also wearing a wedding ring on his left hand. Frankly, I was relieved about the wedding ring. That meant, hopefully, there'd be no sexual tension between us. I wasn't exactly sure about how all the rules worked these days for women in the business world, but I was pretty sure that propositioning someone during a job interview was considered inappropriate behavior.

"How much do you know about our West Coast Media company?" he asked me.

"Well, I know it's on the West Coast. I know it's a company that has something to do with media. And . . . that's pretty much the extent of my knowledge about it at the moment."

"We are a major production company that works with the networks and big TV studios to provide content for on-air production. In other words, we put shows on television. Entertainment shows. News shows. Talk shows. We're based in Los Angeles but we also have offices around the country and around the world."

"Good for you."

"We've been following your career, Ms. Carlson," he said as a black-jacketed waiter brought our lunch order to the table. "Following it for a while now. You've broken big stories. And all the attention you got for your . . . well, your mea culpa, I guess you'd call it about the Lucy Devlin story. So when you got this latest big exclusive about Charles Hollister and the arrest of his wife, Laurie Bateman—scooping everyone else on this—we decided it was time to talk to you. We'd like you to come work for us, Clare."

I noticed how he'd switched from calling me Ms. Carlson, which he did at the beginning, to Clare now. A clever ploy. Start out all businesslike, then switch to a friendly, familiar mode. Mitchell Lansburg was a pretty good operator.

"Doing what?" I asked him.

"Starring on a new talk show we're creating."

"Talk show?"

"Yes, a daytime talk show that is in the planning stages. It would be syndicated around the country, and appearing on all the major channels. You would be perfect for it."

Lansburg had ordered something called a Colorado lamb chop, which looked like any other lamp chop except much bigger. Me, I'd gone for a lunch entrée of creamy chicken hash. And then, since Lansburg was picking up the tab, I added an appetizer of truffle mac and cheese. It was a lot different from the tuna fish sandwiches I usually had for lunch. Maybe I should come here to 21 every day. That way I could work my way through the entire menu. Or at least keep eating until I exploded.

"Has anyone told Ellen yet?" I asked him.

"Excuse me?"

"Well, if I'm going to be replacing Ellen DeGeneres on her talk show . . ."

Lansburg smiled now. The first smile I'd seen so far. That was a good sign. I always appreciated a good audience for my jokes.

"You won't be replacing Ellen at the moment," he said.

"Dr. Phil?"

Another smile.

"We envision a panel show. More like *The View*. Or *The Talk*. Out of our studio in Los Angeles. You'd be part of a group of people like that talking about the news of the day. Lots of it would be entertainment, but we expect to focus on news, too. We'd want you to break stories on the show. Like you do now on local TV. Only you'd be doing it for a national audience. You're a terrific personality, Clare. I could tell that from watching you on air, and I can tell it even more now that I've met you in person. We want to introduce you to a bigger audience. We want to turn you into a big national star, not just a star here in New York. All you have to do is be yourself. Just be Clare Carlson."

"I could do that."

"So you're interested in pursuing this?"

I decided it was time to bring this conversation back to reality.

"Look, Mr. Lansburg . . ."

"Call me Mitchell."

"The truth is, Mitchell, I'm not that good on the air. Sure, it seems great when I'm breaking a big story on air. But those were special moments. Not day-to-day, on-air reporting. When I started out on Channel 10 as an on-air reporter, I bombed. Everyone said I was too grating and too intense and . . . well, too unlikeable on-screen. That's how I wound up working behind the scenes and eventually as news director. Your viewers aren't going to like me any more on air than Channel 10 viewers did back then."

"That was then, Clare. Times have changed."

"What do you mean?"

"Back then, everybody thought it was important that viewers 'liked' the people they were watching on TV. But now, with all competition from hundreds of places on cable and social media and the rest for viewers' attention, it doesn't matter as much. It's all about getting that attention away from the other sites and putting it back on us. Look at how many major news journalists these days—like on the 24-hour cable news channels—have made a name for themselves by being obnoxious and over the top with their actions and opinions. People might love them or hate them. That's what we'd be looking at with you. A personality the viewers wanted to tune in to watch and hear what the hell you were going to say and what big story you were about to break. You'd be must-watch TV, Clare."

"You're saying you'd want me to act outrageous on air?"

"We'd expect that."

"How outrageous?"

"Whatever it takes to attract an audience."

"Can I take my clothes off during a show?"

He smiled again. I was starting to like this guy.

"No, I'm afraid that's one pretty hard and fast rule we stick to— you have to keep your clothes on while you're on the air."

"I guess I can live with that," I said.

CHAPTER 15

"Los Angeles?" Janet asked.

"That's where the job would be."

"You're thinking of moving to Los Angeles?"

"Hooray for Hollywood," I said.

"Are you sure about this?"

"It is kinda far away, isn't it?"

"Three thousand miles."

"We could talk on the phone. Exchange texts every day. Maybe even video chat with each other, if I can ever figure out exactly how to do that on my computer."

"No, I mean are you sure about you being in Los Angeles? You're much more of a New York City person."

"I could change my lifestyle. Eat yogurt and rice cakes instead of pizza. Take up meditation. Join a health club. This could be a whole new me we're talking about here."

"Clare, I think it's more likely you'll spend your time working your way through every fast-food place from San Diego to Santa Barbara."

"I do hear those In-N-Out burgers are pretty tasty," I admitted.

We were sitting on a wooden bench inside a courthouse near Foley Square in downtown Manhattan. Janet was on a break from a case. I'd come down there specifically to tell her about my conversation with Mitchell Lansburg. I didn't tell her beforehand why I wanted to see her, but I think she figured it was pretty significant. When Janet and I meet up for dinner or drinks or anything else socially, we try to stay away from serious topics most of the time. But, when we need to talk business, we go to each other at work. Like Janet did by coming to Channel 10 to talk to me about Laurie Bateman and her divorce plans. And that's why I was here in Foley Square with Janet right now. I needed to tell somebody about what had happened, so why not my best friend?

"When would all this happen?" Janet asked.

"There's no actual job offer yet. He said they're still in the planning stages—getting network and advertising interest and a bunch of stuff like that. He was going to get back to me once it was more nailed down that the show would be a go. After that, I'd have to move to LA."

"Weren't you talking about writing a book one day soon? About all the big stories you've worked on? Lucy Devlin and the rest? Hard to do that if you're gonna make this kind of a big career move."

"People don't read books anymore."

"That's an exaggeration."

"Okay, but twenty-five years from now, it probably will be true."

"Twenty-five years from now you'll be too old to care."

"Thanks for cheering me up with that little piece of wisdom."

We were sitting side by side on the bench. Outside a courtroom where Janet was representing a client in a wrongful injury suit. I had a cup of coffee in my hand, and she was drinking tea. Janet might be the only person I know who drinks tea every morning instead of coffee. Me, I was already on my third cup of coffee for the day. I started to try to take a sip of it now. But Janet suddenly poked me in the ribs, almost making me spill it.

"Uh-oh," she said, "ex-boyfriend approaching."

"Which one?"

This was not an idle question for me. I've been with a lot of men. Married three times. And plenty of others along the way that I've shared passion and heartbreak with as well. Long-term relationships were definitely not my strong suit.

"Wild Bill Carstairs."

"Damn."

William—Wild Bill—Carstairs was an assistant district attorney with big political ambitions. He took the nickname from Wild Bill Hickok. Carstairs said he saw himself as a modern-day gunslinger lawman, cleaning up New York City the same way lawmen like Hickok cleaned up the Old West. He was constantly in the newspapers or on TV. The media loves that kind of stuff.

I'd gone out with him for a while, but it ended badly.

Extremely badly.

One day I unexpectedly walked in on him in bed with a woman police officer. She'd handcuffed him to the bedposts and appeared to be "interrogating" him—using her lips and fingers on various parts of his body and asking him which position felt the best. He was moaning in ecstasy until he saw me. "Clare, I can explain this!" he yelled as I stormed out the door. Needless to say, he couldn't. Handcuffed in bed with another woman is not an easy one to explain. All in all, it ranks right up there as one of your basic relationship busters.

"Where is he?" I asked Janet now.

"Turned the corner and coming down the hall toward us."

I had three choices. I could ignore him; I could dive under the bench and hide—or I could talk to him. I decided to talk to him.

"Clare, you're looking great," he said when he saw me. "You're still the best-looking journalist in town."

"So what do you call that anchorwoman over at Channel 5 you've been dating? The second-best looking?"

He laughed and shook his head. "Same old Clare."

"Same old Billy," I said. "By the way, are the handcuff marks on your wrists healed yet? I hear those suckers can really chafe."

I heard Janet doing her best to try to stifle a laugh next to me. But Carstairs didn't seem to notice. He didn't pay any attention to her at all. He seemed to be interested only in me. Lucky me.

"I've been following your stuff on Laurie Bateman," he said.

"Are you involved in that case at all?"

"Involved? It's my case. I'm going to be the lead prosecutor against Laurie Bateman."

Of course.

"Could we talk about the DA's case against Bateman?" I asked him.

"It depends."

"On what?"

"Just be nice to me."

"How nice?"

"Have a drink with me."

"I'd prefer to keep this on a professional basis."

"Have it your way." He shrugged. "Well, I gotta go. I'm on my way to tell what I know about Laurie Bateman to someone else who wants that information."

"Who is that?"

"The anchorwoman at Channel 5." He smiled.

I stared at him. I couldn't believe this guy. "You're an asshole, Billy. You know that, don't you?"

"C'mon, Clare, don't get mad. What am I supposed to do . . . give all my exclusives to you? Because we had a few good times together?"

"Our times together weren't all that good," I told him.

If that hurt his feelings, he didn't show it. He was still smiling when he walked away.

"Well, that was pleasant," I said to Janet.

"Looks like you're not going to get much help out of the prosecutor's office."

"Which means I need to concentrate on the defense. Laurie Bateman's defense, whatever it is. What about that defense attorney? That woman Donna Grieco you told me about? Can you get me in to talk to her? If I could break a story that gets Laurie Bateman off the murder charge—no matter how improbable it might seem—that would be a huge scoop for me, Janet. And I could stick it to that jerk Carstairs."

"I'm still trying on the interview. I'll let you know. But I gotta say again—this looks like a pretty slam-dunk case against Bateman. I imagine she's going to have to make a plea deal at some point. Everyone is convinced she's guilty—the police, the DA, the media, and the public. You seem to be the only one holding out hope she might beat this charge. Why are you doing this, Clare?"

I watched Carstairs—still smirking I was sure—as he got to the end of the hall and turned the corner, presumably on his way to a meeting with the Channel 5 anchorwoman.

"Hey, if you can't join 'em, beat 'em," I said

CHAPTER 16

THEY HELD THE funeral for Charles Hollister at a church on East 67th Street. The city was festooned with Christmas decorations as I made my way over there. Wreaths. Colored lights. Even a smiling Santa Claus with a sled and reindeer on the lawn in front of the church. Yo-ho-ho. 'Tis the season to be jolly.

The funeral service itself had turned into an A-one media event. Camera crews from all the TV networks as well as the New York stations—including mine—were there, along with throngs of reporters and lots of curious onlookers. Why not? Charles Hollister had been a powerful and wealthy man, a larger-than-life figure, for many years. Now he'd died a violent death, and his beautiful young celebrity wife was in jail accused of the murder. This was big news no matter how you looked at it.

Inside, the church was filled with VIP mourners. The mayor. The governor. Several congressmen and a senator. Some recognizable celebrities, too. There was no Laurie Bateman, of course. We'd done a story the previous night about how her lawyer had petitioned the court to allow her out of jail to attend her husband's funeral. Now that would have been a spectacle, huh? But the request was denied by the court.

I made my way to the section set aside for the media to sit. There was no burial. Hollister, according to his last wishes, had been cremated. So this man who had been such a powerful presence in the world didn't even exist anymore. At least, not in a physical sense. Charles Hollister was gone. Ashes to ashes, dust to dust. All that was left was the mystery surrounding his death.

In the front of the church, I saw a man I recognized from pictures I'd seen as Hollister's son, Charles Jr. Next to him was a woman that someone told me was his sister, Elaine. I wanted to talk to both of them, but it obviously would have to wait until the service was over. I knew their mother was dead, but I wondered if Hollister's previous ex-wife might be there. I found out later that she lived on the West Coast and didn't make the cross-country trip. Made sense, I guess. Their marriage had been a long time ago and ended badly. Like all Hollister's marriages had.

During the ceremony, there was a procession of speakers who gave us eulogies about what a wonderful person Charles Hollister had been. Bert Stovall was one of the speakers. He talked about meeting Hollister in Vietnam when they were young and their long friendship and business partnership since then—as he'd related to me that day in his office. Most of the others said wonderful things about Hollister too. The kind of things you always hear at a funeral about a person who had died. I thought about all the things I'd learned about Hollister in the past few days—and what a cruel and greedy person he had been. It was as if they were talking about someone else.

At one point, Charles Jr. went up to deliver his eulogy. But this one was a lot different from the others. For one thing, he sounded disjointed—his words rambling. He looked kind of out of it too as he spoke. I wondered if he'd been drinking. Well, his father had just died a horrible death. I guess you had to cut a guy a little slack when that happened.

He told stories about growing up as the son of Charles Hollister. Nothing personal or emotional or loving though. Made you wonder what their relationship was actually like. But then it got even stranger. He began to attack Laurie Bateman in the middle of his eulogy.

"This woman—this horrible woman—coerced my father into marrying her. She convinced him to make her the prime beneficiary of his estate. And then, when he realized what an evil person she truly was and told her he was rewriting his will, she murdered him before he could do that. The only solace I have is that she's sitting in a jail cell right now, and I hope she rots away the rest of her miserable life in prison."

It was wildly inappropriate. But he continued to go on like that for a few minutes until the minister in charge of the service gently took him by the arm, led him from the podium and back to his seat. I noticed that when he sat down, he did not look at his sister. She didn't look at him either. She stared straight ahead. The two of them clearly did not have a close brother-sister relationship.

When the service was over and people started filing out, I positioned myself outside on the street so I would be able to talk to Charles Jr. I wanted to talk to the sister as well, but Charles was my priority. He seemed like a powder keg waiting to explode. I wanted to be the one to light the fuse on this guy.

It took a while before he made his way out, but I was ready. Standing between him and the car waiting to take him away. I stepped in front of him as he was reaching for the handle on the car door.

"Charles, my name is Clare Carlson, and I'm with Channel 10 News. I'm sorry about your father, and I know this is a difficult time for you. But I'd like to talk with you about it."

I handed him my card. He looked at me with a glazed expression on his face. I was pretty sure he was drunk now, even though it was barely eleven a.m. Maybe he wanted to get an early start on the day. Or else he was still coming down from a long night of drinking.

"I don't want to talk to you," he said.

"I've spoken to a lot of other people about your father. I'd like to hear from you. We could set something up at a time that's convenient for you and—"

"I told you, I have nothing to say to you."

"Why don't you want to talk?"

"Just leave me alone."

"What do you have to hide, Charles?" I blurted out.

The glazed look disappeared now. It was replaced by one of anger. The same kind of anger I'd seen when he was talking about Laurie Bateman during the service.

"Get out of my way!" he yelled, pushing past me to get to his car. He pushed so hard that he knocked me to the ground. Lying there on my back, I could see video crews recording the whole bizarre scene. My God, I'd come here today to cover this story. Now I was becoming part of the story.

"You goddamned bitch!" Charles Hollister Jr. screamed at me as I got to my feet. "You're like that other bitch that married my father. All you women are bitches. Every one of you. I don't need any of you in my life."

Then someone grabbed him and put him into the waiting car. Once he was there, the car quickly pulled away into traffic.

"Well, that was quite a scene," I heard a voice say from behind me.

I turned around. There was a woman watching it all. Elaine Hollister. Charles' sister.

"I'm sorry about that," I said to her. "I didn't mean for anything like that to happen. I only wanted to talk to him."

"It was Charles' fault, not yours. Things like that always happen with him."

"Clare Carlson of Channel 10 News," I said, sticking out my hand. "Listen, I'm sorry about your father. My condolences."

She shook my hand and nodded.

"How come you didn't leave in the same car with your brother?" I asked her.

"We generally go our separate ways," she said. There seemed to be a touch of sarcasm in her voice. I wanted to find out more about that relationship. I wasn't sure why I cared, but it seemed like it might be relevant. And, of course, I wanted to hear more about Elaine Hollister's relationship with her father. And why she'd apparently been estranged from him all these years.

"Could we go somewhere and talk for a while?" I asked.

She shook her head. "I don't think it's a good idea for me to talk with anyone in the media about all this. I'll be a lot nicer about it than my brother, I promise. But the answer is still no."

"We could just get coffee for a few minutes."

"No, I've got to be going."

"I'll even buy the coffee. How can you turn down an offer like that?"

Elaine Hollister smiled. "You are persistent, aren't you?"

"It's one of my most endearing qualities."

CHAPTER 17

WE WENT TO a coffee shop and sat in a corner table by the window. The street outside was filled with people walking by carrying Christmas packages. On the corner was a man dressed in a Santa Claus suit trying to get donations for the homeless. The guy's beard and outfit were shabby and he looked as though he could be one of the homeless himself. I'd dropped a dollar in his pot as we walked by, figuring it would get to someone who needed it one way or the other.

"Are you in New York just for the funeral?" I asked her once we sat down.

"That's right."

"Where do you live?"

"Oh, I've lived in a lot of places. London. Rome. Even spent a few years in the Far East in Tokyo and then Bangkok. But for the last few years I've been living in Paris. I run a shelter for battered women there. I finance it, I run it, I work with the women myself."

"That sounds like important work. It must be rewarding for you."

"I figure I should make sure something good comes out of my father's money."

"Have you talked yet with Charles about what will happen to the company now that your father is gone? Especially if Laurie Bateman is convicted of murder and can't claim any of the inheritance . . ."

"I have not talked to Charles. I don't want to talk to Charles. If I wanted to talk to Charles, I wouldn't have moved out of the country and be living in Paris, would I?"

The anger with which she said it surprised me. I think it even surprised her the way it came out.

"You don't like your brother much, do you?"

"Charles isn't an easy person to like."

"Do you have any relationship with him at all?"

"As little as possible."

"Why is that?"

"It's complicated. Let's just say there's a lot of history between Charles and me. Not good history, I'm afraid."

I remembered the story Bert Stovall had told me about Elaine as a little girl and the doll she loved so much that had its head ripped off. How she loved that doll and cried when it was gone. How everyone was sure that Charles destroyed the doll out of anger and jealousy over her getting so much attention from their father.

I asked her about that now, but she just laughed.

"Oh, I'm not still upset about something that happened when I was four years old. Believe me, there've been a lot worse incidents between me and Charles since he destroyed my damn doll."

"Like what?"

"Oh, it's a long story."

I took a sip of my coffee. "I've got plenty of time."

Outside, the guy in the shabby Santa suit had packed up and gone home for the day. His place was taken by a guy holding a cardboard sign saying he needed $88 to get home to Florida. Probably a prime business location.

"When I was twenty-two years old, I graduated magna cum laude from Princeton," she said slowly. "I won a Rhodes Scholarship to study in England for a year. It was a tremendous honor. I came home to tell my father. I thought he'd be as happy and proud as I was. But he wasn't. He was more concerned about Charles than he was proud of me.

"You see, Charles had been turned down for admission to Princeton. His grades weren't good enough to get in. And the admissions interview had not gone well. In fact, it was so bad that the Princeton admissions office wrote a memo that said 'Definitely should never be allowed to come to Princeton.' Even my father's money and influence weren't enough to get Charles into Princeton.

"After I graduated and got the Rhodes Scholarship, there was a party at my parents' house. Maybe a hundred people were there. All of them important and rich and powerful. My father humiliated Charles in front of them. Talked about my graduating magna cum laude and about my winning the Rhodes Scholarship and about all my other achievements at Princeton. Then he compared all this to Charles. Complained bitterly about how his son couldn't even get in the front door of Princeton. It wasn't like he was proud of me. He used everything I did as a weapon—a weapon to show his displeasure with Charles in front of all those people. I was embarrassed, of course. But Charles . . . Charles got madder and madder. I could see the look of pure anger on his face. He couldn't be mad at his father, of course. He wasn't man enough to do that. So Charles directed all of his anger at me.

"That night, after everyone was asleep, Charles burst into my room. He was yelling how much he hated me. How I'd ruined his life. Then he hit me. I fought back. That enraged him even more. He hit me again and again. By the time he was finished, I was bloodied and unconscious and badly injured.

"I never did get to study in London on that Rhodes Scholarship. I spent the next few months in the hospital. Getting extensive plastic surgery. Learning to walk again. That's how badly I was injured. But that wasn't even the most painful part. It was the damage that had been done to me inside that hurt the most.

"You see, when I was in the hospital right after the attack, my father came to see me. He told me that I was never to tell anyone what Charles did. If I did, he would cut me off without a cent. He said I should just tell people I'd been clumsy and fallen down the stairs in the dark. He said Charles was his only son and the future for the Hollister empire. He said he'd pay any price to protect him. Even if that meant losing his daughter. He didn't say it that way exactly, of course. But that was the meaning.

"And so that's what happened. When I got better, I moved as far away from all of them as I could. I still take my father's money. Most of it goes to various charities and humanitarian causes I'm involved in. Like the battered women's shelter. Doing that makes me feel better."

I wasn't sure at first why she'd told such a personal story to a journalist like me. And a journalist she'd only met a few minutes earlier. But then I realized it didn't have anything to do with me. It was something she wanted to unburden herself of after she lost her father and her encounter with Charles at the funeral. I happened to be the one she was with right now.

"What did you think of your stepmother, Laurie Bateman?"

"I didn't know her very well. My father had moved on with his life once he married her. I was in the past. So I had no relationship with her at all other than what I read and heard in the media about the two of them. Of course, I never believed all the lovey-dovey happy marriage stuff they kept talking about. But that's only because I knew my father. I figured behind the scenes the marriage was probably as bad as the one he had with my mother. And his wife before that, too."

"What was your relationship like with your father at the end? When was the last time you talked to him?"

"A week or so ago before his death. He called me. I was surprised because he hadn't done that in a long time. But he even talked about coming to Paris to visit me. Looking back on it now, he seemed to be reaching out to me. More than he ever had in years. He talked about wanting to get closer to me again during that last conversation. He definitely seemed different. Nicer. Kinder. And well . . . more like a father. I wondered what had changed him. I figured I'd find out when he came to see me in Paris. But now I guess I'll never know . . ."

The waitress came by and refilled our cups. We sat there talking for another fifteen minutes or so. I asked her if I could interview her on camera talking about her father. She said no. She said she didn't want to do anything publicly as a member of the Hollister family. She wanted to fade back into the background and be left alone.

I liked Elaine Hollister. She seemed like a good person. Maybe too good for the Hollister family, from everything I'd heard. I took out a Channel 10 business card with my office number on it. I wrote my home number on it.

"Call me if you ever want to talk more," I said.

"You mean about my father?"

"About anything."

She smiled and put the card in her pocket.

"Maybe I will."

*   *   *

After we split up, I decided to walk for a while. The city was alive with that special feeling it gets around Christmas time. I wanted to be a part of it. The street was crowded with people coming out of stores, but few of them were rude or obnoxious. Everyone seemed cheery and filled with Christmas spirit. Not like a normal day in New York.

I walked downtown to Fifth Avenue. Past Central Park, Saks Fifth Avenue, and Tiffany's. I window-shopped at Tiffany's for a bit, dreaming about finding one of the baubles there under my tree on Christmas morning. Fat chance. No one was going to put a $10,000 bracelet under my tree.

After that, I walked down to Rockefeller Center. That's where New York truly feels like Christmas. There's an eighty-foot Christmas tree, people ice skating on the rink, and holiday decorations hanging from all the lampposts. Not far away, people filed in and out of St. Patrick's Cathedral. If you don't feel the Christmas spirit there, you might as well just give up and say "Bah, humbug."

I was on my way to the subway station when I saw a car—a dark blue sedan—driving slowly on the street behind me. Nothing unusual there, except I thought I had seen the same car before when I was on my way to the coffee shop. Hell, there were a lot of dark blue sedans in New York City.

I kept walking toward the subway station. The car was still there. There was a newsstand outside, and I spent a minute or two at it buying a package of mints. When I was finished, I turned around one more time. Nothing now. The blue sedan was gone.

I shrugged and headed down the steps for the subway.

CHAPTER 18

EVERYWHERE YOU LOOKED, the city was practically bursting with holiday spirit now. Especially among the people working in my building—who all had visions of Christmas tips dancing in their heads.

The next morning when I left for work, my super held my front door open, tipped his hat, and gave me a cheery "good morning, ma'am." I knew right away something was up. The last time he'd spoken to me was in August, when I'd come back from the shore lugging three heavy suitcases and asked for a little help. He told me he was much too busy. What he was busy doing was devouring a two-foot-long Italian submarine sandwich, so I suggested what he could do with it. Our relationship had gone downhill since then.

Now though, with December 25 approaching, we were fast friends. Pals. The Christmas spirit, it's wonderful. Same thing with the mailman. As a special holiday feature, he didn't mix up any of my neighbor's mail with mine like he usually did or jam stuff in my mailbox so I couldn't get it out. Service with a smile all the way.

Outside, it was not exactly a White Christmas yet. It was more of a wet Christmas. An icy cold rain was pouring down, the sky was dark, and the wind bitter. Some Christmas season. It was the kind of day when even Santa Claus would take one look, unhook the reindeer, and crawl back into bed.

But not me.

I had to work.

I knew it was going to be a rough day at the office when I got there and found a message from Jack Faron that told me my normal morning news meeting would have to be pushed back today. He said he wanted to talk to everyone on the staff first. About a "big concept" idea for our news show.

I sighed. TV news should be simple. All you need to do is put on the air the news that people want to know about, right? Except it doesn't always work that way. Instead, things get confused with all sorts of side issues involving ratings and marketing and demographics. The worst part of this though is the "big concept" idea. I'd heard plenty of them over the years. I wondered what this one would be.

A short time later, I found out as Faron talked to the staff.

"I'm pleased to announce that we've hired a consultant to help make our newscasts even stronger than they are," he said.

"Didn't we hire a consultant last year?" someone asked.

"Yes, and that consultant did fine work for us."

"Until Clare slept with him," someone else said with a laugh.

"This is a different consultant."

"Doesn't mean Clare won't sleep with this one, too."

"I'll try to keep my hormones under control," I said.

My romantic escapades—three failed marriages and a host of other disastrous relationships—were a constant fodder for humor by the people who worked at Channel 10. Much of it got blown out of proportion, of course. I mean, I only slept with the consultant guy once.

"The consulting firm has spent countless hours watching our newscasts," Faron said now. "Analyzing our strengths and weak points. Studying our audience. Comparing us with other successful local TV news operations here in New York City and around the country. They are very impressed by what they've seen of Channel 10 News. But they feel there are steps we can take to make our newscast even stronger. One of them is to build a stronger connection between our on-air news team and our viewers. To make our newscast more personal. To make people like us more. To make them feel they're inviting friends into their home when they turn on the Channel 10 News."

"Happy talk," I said.

"Huh?" one of the younger people in the room said. They weren't that familiar with happy talk. I was.

"Everyone giggles a lot on air and makes quips about the news and pretends they like each other. We're all just one big happy family here at Channel 10 News. That's what we're talking about, isn't it, Jack?"

"I call it an effort to build a better rapport with our audience."

"I call it crap."

Happy talk had been around for a long time in the TV news business. It started back in the seventies with one of the New York stations. It's come and gone in popularity over the years. But it always seems to return—like locusts or the plague—whenever a consultant firm is looking for an easy way to jack up ratings.

"C'mon, Clare," Faron said. "This concept has worked at a number of stations all over in recent years. There's nothing wrong in letting people know that we all really like each other here at Channel 10. That's all we're talking about doing."

"Well, I think we have a few problems trying to implement that 'we all really like each other' idea here."

I looked over at Brett Wolff and Dani Blaine. Things had been quiet on the Brett and Dani front since their argument about who would take care of their upcoming baby during one of my news meetings. But I could just see the two of them going at it on air one night if our newscast got too personal. Especially once the baby arrived. Dani would complain about having to get up for the two a.m. feedings. Brett would say he was the one changing all the dirty diapers. My God, the Channel 10 newscast could turn into a friggin' reality TV show.

"I'm for the idea," Wendy Jeffers, our weather forecaster, said. I could understand that. Wendy always wanted to become more of a personality on air, not just a woman talking about cold fronts and storm warnings. Wearing funny hats and outfits, quipping with the anchors, and talking about what she was going to have for dinner that night or whatever. I think she hoped to turn herself into a female version of Al Roker. So this was perfect for her.

Not so much for Steve Stratton, our sportscaster.

"I'm against it," Stratton said. "I don't want to be some kind of buffoon out there every night. I only want to report what's going on in sports. Sports is serious business, not a joke."

"Yeah, no one would ever want to have fun with sports," Faron said.

The bottom line was, I was glad when the meeting was over and I could do my news meeting with Maggie and the others about what we were going to put on the air that night.

That was what I cared about.

The best part of my job.

We talked about a subway derailment, a neighborhood protest about a police shooting, a new initiative by the mayor's office to get homeless off the streets and into shelters, a potential bid for a star free agent pitcher by the Yankees, and the possibilities of us having a White Christmas this year.

But the biggest story on the news list was still Laurie Bateman.

We'd covered the funeral like everyone else, of course. Including my confrontation with Charles Jr. outside. I told them now in the meeting about everyone else I'd talked to over the past few days: Bert Stovall, the Hollister mistress, Endicott the private investigator—and said I planned to do an exclusive update that night on the air.

Then I also said I'd be out of the office for much of the next day because I was still trying to get an interview with Charles Blaine Hollister, the dead man's son. That surprised everyone, especially after watching him push me to the ground on the video from the funeral we had just aired.

"I thought he made it pretty clear that he doesn't want to talk to you," Maggie said. "And he hasn't talked to anyone else either. So why do you think you can pull off an interview with this guy. It seems like a real long shot, Clare."

"That's why it's called an exclusive," I said. "If it was easy, everybody would have it."

CHAPTER 19

AT EIGHT O'CLOCK the next morning, I was standing in front of the Hollister Tower in Midtown.

I drank a large cup of black coffee, ate several donuts from a nearby bakery, and pored through the morning *New York Times*, *News*, and *Post* on my iPad. By the time I was finished, I was well read and well fed. Only thing was, I still didn't know anything more about Charles Blaine Hollister, aka Charles Jr. I was starting to wonder if this was a waste of time. I was also starting to develop a severe case of heartburn from the coffee and donuts.

The air was crisp and cold, but the sun shone brightly and the sky was a bright blue. Perfect winter weather. Nearby, holiday crowds bustled around with somewhere to go and something to do. Last-minute Christmas shopping. See the decorations at Rockefeller Center. Drinking eggnog around a cozy fire with friends and relatives. I stomped my feet on the sidewalk trying to stay warm and drained the last of the coffee from the cup. Still no Charles Blaine Hollister.

I watched the steady stream of people passing by. Women wearing fur coats. Well-dressed men carrying briefcases. Children holding on to their parents with that wide-eyed look of excitement kids get around Christmas-time. A young couple carrying gaily wrapped presents. Lots and lots of people. None of them was Hollister.

It was a little after eleven a.m. when he finally appeared. Unlike most of the other people going in and out of the Hollister building, he was not dressed in business attire. He had on a ski jacket, a pair of baggy jeans, and hiking boots. He wasn't a bad-looking guy, but his hair was askew and it looked like he hadn't shaved recently. He got out of a cab in front of the building and walked slowly toward the door. I didn't exactly get the feeling that Charles Blaine Hollister was a man in a hurry to get to work.

I ran across the street and was right behind him as he headed toward a bank of elevators. He got in one of them and pushed the button for the 12th floor. I managed to get in it before the door closed and pushed "12", too. That got his attention. He turned and stared at me. Glared at me would be more accurate.

"You're a reporter," he said.

"We usually call ourselves journalists these days."

"From the TV station."

"Clare Carlson, Channel 10 News."

"I told you I didn't want to talk to you."

"Yeah, I know."

"Then why are you here?"

"To talk to you."

"You've been following me?"

"You might even call it stalking."

"Why?"

"Because you won't talk to me."

I could have dazzled him with word play like that a while longer except the elevator doors opened. We were on 12. Where I presumed he had an office. He got out of the elevator now. So did I. This was the key moment when my plan was either going to work or not.

"I can call security and have them escort you out of the building," Hollister said to me.

"You could do that."

"You don't think I will?"

"I'm hoping you won't. For your sake."

"What do you mean?"

"You're in some trouble here, Charles. I can help you get out of it."

Now I didn't know that Charles Blaine Hollister was in any kind of trouble at all. I was taking a wild stab in the dark. But the stunned look on his face told me I'd touched a nerve. Maybe he was involved in this deeper than anyone realized.

"I know about the fight you had with your father, Charles," I said, blurting out the first thing that came to my mind.

I fully expected him to say "what fight?" But he didn't.

"How did you find out about that?" he asked.

Holy crap.

I was making this up as I went along.

But there apparently had been a fight.

"It's not what you think happened," he said.

"Why don't you tell me what did happen then between you and your father?"

"On camera?"

"You need to get your story out there, Charles."

* * *

And that's what he did. I called in a Channel 10 video crew, and we shot it right there in his office. He talked about growing up as the son of Charles Hollister. About struggling to find a place in his father's business empire. About the marriage to Laurie Bateman and how his father had written him out of the will for a major chunk of his estate. And about what a cruel and evil man his father could be.

The afternoon before Charles Hollister died, he had gone to his father's office to confront him about everything, Charles said. Yes, they had argued, he admitted. About his role in the company. About his father's will. And, most of all, about his wife, Laurie Bateman. But Hollister said his father was fine the last time he talked to him that day. He adamantly denied that he had any role in the death later. He pointed to Laurie Bateman as the killer, describing her as a "black widow" who would do anything to get her hands on the Hollister fortune, even if it meant murder.

Did he have any sympathy for her now sitting in a cell on Rikers Island?

"I hope the bitch rots in jail," he said angrily.

That was the money quote of the interview, as we used to call it when I worked for newspapers.

The killer sound byte now that I was in TV news.

It would be quoted on every other TV station and newspaper and website in town after we aired it.

I'd lied to Charles Blaine Hollister though.

I'd said I'd help him by putting his story on the air.

But what it did was make him look even more vindictive, greedy, and a candidate for the murder of his father.

Now all I needed was an interview with Laurie Bateman herself.

I wanted everyone to hear her side of this story—and I wanted them to hear it on Channel 10 News.

CHAPTER 20

DONNA GRIECO, THE defense attorney for Laurie Bateman, had handled a number of high-profile cases over the years.

The most famous was a well-known TV star accused of rape who was acquitted after Grieco shredded the woman victim's story and reputation on the stand. Then there was the case of a teenaged girl who confessed to murdering both of her parents during an argument over a video game—but never went to jail because of an insanity defense from Grieco.

All this—along with plenty of other seemingly unwinnable cases where she unexpectedly came out on top—had given her a reputation as a kind of miracle worker in the courtroom. She seemed like the perfect choice for the kind of Hail Mary defense that Laurie Bateman needed right now.

Janet had arranged an appointment for me to meet with Donna Grieco in her office.

Grieco wasn't all that impressive at first glance. She was a small woman, not physically imposing at all as I expected she might be. Plain-looking, with almost no makeup, seemed to be about sixty—although she could have been younger. She had curly brown hair that wasn't combed well, and she was wearing a plain navy-blue pants suit that was wrinkled and out of fashion. Donna Grieco clearly didn't put a lot of effort into her appearance.

I suddenly had an image in my head of a rumpled Peter Falk as Columbo, and I wondered if Grieco had deliberately adopted the same approach. Make people think you're no real threat to them, then go for their jugular when they least expect it. I decided pretty quickly I was right about that after we started talking.

"What media outlet are you with again?" she asked me, even though I was pretty sure she already knew. She had to be aware of all the Laurie Bateman stories I'd put on air in recent days. Plus, Janet had talked with her about me. But I think Grieco was feeling me out, trying to decide whether or not I could help her or not.

"Channel 10 News."

"And what do you do there?"

"I'm the news director."

"Why is the news director out covering a story on her own?"

"I have a personal interest in the Laurie Bateman story."

"Why is that?"

"I was supposed to interview her on the day she got arrested. I still want to get that interview. And I'm not as sure as the rest of the world that she's guilty."

Grieco smiled now. "Then I guess we're on the same side, Ms. Carlson."

"I'm not on anyone's side. I'm a journalist, and I have to be objective. But I've found that a lot of the facts in this story don't add up for me. That's why I'm looking for more answers about what happened to Charles Hollister. I'm hoping that Laurie Bateman can give me those if I talk to her in jail. Can you tell me any more about your defense for her?"

She went through a lot of the things I'd already uncovered, but added more new details.

First, there was the ex-husband of Melissa Hunt, Wayne Kanieski. She'd learned he had a prior record for aggravated assault and battery. "Kanieski badly beat up a guy he caught with Melissa a few years ago—might have even killed him if someone hadn't stopped it in time. We know he was insanely jealous of Hollister for taking Melissa away from him. It's not a huge leap of logic to assume he could have done the same thing to Hollister as he did with the other guy, only this time he killed Hollister. I plan to sub-poena Kanieski, put him on the stand, and see what happens. I think he's an angry, violent man. I want the jury to see that."

Then there was Max Gunther, the businessman who had lost out on a big money deal because of what he claimed were dirty tricks by Hollister. "Did you know Gunther publicly threatened Hollister?" Grieco asked. "Said he wanted to kill him in front of a whole bunch of witnesses. I want the jury to hear about that, too."

She also seemed particularly interested in Hollister's son, Charles. Much as I was. She talked about his troubled history, including the hit-and-run where he killed a person but his father got him off, and also about the things I'd broadcast recently that were potentially damaging and incriminating for the younger Hollister.

"Laurie couldn't stand the kid, thought he was a screwed-up and potentially violent person," Grieco told me. "I mean you saw that performance he put on at the funeral. And then again in the interview with you. Everyone knows he was furious at the last ex-isting Hollister will that put her in power of all the Hollister busi-ness, instead of him. Well, that's a motive for murder if I ever heard one. Oh, yes . . . Charles Hollister Jr. is going to be a big part of our defense. I think I can raise a lot of questions in people's minds about the kid."

But Grieco's biggest surprise came when we started going through the logistics of how and when I'd meet Bateman in jail to do the interview.

"We're also going to reveal that Laurie Bateman was a victim of horrific abuse at the hands of Charles Hollister during their marriage."

"Emotional abuse?"

"Physical, too."

"Hollister was an old man. I have trouble imagining he was even able to have sex with her, much less beat her up."

"Well, he did. He was in good physical condition, worked out every day, and even took karate lessons. Believe me, there was a lot of physical abuse she suffered constantly from him. She kept quiet about it for a long time, protecting the happy couple image they always put on for the media and the public. But she wants to tell the world about it all now. That's where you come in . . ."

I thought about everything Donna Grieco had told me.

"Let me see if I've got this straight," I said. "Your defense is going to be that she didn't kill her husband, and that a lot of other people could be suspects for murdering Hollister. But, even if she did kill him, she had a good reason: self-defense after years of abuse by Hollister. There's a lot of stuff in that defense."

"All I need is one of them to work with the jury."

"And she's going to talk about all this—talk about abuse by Hollister—in the interview with me?"

"She wants to tell the true story about everything."

CHAPTER 21

THERE WAS A car waiting for me when I left Donna Grieco's office and went back outside. Sitting on the street in front of her building. I recognized it. The blue car I'd seen earlier that I thought might be following me before. Except this time, it was doing more than following. The driver got out of the car and walked over to me. He was a good-looking guy with a stubble beard who reminded me a bit of a scruffy Brad Pitt.

"Clare Carlson?" he said.

"That depends?"

"On what?"

"Who you are."

He reached into his pocket and showed me a badge and ID. It said: "Nick Pollock, Treasury Agent." There was a picture of Nick Pollock, Treasury Agent on the ID. He was minus the stubble in the picture. But it definitely was him.

"Treasury Department?" I said. "Did I not pay my taxes or something?"

"I'd like to ask you a few questions, if that's all right with you."

"What kind of questions?"

"We're investigating the death of Charles Hollister."

"Hey, I know you're not gonna believe this. But that's what I'm doing too. What a coincidence, huh?"

He smiled. It was a nice smile.

"Maybe we could exchange information with each other," he said.

"Maybe."

"So let's talk about it a bit."

*   *   *

A short time later, we were sitting in a room at the Federal Building in Foley Square. Pollock had made it clear to me in his car on the way down that my appearance was voluntary. He said he was only hoping he could ask me a few questions that might help him in what the Treasury Department was working on. I was hoping he could help me by giving me information about why the Treasury Department might be interested in the death of Charles Hollister. We hadn't said much on the ride downtown, feeling each other out, I guess, on what we were going to do during the conversation.

Now that we were at the Treasury Department offices, it was time to find out.

"Okay, tell me why you Treasury people are interested in Charles Hollister," I blurted out to Pollock as soon as we sat down.

"If I tell you what I know about Hollister, you'll tell me what you're doing—and what you've found out—about him?"

"The exchange of information is vital in a free democracy," I said.

He smiled again. I sure liked that smile. But I remembered I was here on business.

"Anything I tell you here has to be off the record. Is that acceptable?"

"I can live with off the record."

"I have your word on that, right?"

"Cross my heart and hope to die."

I made an exaggerated gesture of crossing my heart to show him I meant it.

He smiled.

Again.

Yep, I could get used to that smile. But then I've always been a Brad Pitt fan.

"I can't give you a lot of detail," Pollock said. "But we have concerns that millions of dollars have gone unaccounted for in Hollister's businesses. Pension funds that were supposed to be going to workers. Money that he should have been paying taxes on. We aren't sure where the money went. But we believe it might have been moved to secret accounts. We're still in the preliminary stages—that is, we hadn't reached any real conclusions—but we notified Hollister about the investigation. We planned to question him soon. But then he was killed. Before we could talk to him again."

I remembered now hearing about an SEC or Treasury Department. investigation into Hollister's finances from the briefing Maggie had given me.

"Do you think his death had anything to do with your investigation?"

"On the face of it, since his wife has been charged with murder, there doesn't seem to be any connection between that and the missing millions we're trying to locate. But in a case like this you always . . ."

"Follow the money," I said.

"Follow the money," he repeated.

"Just like Woodward and Bernstein did as journalists in Watergate."

"It works in my business too. Look, we have no reason to believe that's the reason Hollister died. Especially since his wife is the one in jail for the murder. But we need to connect all the dots here to make sure. We've already talked to a lot of the same people you've talked to. That's why we started watching you too. And watching what you've said on the air about this. You went to Hollister's mistress. The private investigator he used—and that his wife then hired to spy on him. To Bert Stovall, the Hollister CEO. The Hollister kids. Now Bateman's defense attorney. Everyone thinks it was Laurie Bateman who killed him. Out of jealousy and/or because she feared getting cut out of his estate in a divorce. So what are you looking for?"

"I don't think Laurie Bateman did it."

"What kind of evidence have you come up with to support your conclusion that Laurie Bateman is innocent?"

"Uh, I'm a little short on actual evidence at the moment."

"Then why are you so sure she didn't kill him?"

"My news instincts."

"And your news instincts always turn out to be right?"

"Not always, but I've had my moments."

"So I've heard."

It turned out he knew all about me. Which wasn't that surprising. I'd been in the news recently with a couple of big stories—plus the revelation about my daughter that had turned me into a media star.

But it was clear he'd also done his own homework before meeting me.

We talked about that for a while—and then got back to Charles Hollister.

"Okay, let me see if I've got this all now," I said. "Hollister had a mistress who could have been jealous of his wife. The mistress had an ex-husband who was jealous of her relationship with Hollister. His son was upset that Laurie Bateman was still the primary beneficiary in his will at the time of his death. Hollister had a business rival who had vowed revenge against him for what he thought were dirty business tactics. You can throw a private investigator into the mix too; we don't know what he knew or found out or did in dealing with Hollister and his wife. And now I find out that Hollister and his company were under investigation for millions of dollars in missing money. That sure leaves us with a lot of different scenarios for what could have happened to Charles Hollister."

"What do you make of it all?" Pollock asked.

"Oh, what a tangled web we weave," I said.

CHAPTER 22

THE NEXT DAY, I went to see William Carstairs at the District Attorney's office to try to find out more about the case the DA was building against Laurie Bateman. I didn't want to see Carstairs again. But I knew I had no choice. I had to sublimate my personal feelings for my professional obligations. No matter how much this jerk Carstairs pissed me off every time I talked to him.

The Manhattan DA's office is located at 1 Hogan Plaza, which is downtown—a few blocks from City Hall. The front part of the building, which is on Centre Street, is the Criminal Courts section. It's run-down and dismal. If you go in the building that way, you run into an army of drug pushers, prostitutes, pimps, and other lowlifes waiting for their court appearances. The Hogan Plaza entrance in the back is a lot more civilized. It's used mainly by the DA's people and law enforcement officials and the like. I went in the back.

I'd spent a lot of time in this building over the years. First, when I was a reporter covering crime and court cases for a newspaper. Then, more recently, when I was involved in a big story with the then-DA, a woman named Teri Hartwell. That wound up with a lot of indictments, including her own top aide for taking bribes. Hartwell and the aide were both gone now, and Carstairs seemed to be the rising star in the department. The retired judge who was district attorney now was clearly just a caretaker, and everyone figured Carstairs would be a candidate for the job one day soon.

When I got to his office, the secretary was one I hadn't seen before. She was a pretty blond, wearing an outfit consisting of a short skirt and a low-cut top that didn't leave a whole lot to the imagination. She didn't look happy though. I wondered if Bill Carstairs was screwing her. He liked to screw everyone.

"I'm here to see William Carstairs," I said to her.

"Do you have an appointment?"

"No."

"Does Mr. Carstairs know you?"

"Oh, yes."

"Uh, how does he know you?"

"In the Biblical sense."

"Excuse me?"

"I used to date him."

"So, in other words, you have a personal relationship with Mr. Carstairs?"

"In ways you can only imagine."

She smiled, but not like she thought it was funny. More like it was what she expected from Bill Carstairs.

"Just tell him Clare Carlson from Channel 10 is here to see him."

A few minutes later, I was sitting with Bill Carstairs in his office. It was a corner office and had a nice view of the downtown courthouses and business buildings around them. Much nicer than the office he had when I was going out with him. Yep, this was a guy definitely on the way up. And I knew that he figured the Laurie Bateman prosecution was going to be the next big step in his rise to the top.

"Did you come to see me about that drink, Clare?"

"I came to ask you about the Laurie Bateman case."

"Happy to tell you everything I know about it."

"Good."

"But, like I said the other day, you have to promise me you'll go out for drinks with me."

"Will your secretary outside be coming along with us?"

"Why would my secretary be there?"

"Because I expect we have so much in common. Like you, for instance."

He smiled.

"Is that a yes or no?"

I sighed. I didn't want to go out for drinks with Bill Carstairs. But I'll do almost anything for a story. Even this.

"Maybe," I said.

"C'mon, Clare, we're only talking about a lousy drink here."

"Okay, one drink. But only if you tell me everything you know right now."

"No, not just a drink. An evening of drinks. And I mean real drinks. I don't want you sitting there sipping a ginger ale for thirty seconds and running out on me."

"I promise I'll get totally bombed, jump up on a barstool, and start singing 'Danny Boy.' Now what do you know about the Laurie Bateman story?"

Carstairs leaned forward, looked around in an exaggerated gesture as if to make sure no one was listening, and then said in a conspiratorial-like low voice: "Laurie Bateman murdered her husband . . . end of story!"

Then he began to laugh uproariously.

I told him that I wasn't as convinced as everyone else that Laurie Bateman did it. I pointed out that Charles Hollister had a mistress at the time of his death who might have been angry for him not spending enough time—or money—with her. And that she had an ex-husband who was jealous of that relationship. That Hollister had made a number of enemies in the business world with his cutthroat methods of deal-making. Then there was also his troubled son who was angry at Laurie Bateman for cutting him out of a big chunk of the family fortune. Having Laurie Bateman convicted and sent to jail for his murder would be awfully convenient for him in the estate battle.

"Do you have any actual evidence implicating any of these people as suspects?" Carstairs asked when I was finished.

"Evidence?"

"Yes, that's what we call it in the justice system—facts instead of just speculation?"

"I'm still working on that."

"Right. You have nothing. And so you come here and throw out all these names like an old Perry Mason show in hopes of diverting suspicion away from the obvious suspect who's on trial. Do you think that by just asking a few questions out there you're going to find out more than a team of trained investigators working on a case from this office?"

"I have before," I pointed out.

"Except you had facts before. You had . . ."

"Evidence," I said.

"That's right."

He leaned back in his chair now and looked triumphantly over at me. Gloating about it. I wanted to say something clever back to him, but I couldn't think of anything.

"Me, I've got plenty of evidence," Carstairs said. "Bateman's gun was used to shoot him. She'd just found out from a private investigator that he was cheating on her with another woman. He was about to change his will and leave her nothing. Also, there was a divorce in the works with a very limited prenup settlement for her if he lived. That's a lot of motive and a lot of evidence. Oh, and one more thing . . . the maid, Carmen Ortega, will testify that Laurie Bateman was the only other person there when she arrived and found Hollister murdered on the floor, with the pieces of the broken lamp used to hit him lying all around the body. And that Bateman was attempting to flee the crime scene until the maid called the police. Pretty convincing evidence, huh?"

I had no comeback for him on that either.

* * *

Later, he walked me out of his office, past the blond secretary's desk. She still looked sullen. I felt sullen too. Maybe being around Bill Carstairs did that to you.

"Don't be a stranger, Clare," he was saying. "It's good seeing you again. And don't forget about those drinks you promised to have with me one night soon."

"Will the evening be BYOH?" I asked.

"Huh?"

"Bring your own handcuffs?"

I thought I heard the secretary snickering behind me, but I wasn't sure.

Carstairs just ignored it though and said: "If you find out anything else about Charles Hollister and Laurie Bateman, please come and tell me. I'm always happy to work with the media."

"You'll be the first person I tell, Billy boy."

Then Bill Carstairs walked back into his office.

"Isn't he the biggest asshole you ever met?" I said to the secretary after he was gone.

She was studying her nails. "No comment," she said.

I headed for the door. When I got there, I turned around and saw the secretary smiling—really smiling—for the first time. She gave me a "thumbs-up" sign as I left.

I took that as a yes.

CHAPTER 23

WHEN I GOT back to the office, I found a message that Linda had called me. It always took me a second or two to realize who Linda was. My daughter. I mean I knew her name now was Linda, but I couldn't stop thinking of her as Lucy. The little girl I'd given up for adoption when she was born, who went on to become Lucy Devlin—the most famous missing child ever—until I discovered her again as Linda. Linda Nesbitt.

I was glad to hear from her now. I'd been meaning to call her to tell her the exciting news about my job offer that could make me a national TV star. I wasn't sure how a move to Los Angeles would affect us—since it would put me even farther away from her and my granddaughter, Audrey. But I figured we could talk about it. It was nice having a daughter I could talk with about things like this.

I called her back and she answered on the first ring. Like she was waiting for my call. That should have given me the first tip-off, I guess, that she had something important to discuss with me. But I was too wrapped up in my own big job offer to notice.

"I have news to tell you," I said excitedly.

"I have news for you, too."

"Let me go first because this news is really good."

"My news is not good," she said.

"What happened?" I asked anxiously. "Are you okay? Is Audrey . . ."

"We're fine."

"Well, then, what's the news that isn't good?"

"Let me tell you the whole story."

She said she had recently signed up for one of those genealogy sites where you sent in a sample of your DNA—and they gave you all sorts of information about your family history. She said she had gotten curious after finding out that I was her biological mother. She wanted to find out more about her background. My parents and grandparents, etcetera—and the ones on the side of her biological father, the man I'd had sex with in college that had resulted in her pregnancy. She thought it would be fun to find out more information. But the results she got back weren't fun at all, she told me. They were very serious.

Now she might be my daughter, but she sure didn't know how to put the lead in the first paragraph of a story, as we used to say when I worked at a newspaper.

I kept waiting until she finally got to the real news.

The results of the DNA test.

"The DNA test showed I have something called BRCA1. It's a heredity gene that can result in breast cancer—or cancer in the ovaries—as a person grows older. Only about one in five hundred people have this gene. But, if you do have it, there's a fifty-fifty chance you pass it on to your offspring. In my case, it dramatically increases the chance of me developing breast cancer as I get into my thirties and forties."

"Are you all right now?" I asked anxiously.

"I'm fine. I went to a doctor who confirmed the results this morning. That's why I'm calling you. There's no indication of cancer at the moment. But I have to realize I'm in a high-risk category—and maintain surveillance on this as I get older. I'm twenty-nine right now, so I'll move into the real danger range in a few years."

"And Audrey? You said it was a heredity gene? Does this affect her? Does she have the gene, too?"

"No one knows for sure. She's too young to be tested for it at the moment. But, like I said, there's a fifty-fifty chance that it was passed on to her. She'll need to be tested when she gets older."

I squeezed hard on the phone, trying to absorb everything she was telling me.

It was all pretty much of a shock.

But not as much of a shock as what came next.

Because I was the one who had missed the real lead of this story.

"We need to talk about you now," my daughter said.

"What about me?"

"The gene is passed down from your parents. I have it. I may have passed it down to Audrey. But that means I got the gene from my parents. I either got it from you—or from my biological father. Whoever he was."

We had never talked much about Doug Crowell, the man I had sex with the night she was conceived. He never knew he was the father of a child, because I left college right afterward without telling him. I found out many years later that he had died in a traffic accident. But Doug Crowell didn't seem important to me. Now suddenly he was.

"Men can carry the gene too," she said. "And they can pass it on to their children. Because I have it, that means it was my parents—either him or you—who carried the BRCA1 gene and passed it on to me. So you need to get tested. Remember what I told you about the risk factor increasing as you get older? It gets worse in the thirties—but a woman in her forties or fifties has the greatest chance of it developing into breast or even ovarian cancer. That's you. So please get this checked out with a doctor right away."

"I had a complete physical earlier this year. They give it to us as part of one of the health plans we have here at work."

"That's not good enough. The BRCA1 gene doesn't show up in routine blood tests. You need to take a specific test for it if you think you might be at risk. That's what I did. And you should do the same thing."

All I could think of was that I didn't have time for this. I didn't have time to go to a doctor and deal with a blood test or whatever else was involved. Suddenly having a daughter—and having to deal with the problems that went with it—didn't seem like such a good thing anymore.

"There's something else," my daughter told me. "If it turns out you don't have the BRCA1 gene, then it means that it came from my father. If he had any other children after me, we have a responsibility to notify them about this. And what about your own parents? I know they're both dead now. But do you know anything about their medical history? Can you find out if they might have had this gene? I want to know about my family—I want to know everything. For better or worse, I want to find out. Don't you?"

I mumbled a response, but I'm not sure what it was.

I kept thinking about that long-ago night when I got drunk and jumped into bed at a fraternity party with a good-looking guy who I would never see again.

I'd thought it was just a one-night stand.

But I'd paid a hefty price for that irresponsible moment a long time ago when I was very young.

A price that has haunted me for my entire life.

And a price that I was still paying . . .

CHAPTER 24

THAT NIGHT I had a lot of trouble falling asleep. I lay in bed for a long time thinking about the conversation I'd had with my daughter.

About the potentially deadly gene she—and maybe Audrey too—were now carrying.

About the questions she had concerning her biological father, who might have put people at risk too.

And especially the part she'd brought up about my own mother and father.

"I want to know more about my family," she had said. "I want to know everything. For better or worse."

Well, good luck with that.

Me, I already knew too much about my own damn family.

I hadn't thought about my mother and father for a long time because . . . well, it wasn't a pleasant memory.

I got out of bed, poured myself a soft drink in the kitchen, and turned on the TV. There was a situation comedy on one of the channels. I tried to watch it for five minutes or so, but the words didn't mean anything to me. There was a good-guy father, a smart, attractive wife, and a couple of wisecracking kids. Seemed like a decent enough family. But then so did the Huxtable family when

I was growing up in the eighties. And look how things turned out for Bill Cosby.

I switched off the TV and walked into the study area I have in my apartment. There's a desk, a computer, bookshelves, and a filing cabinet. In the bottom drawer of the filing cabinet was a large brown manila envelope. I'd stuffed it underneath a lot of other stuff and hadn't looked inside for a long time. But I fished the envelope out now.

There were maybe twenty-five or thirty snapshots there. They weren't mounted or anything. No one in my family had ever gotten around to doing that. Many of them were a bit worse for wear—curled up at the corners and bent in a couple of places— because of the years that had gone by since they were taken.

But you could see them well enough—that is, if you wanted to.

There was a little girl in all of the pictures. That would be me. Then my mother and father. They looked young and vibrant and attractive in those days—the way people look when they still believe that the future holds good things ahead for them.

A few of the pictures show me as a baby growing up inside the house where we lived. In others I'm a little older and playing in the backyard. Then there's all of us at a summer vacation cottage on a lake. I was nine years old then. My favorite picture shows me standing between my father and mother next to a sailboat on the shore of the lake. God, I still remembered that day. In the picture, my mom and dad were looking at my Uncle Mike—who was taking it with his camera—but not me. I was looking up at my father. It was the look of a little girl who thinks that her father is the greatest person in the world. A lot of little girls think that. But then they grow up.

For me, the growing up culminated when I came home from college and told my parents that I was pregnant. "Hi, Mom and

Dad, here I am back from college. I got drunk and wound up having a one-night stand with this good-looking fraternity guy named Doug Crowell. Jeez, it all happened so fast that I barely remember it now. But guess what? I'm pregnant."

Okay, the conversation between me and my parents didn't go exactly like that, but it was just as bad. My father ordered me to have an abortion. Most young women in that situation would have done that, and I might have too. Except the more he yelled and screamed at me to have the abortion, the more I resisted. Looking back on it now, I suppose that was the reason I did not have an abortion. Because my father wanted me to so badly.

I had the baby, gave her away for adoption at birth, and she grew up to be Lucy Devlin first, then Linda Nesbitt—which is how I got to where I am today.

My father died without us ever repairing the rift between us over that incident. My relationship with my mother was a bit better, but still never what it was before because she always supported my father in whatever he said and did. I never was able to totally forgive her for her lack of support when I needed it, just like I was never able to forgive my father for his demands. Now they're both gone, taking with them whatever secrets they might have had that could be a life-and-death medical clue for me, my daughter, and my granddaughter. Did they pass on the potentially deadly cancer gene to me, and did I then give it to my own daughter—and possibly my granddaughter?

The guy in the fraternity house, Doug Crowell, was never a part of any of this drama for me. To him, I was nothing more than another roll in the sack with a naive young coed.

There was a picture of Crowell in the envelope too. A couple of pictures. I'd found them online from a college yearbook and printed them out a few years back. One of the pictures showed him goofing around in front of the fraternity house in a sweat-shirt and shorts. The other one was of him in his ROTC uniform. He looked very handsome, very sexy—and I could see why a nineteen-year-old me had jumped into bed with him.

He went into the Air Force after college, then became a commercial pilot. He survived all that, but died in a senseless car accident several years back. Yep, I looked that up online about him. Not sure why. I guess I was just curious.

I put the pictures inside the envelope again and stuck it back in the filing cabinet where I'd found it. Every time I did this, I told myself I should throw the damn things away. Get rid of the memories. Make a clean break with the past. But I'd never done that. Not yet.

And now I had to go back in time and search for answers amid these memories. About my parents. And about Doug Crowell. To find out if any of them carried the deadly gene that threatened my family today. I'd found out from the obituary I'd looked up on Doug Crowell that he had been married and had a son and two daughters. My parents still had relatives too. I needed to find these people and open up the past—theirs as well as mine—all over again.

My apartment is on the 11th floor of a building overlooking Union Square, which runs along 14th Street between Broadway and Fourth Avenue. I looked out the window next to my desk. Even though it was late, there were still people out there. Sitting on the steps on the edge of the park. Walking along the streets. Straggling out of the clubs and bars in the area.

I looked north and saw the Empire State Building and the skyscrapers of New York City. The lights twinkled brightly from them in the clear, crisp December sky. The city that never sleeps.

I thought about how much I loved the bigness of New York. A person can lose themselves in it.

I'd run a long way to get away from the memories of my past.

But not far enough.

The past always catches up with you.

CHAPTER 25

THE TOUGHEST THING—AND maybe the best—about running a TV news operation is that you never know what's going to happen.

I mean you spend all day figuring out what your top stories are going to be, the order you'll put them on the air, what the reporters and anchors will say about them—and then in a few seconds everything changes.

Because big news breaks.

The best-laid plans and all that . . .

Maggie burst into my office just as I was wrapping up my schedule for the 6:00 p.m. newscast.

"Carmen Ortega is dead," she yelled.

"Who?"

It took me a second or two to recognize the name.

"Carmen Ortega," Maggie said. "The maid for the Hollisters."

"The one who found Charles Hollister's body?"

"With Laurie Bateman there."

Damn.

Carmen Ortega had been a part of the story from the beginning, but a small part. I'd never paid much attention to her. She'd showed up for work that morning, seen the dead Charles Hollister on the floor with his wife trying to leave the apartment—and called the police. End of story. There didn't seem to be much more to say about Carmen Ortega than that. The other players in this story had been much more interesting to me. Hell, I hadn't even included her on my list of people to talk to about the case.

But everything was different now.

Now I had a million questions about Carmen Ortega.

"How did she die?" I asked Maggie.

"She was hit by a subway train."

"Accident?"

"At the moment. That's what the authorities are saying. But the timing is pretty incredible. Key prosecution witness dies before she can testify in court against Laurie Bateman. That's a big story."

*   *   *

The details went like this. Carmen Ortega had been waiting for a subway at Grand Central Station. She was standing on the platform when a #7 train rolled in, the one that took her to her home in Woodside, Queens. The platform was crowded, and there was a lot of pushing and shoving from people trying to get into position to get aboard the already crowded train. No one was sure exactly what happened next. But suddenly there were screams, and witnesses saw that a woman—Carmen Ortega—was lying on the tracks. It was too late for the driver to stop, and the train hit and killed her.

It's not uncommon for people to be hit by subway trains. The platforms are close to the tracks and they can be dangerous—especially with big crowds. It is normally a news story when someone dies like that, but not necessarily a big news story. Except this time, it was different. Because of who the victim was and the fact that she was about to be a witness in a high-profile murder case.

At a hastily called press conference after Carmen Ortega's death, the police commissioner—flanked by transit police officials as well as a stunned-looking William Carstairs from the DA's office—faced the media.

"We are pursuing three different possibilities in our investigation," the police commissioner said. "1) Carmen Ortega's death was accidental—she either fainted, was inadvertently pushed by the crowd, or fell onto the tracks accidentally for another reason; 2) she committed suicide by jumping in front of a subway train; or 3) someone deliberately pushed her onto the tracks to kill her. At the moment, we are leaning toward 'accidental death' as being the most likely scenario. But our investigation is continuing. So if you were on that subway platform and saw or heard anything, please contact the police immediately."

Carstairs spoke to the press next and he tried to put the best face on the shocking news of his star witness's death. He said that they still had a strong case against Laurie Bateman; that they did have Carmen Ortega's account of what happened that morning on video; and that he believed they still had overwhelming evidence—even without Carmen Ortega's courtroom testimony—to get a conviction of first-degree murder.

But there was no question that his case against Laurie Bateman had suffered a significant blow with the death of the Hollister maid who claimed she'd confronted Bateman running out of the apartment with her dead husband's body inside.

I did the story myself on air.

I'd decided I wanted to report everything about this case myself.

That's the way I am on a big story—I make the story my own, even if I am supposed to be the news director.

Jack Faron wasn't happy with me reporting this story myself—he rarely is when I do it. When I told him my plan to continue reporting about Laurie Bateman until the story was over, one way or another, he asked me if it wouldn't be better for me to hand the story off to one of the other reporters. I said no. He asked me if there was any way he could get me to change my mind. "Have we met?" I asked Faron. He gave up after that.

We followed up the original report with a dramatic interview with Ortega's family. I did assign a reporter to do that. Ortega had a husband and three children—between the ages of seven to fourteen—who lived in Woodside. The husband cried on camera when he talked about how he had kissed her goodbye that morning just like any other day. The three children were crying, too.

The husband also talked about the day his wife found Laurie Bateman with Charles Hollister's body. He said she'd gone to work at the Hollister apartment an hour early that morning—she didn't usually start until ten a.m.—but she wanted to leave early to help celebrate one of their children's birthdays. He said sadly that someone else might have discovered the Hollister crime scene if she'd gotten there later at ten. And then she wouldn't have become a key person in the murder investigation. He said he didn't know if that had anything to do with her death now, but he couldn't help wondering if she might be alive today if that hadn't happened. It all seemed so senseless, he sobbed.

Yes, it was all very sad.

But it was also great television news.

CHAPTER 26

A GROUP OF us from Channel 10 were sitting in a bar next to the station after the 6:00 p.m. newscast was wrapped up. Maggie, Brett, Dani, Wendy Jeffers, Steve Stratton, and other on-air reporters and production staff. We were telling stories about how crazy the TV news business is, inspired, I guess, by the latest announcement from Jack Faron about another consultant being hired.

I said that one of my favorite TV news stories ever was the one told by Linda Ellerbee in her book *And So It Goes*.

"They tell a woman news reporter at this station that they want her to cover cooking stories," I said. "Not as fluff, the producer tells her. But they had come up with the concept of 'hard news' cooking stories—food as news. Did she understand? She said that she did.

"'If a 707 crashes this afternoon, you want me to take a video crew to the pilot's house, and when his wife comes to the door, you want me to ask her what she would have cooked him for dinner if he was coming home. Is that right?'"

Everyone around the table laughed. Maggie talked about another book on TV news—*Too Old, Too Ugly, and Not Deferential to Men*, by Christine Craft, a TV reporter in Kansas City.

"This consultant shows her a tape of women anchors from around the country to show her the way she should look and act on the air. They're all interchangeable—almost identical in appearance, same hair, same clothes, same way they all talk. Finally, there's a woman who appears on the tape that seems different, Craft says. She's insightful, streetwise, spunky. 'Oh no,' the consultant says, 'I don't want you to see her—she's too assertive.'"

It was fun to be out of the office with Maggie; she was always so serious at work. Nice to socialize with Brett and Dani too. They sat there holding hands and seemingly having a good time, even though most of the rest of us were drinking. Dani wasn't drinking, of course, because she was pregnant—and Brett said he didn't want to make her feel bad by drinking in front of her. But it was also because they still had to go back and do an 11:00 p.m. newscast. I worked at a station once where the anchor was fine on the 6:00 p.m. newscast, but was wobbling and slurring his words a lot of nights by the 11:00 p.m. show. I couldn't even imagine what Brett and Dani might be like on the air after drinking. On the other hand, it might be a lot of fun.

Steve Stratton had worked at quite a few TV stations over the years. He'd seen a lot of consultants come and go. He remembered one of them who liked to write memos to the on-air people. One of the memos to a woman reporter said she needed a "new look"— something fashion wise that would make her stand out to the audience. So she went out and got a $300 perm at a fancy salon and bought a hat. A big white hat that made her look like a cowgirl or a female country singing star. She figured the hat would be her trademark—her new look.

"Except the first time she went on air with the hat, it was a windy day and the hat kept threatening to blow away. As she was doing a remote, she kept holding onto the hat at the same time she was talking into the microphone. At first with one hand. Then two. By the end of the appearance, she was pretty much holding onto the hat for dear life. The next time she came to work, she found a memo from the consultant to her. It said: 'Love the hair, lose the hat.'"

There was more laughter and a lot more stories. At one point, I asked Dani about her craziest newspaper moment. She said it had been at the *New York Post*. Dani had worked as a reporter at the *Post* before I hired her away for TV. I liked hanging out with newspaper people, the way I did when I worked for a paper in New York. Maybe that's why I liked Dani, despite all the problems she caused for me because of her volatile relationship with Brett.

"The *Post* was—and is, as you know—a pretty sensational publication. When I was there, all of us reporters would do anything for a story. So one day I get a tip that this married congressman is shacking up with his girlfriend at a Midtown hotel. I go to the room, knock on the door, and say I'm from the *New York Post*. I can hear a lot of frantic scurrying around behind the door.

"Finally, the politician opens the door and I say to him: 'Where's the girl?' He insists there's no one else in the room. I look over at the bed and see a pair of panties and a bra. I say: 'So whose are those?' He thinks about it for a second and then blurts out: 'They're mine.' I tell him: 'Congressman, the voters might forgive you for cheating on your wife. But there's going to be an awful lot of jokes if they think you're a transvestite. Are you sure you don't want to reconsider that answer?'

"The congressman mulls that over for a while, and finally he says to me: 'Well, maybe the maid left them.'"

I was going to miss all this—I was going to miss the people at Channel 10—if I wound up moving to Los Angeles for the big new talk show job.

Before we left, Maggie asked me about the Laurie Bateman story. I told her about my meeting with Donna Grieco and my hopes of getting an interview with Bateman herself soon. All the time I was doing this I kept thinking about how much I liked talking about stuff like the Laurie Bateman story. Because it kept my mind off all the other things going on in my life right now. I wondered if a young woman like Maggie had such worries on her mind.

"What do you want to do—what's your goal, Maggie?" I asked her now.

She looked at me strangely.

"I want to go home and get some sleep so I'll be wide awake at work in the morning."

"No, I mean what do you want to do with your life?"

"I work on that from day to day, Clare. My goal is to put out the best news show that I can every day. Then do it all over again the following day. Someone taught me how to do that. Taught me how to live for that day's news—then worry about the rest of it later. Someone I respect a great deal in this business. That was you, Clare."

Maggie was right. That was the rule I'd lived my life by and passed that on to others like her. But Maggie was still in her twenties. She had a lot of time yet to make decisions about her life. Me, I was running out of time.

I had decisions to make about my career—plus the decisions involving my family life with my daughter and granddaughter.

And I was going to have to make those decisions very soon.

My phone buzzed. I took it out and saw I'd just gotten a text message. From Donna Grieco. It said: "The interview with Laurie Bateman is on for ten a.m. tomorrow at Rikers Island. I'll be there waiting for you."

CHAPTER 27

GOING TO RIKERS Island prison was not something I looked forward to doing, even for a big exclusive with Laurie Bateman. I'd been to Rikers a few times in the past, to interview other prisoners when I was a newspaper reporter, and it was always a depressing experience.

First off, it took a long time to get there. Rikers Island, like the name implies, is located on an island in the East River. To get there, you have to go to Queens—then take a bus or drive across a bridge to reach the prison, which is technically in the Bronx. Then, when you get there, you find yourself in one of the biggest and most depressing prison complexes in the U.S. It houses more than ten thousand inmates, many of them awaiting trial on murder and other serious charges.

I was uncomfortable just walking into the visitor's area with a camera crew from the station.

So, I could only imagine what it must have been like for Laurie Bateman locked up in a jail cell in the place.

Donna Grieco was waiting for us there. I still wasn't convinced even now that Rikers officials would give us permission to shoot a television interview with a prisoner. It's been done before, but not often. Grieco assured me again that not only the warden—but also the city's corrections commissioner—had given her their personal confirmation we could do a TV interview with Bateman.

I guess Grieco was really good at her job. Or maybe the Rikers officials wanted to be transparent about the Bateman case, to put the right PR spin out on it—because Laurie Bateman was such a high-profile prisoner. Whatever it was, I was going to get my exclusive by putting Laurie Bateman on the air for Channel 10. That worked for me.

A correction guard led us to a conference room. There were no bars or glass partitions to talk through like you might expect. But a guard would be present during the entire interview, we were told. I said that was fine.

A few minutes later, another guard—a female one—led Laurie Bateman into the room to meet with us.

Except for that brief time outside her building when she was being arrested after her husband's death, I'd never seen Laurie Bateman in person. Just in movies and on TV and print commercials where she always looked beautiful, glamorous, stylish, and poised. She looked a lot different from that woman now. She was wearing an orange prison jumpsuit that didn't fit her. She had no makeup on, her hair was uncombed, and she looked scared.

When she came into the room, she ignored me at first and went directly over to talk to Grieco.

"Is there any news about my bail?" she asked anxiously.

"I'm working on it, Laurie . . ."

"You've got to get me out of here!"

"That's why I brought Ms. Carlson here to see you today."

"Will she help me?"

"She'll get your story out to the public."

"What am I supposed to say?"

"Just tell her the truth."

"All of it?"

"Everything."

Grieco introduced me to Laurie Bateman. When she got closer to me, I could see she looked tired with dark circles under her eyes. Her hand trembled slightly when she reached out to shake mine. Prison had already taken quite a toll on Laurie Bateman.

I asked Grieco if she wanted us to put makeup on Bateman or fix her hair or anything else before we put her in front of the camera. But Grieco shook her head no. I think she wanted viewers to see her like this, rather than the glamorous figure they'd known in the past. To make her seem more sympathetic in the public eye. It was a good strategy. I realized again how smart Grieco was. She played every angle.

Once the cameras were rolling, I hit her with the most obvious question first:

"Did you murder your husband, Laurie?" I asked.

"No, I did not murder Charles," she said, looking directly at the camera and seeming very believable. "I've never killed anyone. I couldn't kill anyone. This is all a horrible nightmare for me—being accused of my husband's murder and now locked up in this place. I just want it all to be over."

That was pretty much the answer I expected from her.

It was her follow-up to that question that was more shocking.

"But I wanted to kill Charles. I didn't do it, but I wanted to. There were many times I wanted that man to be dead. Because of all the terrible things he did to me."

I looked over at Grieco. She didn't say anything. I guess she knew this was coming. And I knew it was a perfect time to segue into the domestic abuse stuff she'd told me about in her office.

"What exactly are you referring to here?" I asked Bateman, even though I knew the answer.

"Abuse. He abused me."

"Emotional abuse?"

She nodded.

"Physical abuse, too."

"Charles Hollister was an old man," I pointed out.

"He was still in good physical shape. Good enough to beat up on me. He did plenty of that. Whenever he lost his temper, he used his fists on me. Never on the face though. He was careful about that. He always hit me on the body below my neck, so no one would ever see the bruises when we went out in public. I've kept quiet about it all this time, but not anymore. Now I want the world to know the truth. The true story of my marriage to Charles Hollister. I suffered all this time with him, and now I'm being blamed for his murder. It's not fair."

She kept talking about the abuse she'd suffered at his hands. At first, she went through the details of it all with calmness and determination to tell the story as she looked directly into the camera. But, as she continued, she became more and more emotional. By the end of the interview, she was crying on camera.

"I don't belong in here," she said, sobbing. "I didn't do anything wrong. I didn't kill Charles. I'm a victim here too . . ."

It was powerful stuff that was going to give us blockbuster ratings when it aired on Channel 10.

But that's not what I was thinking about at that moment.

I was thinking about what it must have been like living with Charles Hollister. Oh, I'd heard the stories about what a bad person he was from a lot of the people he did business with over the years. I knew he wasn't a nice man. But this was much worse than that. I couldn't even imagine what it must have been like to live with him—terrified that he would erupt in violent anger at any second.

I'd never experienced anything like that.

Not really.

I had a man I was in a relationship with hit me once. Only once. I stopped seeing him after that happened. He apologized profusely and vowed it would never happen again. Maybe he was telling the truth. But I knew I could never be with a man who did anything like that to me. Not all women in that position—battered women desperate for a way out—can just walk away. Mostly it's because they don't have the money to leave or nowhere to go or are afraid of being alone. Laurie Bateman certainly had the money to leave. But, like many women, she had made bad decisions about a man who had abused her. She'd stayed with him and continued to be abused until the end. And now she was being blamed for his murder. A murder she insisted she didn't commit.

I believed her. About the abuse. And about not killing him.

A journalist is supposed to be objective on a story, but I wasn't feeling very objective about Laurie Bateman at that moment.

I was going to help her.

I was going to help her get out of this horrible place.

And then I was going to help her prove she was innocent.

CHAPTER 28

IN ANOTHER TIME, another era—maybe even just a few years ago—things might have happened differently after Laurie Bateman made her allegations of emotional and physical abuse while married to Charles Hollister.

Oh, there probably would have been some sympathy expressed for her and outrage directed at the dead Charles Hollister—except it would have taken much longer to develop, and would not have become THE story of Hollister's murder the way it did.

But this was the age of #metoo and viral social posts that reach hundreds of thousands of people immediately and set in motion forces to change public opinion in a matter of hours—or even minutes.

By the time our newscast ended that night with the emotional interview I'd done with Laurie Bateman at Rikers Island, the station had started receiving texts, tweets, emails, and phone calls—most of them expressing compassion and sympathy and support for her. It was pretty amazing. Laurie Bateman had gone from a greedy murder suspect—a deadly gold-digger out to snare her husband's fortune—to a wronged woman.

She had become the victim.

Maybe even more than Charles Hollister who was the one who died.

Bateman still denied that she was the person who murdered Hollister, even if she felt she was in physical danger from him and would have been justified doing whatever it took to defend herself. But the public didn't seem to care whether she did it or not anymore. She was an abuse victim; they were on her side now, no matter what had happened.

Charles Hollister was a monster—just like Jeffrey Epstein, Harvey Weinstein, Bill Cosby, and the other men who had abused women like Laurie Bateman in the past—and there was no sympathy for him.

Only for his wife sitting now in a jail cell.

At the same time as all this, the prosecution's case against Laurie Bateman—which they, and everyone else, believed so airtight at the beginning—was beginning to show more cracks.

First, of course, there was the sudden death of the maid, Carmen Ortega, who said she'd arrived to find Bateman attempting to flee the apartment with her husband's dead body inside. That seemed to be pretty damning testimony. Except Bateman denied she was running away. She admitted she was in the apartment, but said she arrived there after her husband had been killed. She said she was in such total shock that she didn't remember exactly what she did next, only that she knew she had to get help. That's all she was doing when the maid saw her, she maintained—trying to get someone to help her. This was much vaguer than the maid's version that she was fleeing. The prosecution could still introduce the maid's recorded testimony, but that made it harder for the prosecution to back up the now dead Carmen Ortega's account.

Then it was also revealed that there were none of Laurie Bateman's fingerprints on the gun. No prints of any kind were there, it turned out. The prosecutor said she must have wiped them off, but there was no proof of that either.

Also, there were now a lot of other potential suspects out there as more information came out—from me and others—about Hollister's nasty business relationships, his affair with a married woman, and even his fight/argument with his own son on the day before he died. There were plenty of people who could have wanted Charles Hollister dead besides just his wife, Laurie Bateman.

At the same time, other women from Hollister's past began to come forward, making claims of abuse and inappropriate sexual actions by him. They said they had been afraid to say anything earlier because Hollister was so powerful and vindictive that they feared retaliation by him and his influential friends. But now they had been inspired by the courage of Laurie Bateman to tell their own story too. A few of these women were likely opportunists out to get free publicity or make a quick buck. But many of the stories sounded authentic. No question about it, Charles Hollister had a lot of skeletons in his closet.

All this attention put a new light on the people prosecuting Laurie Bateman—especially the lead prosecutor, my old pal, William—Wild Bill—Carstairs. Carstairs' own track record with women came under scrutiny, and it wasn't long before there were numerous allegations of his own inappropriate sexual activity in the workplace and elsewhere making the rounds. It became so intense that several media outlets actively demanded he recuse himself from the Bateman case.

"You screwed me, Carlson!" he screamed at me after that when he called me up to rage about how I'd done all this with my interview of Laurie Bateman.

"Probably not the best choice of words," I pointed out.

"You're destroying my career. Everything I've built up here. All the respect I've built up over the years—that's all gone because of you."

"Oh, I don't think all that many people respected you that much anyway, Billy," I said.

"Is this because I stopped going out with you?"

"Uh, I think I stopped going out with you."

"This is all about revenge, isn't it? You nasty little bitch!"

"Again, I don't think 'nasty little bitch' is acceptable language in these enlightened times of male/female relationships. So, as much fun as this conversation is, let's get down to business. Are you going to recuse yourself from the Laurie Bateman case like everyone is speculating?"

"No way! I'm not going to be bullied by you and a lot of radical zealots from doing my job. I'm staying on the case. I'm going to prosecute Laurie Bateman and put her away in jail for life. And nothing you—or anyone else—can do will change that."

Which wasn't true, of course.

I think even Carstairs knew that at this point, but he needed to put up this show of bravado for his own self-esteem.

Not long afterward, the District Attorney called a press conference to announce that William Carstairs had stepped away from the Bateman case to concentrate on other pressing—although unspecified—matters in the office. He introduced the new lead prosecutor—who just happened to be a woman.

Meanwhile, Donna Grieco held her own press conference to say that—based on all these new developments in the case—she planned to petition the court for a new hearing to seek bail for Laurie Bateman and also to demand anew that all the charges against Bateman be dropped.

*   *   *

"Well, you've certainly had a big week for yourself," Maggie said to me at the news meeting.

"I am the talk of the town," I admitted.

"Our ratings numbers—the big boost we got at Channel 10 News from your Laurie Bateman interview and all the other news you've broken about the story—are pretty impressive."

"Yep, the viewers love me."

"That must make Jack Faron happy," said Brett.

"My boss loves me."

"Our owner, Barry Kaiser, must be pretty happy about it all too," added Dani.

Not to mention West Coast Media, the media company looking to hire me away to make me a national star, I thought to myself. Mitchell Lansburg and West Coast Media must be damn happy with me. But I hadn't told anyone at Channel 10 about the new job offer yet. Not yet.

"Everybody loves me," I said.

We were discussing the Laurie Bateman story—and what might come next—following the dueling press conferences between the District Attorney's office and Donna Grieco.

A judge had just granted Grieco her request for a new bail hearing.

"Do you think Bateman is going to get out on bail because of all this?" someone at the news meeting asked.

"The word I hear in legal circles is yes," Maggie said. "And a lot of people think the charges against Laurie Bateman could even be dropped altogether."

The hearing was scheduled for the following day.

Even better, Grieco announced that she was going to call Laurie Bateman to the stand as a witness to testify on her own behalf.

"Bring your popcorn," I said as we discussed our plans for covering it all in court. "This is gonna be a helluva show."

CHAPTER 29

THE HEARING WAS a circus, right from the start. Crowds of people lined up outside the courthouse in downtown Manhattan hoping to get in to watch. Large groups of demonstrators—holding signs and chanting slogans demanding Laurie Bateman's release from jail—clogged the streets and blocked traffic. And, of course, media everywhere scrambling for video and pictures. Including me and a news crew from Channel 10.

Laurie Bateman was the star attraction. They brought her into the building in a van from Rikers Island—escorted by a lot of other police. You couldn't see into the van as it pulled in the courthouse. But the crowds knew she was in there and cheered loudly as the vehicle passed by them.

Laurie Bateman wasn't the only one the crowd was interested in.

I was the center of attraction too.

I'd just been on television doing the Laurie Bateman interview from jail—and many of the people recognized me as the person they believed responsible for getting this new hearing called on the case.

"Freedom for Laurie!" they shouted at the passing van.

"You go, girl!"

"Women power! We women fight back now against sexual predators like Charles Hollister."

And there was even one sign that said: "Let's put Billy Carstairs in a jail cell—not Laurie."

Inside the courtroom, things were just as crazy. The place was packed with spectators and press. I wasn't sure the judge would be able to get everyone under control in order to start the hearing, but he finally did after a long period of banging his gavel and admonishing everyone to quiet down.

The prosecutor who'd replaced Carstairs on the case was a tall, striking-looking African American woman named Karen Sanders. As a woman, she clearly presented a better image for the DA's office in a case like this rather than a man with a checkered sexual past himself like Carstairs. But Sanders was already in damage-control mode because of everything that had happened.

She did her best to run through the case against Laurie Bateman that had once seemed so airtight and strong. The maid seeing Bateman trying to flee from the apartment with her husband's dead body inside. The fact that her gun was used in the murder. That she had no alibi. And also that she had strong motives for killing him. Finding out from the private investigator that her husband was secretly carrying on an affair with his mistress, Melissa Hunt. And also that Charles Hollister had made it clear that he planned to change his will—and leave her only a small portion of his estate, the minimum required by the prenuptial agreement they had signed.

Based on all that, Sanders told the judge, Laurie Bateman should continue to be held without bail on a charge of first-degree murder.

Boos and catcalls filled the courtroom as she finished her presentation and sat down at the prosecutor's table. The judge had to warn everyone all over again that he would close the courtroom if these kinds of outbursts continued.

Donna Grieco then presented the case for Laurie Bateman. Grieco was definitely in killer mode now, going for the jugular. She expertly destroyed point by point much of the prosecutor's argument. Pointing out that Carmen Ortega the maid was no longer alive to testify in person—and there would be no opportunity for the defense to cross-examine her about what she saw or didn't see that day. Also, the fact that there were no fingerprints—Laurie Bateman's or anyone else's—found on the murder gun.

"Laurie Bateman was simply a woman who panicked when she found her husband dead on the floor," Grieco said. "Just like you or I might have panicked in that kind of stressful situation. She was not attempting to run away. She was only instinctively trying to get help from someone or somewhere as quickly as she could. Just like Carmen Ortega eventually did when she called the police. That is all that happened. Mrs. Ortega was simply mistaken in her original testimony."

Grieco then went through the long list of other potential suspects who might have wanted Charles Hollister dead. Business rivals, jealous men of women he'd seen—and possibly even a member of his own family, angry because of being left so little in his will. She specifically zeroed in on Charles Jr, detailing all his past violent acts and his anger over losing control of his father's company to Bateman in the current will.

She also brought forth a long line of character witnesses, who took the stand to testify that Laurie Bateman was a fine, upstanding, and law-abiding person who they couldn't believe would ever murder anyone. I didn't recognize all of them, but one was a surprise to me—Bert Stovall, the Hollister CEO and Charles Hollister's lifelong friend. Asked about Laurie Bateman, he responded: "Laurie Bateman is innocent of this. I am absolutely sure of that. She does not belong in jail." Others talked about the suffering—both physical and emotional—she had suffered at the hands of Charles Hollister.

Yep, it was a simple, yet effective strategy: My client didn't kill her husband. But, even if you think she did, she would have had a good reason—self-defense against a man who had been abusing her.

But the real highlight—definitely the most dramatic moment—came when Laurie Bateman herself was called to the stand to testify.

She looked different than the day I'd met with her on Rikers Island. For one thing, she wasn't wearing a prison jumpsuit. She was dressed in a stylish blue pants suit and high-heeled shoes. She'd been allowed to wear her own clothes for the court hearing. Her hair was combed now, and she had on makeup. Not enough to look glamourous like a celebrity, but, still, it made her look more like the Laurie Bateman we knew. I had no doubt that Grieco had spent a lot of time and preparation here to make sure she presented the right appearance for this date in court.

Under quiet questioning by Grieco, she told the same story she had earlier about the morning of the murder. How she had not stayed at their Fifth Avenue townhouse after the fight with her husband the previous night at the charity event. How she'd woken up in her Greenwich Village apartment the next morning, then went back to the townhouse because she was scheduled to meet me there. And how she still was not sure what had happened to her husband. She insisted over and over again that she had not killed him. She could never do that, she said. Even after the horrible things Charles had done to her.

Grieco asked her to talk more about the abuse she'd suffered during her marriage.

Bateman's entire demeanor changed then. She'd been calm and in control until that point. But now she became very emotional.

Her voice broke several times as she tried to talk—and tears formed in her eyes.

She told the same story she'd told me during our TV interview at Rikers—but this time with even more details.

"I was a victim of domestic abuse that went on for much of my marriage," she said. "I was embarrassed to tell anyone at the time, ashamed that I allowed myself to be put in such a position. For a long time, I blamed myself for what was happening. That I needed to be a better wife to Charles. I've since learned that this is a common theme for women who are in an abusive situation. And so I put up with it for a long time. Desperately trying to keep up the happy image Charles wanted for us in public as the perfect couple. But eventually, I was forced to confront the truth. My husband was abusing me, he was cheating on me, and everything about our marriage was a lie. I was living a nightmare with no way out."

She said the abuse against her was not violent at first, but more emotional. He tried to control what she wore, what she said, who she saw, and what she did in her life. Just like she was one of his employees. Charles Hollister, the tyrannical businessman, was just as demanding behind closed doors with her, she said.

"I'm not sure exactly when it turned physical," she said. "But I remember one day he slapped me. Slapped me hard enough to make a mark on my cheek. I thought it was just a onetime occurrence. But when he did it again the next time, we had an argument. Soon he started punching me, knocking me down, kicking me. Once he picked me up bodily and smashed me into a wall, knocking me unconscious.

"Charles was in extremely good shape for his age; he worked out every day—lifting weights and other kinds of gym exercises. He was fanatic about being in fit form. I was an easy target for him. I couldn't fight back because he was so much stronger than me. I simply had to bear it until his anger subsided.

"Afterward, he would always apologize, tell me he loved me, and promise it would never happen again. But it did, over and over. My clothes covered up most of the bruises, but I had to wear long-sleeved tops and make sure I never had any bare shoulders showing either that might let people see the damage he'd done. He was careful about my face, and I was able to use makeup to conceal any bruises there.

"I was living a lie. My marriage was a public relations charade at this point. I thought I loved Charles once, but by the end I hated him. Yes, I hated my husband and I hated everything he'd done to me. But I didn't kill him. I had plenty of reason to want him dead. But so did a lot of other people."

She looked pleadingly at the judge now.

"I'm innocent! I'm not a murderer! You have to believe me!"

She broke down in tears now.

"Please, don't send me back to that horrible jail again. Please, I beg of you . . ."

It was an incredibly dramatic moment that would be played repeatedly on TV news and in newspapers and on social media in the hours and days afterward.

Finally, Grieco led Laurie Bateman from the stand back to her seat.

Grieco put her arm around her and comforted her as best she could.

She was still sobbing uncontrollably.

There were tears in the eyes of a lot of people in that courtroom at that moment.

Including mine, although I made sure no one could see them.

Objective reporter, my ass!

CHAPTER 30

THINGS BEGAN TO happen very quickly after that.

At the end of the hearing, the judge issued his ruling on Donna Grieco's appeal to obtain bail for Laurie Bateman. He said that Bateman did not appear to be a flight risk and—based on this and her standing in the community and absence of any previous criminal record—she did not belong in jail while the prosecution prepared a lengthy case for trial against her. He set bail at $1 million, $250,000 of which had to be put up front with a bond.

This was a dramatic departure from the original judge's "no-bail" ruling, and court observers pointed out afterward that there had been no significant change in the actual evidence against Bateman since then.

But her emotional testimony about the domestic abuse that she suffered and all the rest clearly had a big impact on the judge—the same way it did with me and other spectators in the courtroom that day.

And the judge—who some people noted had his own political aspirations for the future—couldn't help but be aware of the overwhelming public support for Laurie Bateman that had grown exponentially both inside the courtroom and outside during recent days ever since that first interview with me.

But there was more. During his bail ruling, the judge said he would also take under consideration Grieco's motion to have the murder charge against Bateman dropped entirely because the District Attorney's office had not provided a substantial argument for her prosecution. He said he would rule on that later after going over all the evidence and testimony from the hearing in his chambers.

As for Laurie Bateman's bail, no one figured she'd have trouble raising the bond money, and they were right. Bert Stovall promised he would be able to provide the $250,000 bond within a matter of hours—so that Laurie Bateman could be released from Rikers Island as soon as possible.

But it turned out Stovall didn't have to post the bond at all to get her free.

Later that same day, the judge—after retiring to his chamber to consider the evidence for just a few more hours—shocked everyone when he quickly announced his second ruling.

He said he had decided to grant Grieco's appeal to dismiss the murder charge against Bateman "based on the latest evidence and testimony disclosed during the court hearing in which the district attorney's office failed to provide a compelling case for prosecuting Laurie Bateman on the crime of murder."

Had it been the evidence that had convinced the judge? Or was it Laurie Bateman's emotional testimony? Or the groundswell of public opinion that now supported her? Or, as was most likely, was it simply a combination of all of these things? Whatever, Donna Grieco had managed to work her magic in the courtroom one more time—turning a seemingly unwinnable case into a stunning legal victory for Laurie Bateman.

The DA's office tried to put the best face on it. "We presented a formidable case to uphold the murder charge against Laurie

Bateman," Karen Sanders said at a press conference after the ruling. "Yes, there were still unanswered questions, but we believe the evidence was more than enough to take her to trial for murder. Instead, the judge in this case—bowing to emotionalism and public hysteria instead of carefully examining our evidence—prevented justice from being carried out in the brutal murder of Charles Hollister. We will continue to investigate this case, and we will continue to investigate Laurie Bateman—until justice is done and we are able to obtain a conviction." But she gave no specific details on how they planned to do that—and it seemed unlikely they would be able to go after Laurie Bateman again.

A short time later, Bateman gave her own press conference as she emerged from Rikers Island following her prison ordeal.

"I had a tough time in there, but I survived," she said. "I'm a strong woman. I want to thank all the other strong women who helped me win my freedom. And, no matter what he did to me, I still want to see justice done in the death of my husband. I will work with the District Attorney's office and the police in any way I can to assist them in finding out who really did murder Charles. I want them and all of you to know that. Now I just want to go home."

We broadcast it all, the courtroom appearance and her press conference—like the rest of the media did. But we—and to put modesty aside, it was really me—were the only ones who could say we exclusively played a key role in getting Laurie Bateman out of jail.

"And so," I said on our newscast, "Laurie Bateman is a free woman again. We will continue to report on this breaking story all evening. This is Clare Carlson, Channel 10 News."

* * *

Laurie Bateman threw herself a party—a "victory party," I guess you would call it.

She invited friends, political figures who had supported her in her fight to get free, and also a number of the women's group leaders that had supported her so voraciously. The media was not invited. Well, that's not totally true. One member of the media was invited—and attended—the party. That would be me.

"This is a gathering of my friends, the people who were there for me when I needed them the most," she explained. "And you're one of them, Clare. I couldn't have done this—I would still be in jail—if not for you. I'm so grateful."

I wanted to tell her that I was just doing my job. That a journalist wasn't supposed to take sides on a story. But the truth was I liked her. I was glad she was free again. And I was glad I'd been the one who helped make that happen.

The party itself was in the same apartment where Charles Hollister had died. Which seemed a bit weird to me at first. But it was where she lived—the home she went back to—so I guess this was the obvious place for her to do it. Still, even as I stood in the living room holding a drink and talking with her other guests, I couldn't help wondering if I was standing on the same spot where her husband had been found dead.

I wasn't allowed to bring a video crew in with me. But I was able to take pictures and video with my phone—and report on it for the 11:00 p.m. newscast that night. It was another big exclusive for me, the latest on this story, which was great for me and my career.

I was also a bit melancholy about it all though.

The story was winding down for me now.

At least the Laurie Bateman part.

Oh sure, sooner or later someone would be arrested for the Charles Hollister murder, and that would be a big story. But I figured this would be the last time I'd spend much time with Laurie Bateman. My brief inclusion in her celebrity world would be over once this party had ended.

"That's not true," she said when I mentioned this to her that night. "I want to continue to be friends with you, Clare. You and me, we have a real bond. We're going to stay in touch. I promise you, girlfriend."

Girlfriend. I was Laurie Bateman's girlfriend. At least for the moment.

I nodded and said that was fine.

But I didn't believe it.

I knew what happened for me when a story was over. The story, and all the people in it, would disappear—and I would go on to the next story and the next cast of characters. I always felt like this at the end of a story and it made me a bit sad. But that was how it was. People—and the stories I covered about them—moved in and out of my life very quickly. Nobody stayed around after the curtain went down.

"You're not going to get rid of me so easily." Laurie Bateman laughed now. "I'm not going to disappear from your life. You and I will be talking again real soon. Trust me on that, girlfriend."

It turned out she was right about that.

And I was wrong.

But I didn't find that out until later.

PART II

KATIE, BABA WAWA & ME

CHAPTER 31

JANET AND I were playing a game we'd played a lot of times in the past. It was a silly game. But it had become kind of a ritual whenever something good happened to one of us, like all the media acclaim I'd gotten from the Laurie Bateman story. We called the game "What If?"

"What if I become a really big star from all this?" I said.

"You are a big star."

"Even bigger than I am."

"How big?"

"Let's just say I'll be a legendary newswoman."

We were having a drink at the Rock Cafe in Rockefeller Center. It was really starting to feel a lot like Christmas in New York City. The Rockefeller Center Christmas tree. The ice skaters on the rink outside where we were sitting. Radio City Music Hall next door with its Christmas show and the Rockettes dancing. Sure, the area was flooded with tourists during the holiday season. But Janet always thought that battling the crowd and the shoppers and all the rest was worth it, and she generally managed to drag me along with her.

"Do you think you'll be bigger than Connie Chung?" she asked me now.

Connie Chung was one of the first female news anchors at CBS News back in the eighties. She was a personal favorite of mine because of that, and Janet knew it. Although Connie had lost points in my estimation with the whole marriage to Maury Povich.

"Bigger," I said.

"Katie Couric."

"Bigger than Katie Couric."

"C'mon, Katie Couric was a CBS News anchor. She was the cohost of the *Today Show* for years. And she even had her own talk show like you're going to have if this all works out. How can you go wrong with Katie Couric?"

I thought about that. If I wanted to pattern myself after a female legend in the news business in this fantasy, I needed a real legend.

"Barbara Walters," I told Janet.

"Really?"

"Sure. She was the first female news anchor in TV news history for ABC. She did all those great interviews over the years with celebrities and political figures. She had her own incredibly popular talk show with *The View*. And, even better than that, she became famous as Baba Wawa when Gilda Radner did that great imitation of her on *Saturday Night Live*. After all this time, she's still Baba Wawa to a lot of people. Now that's fame. That's a legend. That's what I want to be. I'll be just like Barbara Walters."

"What happens then?"

"Well, my show is a big hit. It wins an Emmy. I win an Emmy. Everyone wins an Emmy. I get offers for TV and movies. I'm on the cover of *People* Magazine . . ."

"Okay, you're a big Hollywood star. Everyone loves you. In the midst of all this, you have a torrid love affair with a big star out there. But who?"

"Give me some choices."

"Ryan Reynolds."

"Someone better."

"Uh, Ryan Gosling."

"How about someone not named Ryan?"

"George Clooney then."

"I don't know, he's a bit long in the tooth, isn't he? I mean he's no kid anymore."

"Neither are you," Janet pointed out.

"Yeah, that's true. All right, I fall in love with and marry George Clooney."

"And live happily ever after?"

"Wrong. The marriage breaks up because I start playing around with another Hollywood star . . ."

"Who?"

"Bradley Cooper!"

"All right!" Janet laughed and the two of us sat there giggling like a couple of schoolgirls.

I took a drink of my wine and looked at everything around us. The Christmas tree. The ice-skating rink. The happy holiday families milling around. I'd been to Rockefeller Center many times since I'd moved to New York City. But I was here even before that.

"The first time I ever came to Rockefeller Center I was eleven years old," I said to Janet. "I won a big national contest for a school essay I wrote about 'What I Want to Be When I Grow Up.' I wrote about wanting to be a journalist. Even then, it was like I knew what I was destined for. Anyway, the prize was a trip to New York City. Me and a couple of other kids got to see the sights here. The Empire State Building. The Statue of Liberty. And they brought us to Rockefeller Center. For me, because I wanted to be a journalist, I got a tour of NBC News. I met Jessica Savitch that day."

"Who?"

"Jessica Savitch was the golden girl of news then. A female newscaster who was blazing a pioneer trail in the news business for all who would follow. She had it all. Everyone figured she'd wind up being a female network news anchor one day. Just like Barbara Walters, Connie Chung, Diane Sawyer, Katie Couric. Except it all fell apart for her."

"I sort of remember the story. What happened? She had a drinking problem or something?"

I nodded and drank more of my wine.

"She went on the air one night and began slurring her words. She was almost incoherent. It seemed to everyone who saw that live broadcast that she was either drunk or on some kind of drugs. That pretty much destroyed her career ambitions and then, just a few weeks later, she drowned in a car accident. She wasn't driving, but I always thought there had to be a connection between her on-air disaster and then the fatal car crash. I mean it all happened—the meteoric rise and then the sudden fall from grace—so fast. Her career. Her life. She lost everything in an instant. You know, she was so nice to me that day I met her. She told me that one day I could grow up and be a big TV news star like her. And that's sort of what happened, I guess. Maybe that's why I still think about Jessica Savitch. I think about Jessica Savitch a lot."

"Wow, that's pretty heavy-duty stuff coming from you. I'm more used to the jokes. But you're not going to wind up like Jessica Savitch, Clare."

"No," I smiled, "I'm going to be like Katie Couric and Barbara Walters."

*   *   *

The new "happy talk" format at Channel 10 News had gotten off to a rocky start. I wouldn't describe it as a complete disaster. But it sure wasn't working out as well as Jack Faron and the consulting firm had hoped.

One of the biggest problems was our anchor team of Brett Wolff and Dani Blaine. Brett and Dani did all right making routine—and fairly obvious—quips on most of the innocuous stories. Like saying how adopting a cat at a local shelter was the "purr-fect" gift at Christmas. Or exchanging banter with a re-porter at a pie-eating contest like how it "must have taken a lot of crust" to cover that assignment.

But when the exchanges got more personal between Brett and Dani, they looked tense and uncomfortable and even a little bit angry at each other.

"Why aren't Brett and Dani happy on air?" Faron wanted to know.

"They are married," I pointed out.

"Can't married people be happy?"

"Not in my experience, no."

There'd been a particularly awkward on-air exchange between them the night before. Brett made a remark about how much food the pregnant Dani was eating every day—and also joked about the weight she'd put on. Dani then made a "joke" suggesting that Brett's performance in the bedroom was pretty lackluster these days. It was like watching a reality show to see the two of them going after each other like this.

I found out later what the real problem was between them— the one that had started all this bickering. I brought them into my office and listened as they told me how they'd been arguing for days about what to name their baby. They knew it was going to be a girl. Dani wanted to name her Elizabeth because that had been the name of her beloved grandmother. Brett liked the name Anne. Neither of them was budging in their position.

"What about naming her Elizabeth-Anne?" I suggested.

They both looked at each other.

"I can live with that," Brett said.

"Me too," Dani agreed.

Ah, Carlson, you silver-tongued genius you! The great compromiser. I'm telling you I should get a job after this negotiating peace treaties in the Middle East. Or going down to Washington to straighten out all this bickering between the Democrats and Republicans. Carlson's the name, diplomacy's my game.

Not all of it was this easy though. It's dangerous when people are talking live on air without specifically following a script. The worst on-air gaffe came from Cassie O'Neal. I mean I could have predicted this would happen. Giving Cassie the freedom to ad-lib anything she wanted on air was like handing her a loaded gun. You knew it was going to go off—you just didn't know when.

It happened while she was covering the opening of a school for special-needs students and decided to banter with Brett and Dani about it at the end of the report. "You'd have to be retarded not to be impressed by what's being accomplished here with these kids," she said with a laugh. Yep, I know. Well, we were deluged by viewer complaints and had to issue an apology on air the next night.

After that, Maggie and I started writing the quips people could say into the actual script. So they weren't actually impromptu anymore. That might have taken away from some of the realism of the "happy talk" idea—but it seemed safer to us if we knew exactly what people were going to say.

Maggie asked me how long I thought we'd have to keep doing this.

In other words, when would this damn happy talk idea go away so we could just concentrate on the news again?

"As soon as another big story breaks," I said. "Happy talk only works when there's nothing serious going on. It's no good when you're covering a sensational murder or a plane crash or a big corruption case. You don't have to joke about that to get the viewer's interest. A big story will solve our problem."

"A big story, huh? God, I hope you're right."

"A big story always makes everything better," I told her.

*   *   *

That big story didn't seem like it was going to be the Charles Hollister murder.

It—along with Laurie Bateman's arrest—had been a media sensation when it happened, but now everyone had moved on. That's the way it was in the news business. Stories—even big stories like that—don't have a long life span. Especially in this era of instant news with Twitter and other social media.

Sure, the story would be big again if they arrested someone. But the police didn't seem close to doing that. And there were other big crimes happening all around at the same time in New York that we had to cover.

I hadn't heard from Laurie Bateman since the party that night after she was freed from jail. I'd tried calling her once or twice, but never got a return call or text. Which didn't surprise me. I didn't really believe what she'd said that night about us wanting to be "girlfriends" and all that crap. Laurie Bateman operated on a whole different level of celebrity than me, and we didn't have much to talk about with each other except for that interview I did that helped her go free.

I did read in the *Wall Street Journal* how Laurie Bateman had taken over the controlling interest in Hollister's business holdings. The story pointed out again how Hollister had never had a chance to alter the will—i.e., write her out of it—before his death. So the original will he'd drawn up at the beginning of their marriage was still valid, which gave her power over all her husband's holdings.

I wondered what that meant for Charles Jr.

Or Bert Stovall.

I thought about Elaine, his estranged daughter, too, and about Melissa Hunt, his mistress, and the rest of the people in Charles Hollister's life.

He'd been living a soap opera.

*   *   *

My daughter wanted to know if I was coming to their house in Virginia for Christmas.

"Christmas?" I said. "Bah, humbug."

"I was hoping we could spend it together as a family. Our first Christmas together," she said.

"I don't think I can get away from work for long enough to do that."

The truth was that I've always hated holiday family gatherings. Have ever since I was growing up. I suppose that's because Thanksgiving and Christmas and all the rest was such a tense, unpleasant time for me with my parents. Looking back on it, I realize now that I didn't have a happy childhood. And it ended badly when my father kicked me out of the house once he found out I was pregnant with the child who turned out to be Lucy. My parents and me . . . well, we never resolved our issues before they both died.

Of course, I did have my own new family now to spend the holidays with, if I wanted. I'm sure Jack Faron would let me have time off to do it. But saying I had to work was a good excuse not to have to deal with my holiday anxieties. I had been down to Virginia for Thanksgiving with Lucy and her husband and Audrey. It was fine, but I still felt a bit uncomfortable. Like I didn't really belong to that family yet. Maybe next year.

That's why I was happy to spend Christmas alone in my apartment, eating take-out food and watching *A Christmas Story* or *It's a Wonderful Life* or *Miracle on 34th Street* on TV like I usually did.

"Are you sure you're going to be all right?" Lucy asked me.

"If I start feeling suicidal," I said with a laugh, "you'll be the first person I call."

And then there was the whole issue of the breast cancer gene that Lucy had discovered she was carrying—and presumably passed on to Audrey.

Did I have the same gene in me?

Was I responsible for that?

Did I really want to have to deal with one more thing I felt guilty about with Lucy—and all the mistakes I'd made since that long-ago day when I'd given birth to her as a nineteen-year-old college freshman?

I've never been good with medical issues, putting things off for as long as I could. And this one was no different.

I had finally gone to a doctor, told him the story, and taken the test to discover if I had the BRCA1 gene inside me or not. The test itself was relatively simple. But it would be a few weeks before I'd know the results, they told me. I didn't want to think about it until then. I didn't want to talk about it. I didn't want to deal with it.

I also had not dealt with the other part of this. Doug Crowell. The guy I had a one-night stand with nearly three decades ago that resulted in the birth of my daughter. Crowell was dead now. But, if it turned out I was not the one carrying the gene, then he had been. That meant his children were at risk. I was the one who could warn them to get tested, if things turned out that way. But I hadn't reached out to his family since I got the news. Not yet.

I was procrastinating on that, too.

I'm really, really good at procrastinating.

It's one of my specialties.

When it comes to procrastinating, I'm right up there with the best of them.

Meanwhile, there wasn't much happening in my romantic life.

Just out of curiosity, I looked up the number of Nick Pollock, the guy from the Treasury Department. I called him. I wasn't sure what I was going to say if he picked up the phone, but he didn't. I didn't leave a message. No reason to think he was interested in me. Just because a Treasury agent picks up a woman and takes her back to the Federal Building to interrogate her doesn't mean he's hot for a romance with her, right?

Anyway, it looked like I was not going to find out the answer to that.

Which was okay.

He sure was good-looking though.

I'd had a few more exchanges with my ex-husband Sam Markham about the Hollister case, but he seemed happily married now with his new wife and new baby. So he was out of the picture.

So was Scott Manning. Manning was the ex-NYPD homicide cop who now worked for the FBI. I'd slept with him two times—once when he was on the NYPD and again last year when we worked together to capture a serial killer. But he was married, too, and thus unavailable.

So where did that leave me?

I could try Wild Bill Carstairs again. He probably had a lot of time on his hands now that his star in the DA's office had fallen so far.

But I wasn't that desperate.

Not yet anyway,

*　　*　　*

And so I was sitting there alone in my apartment when an old Laurie Bateman movie came on one of the cable channels.

It was one of the best ones she'd made. She didn't make a lot of good movies, but this one was worthwhile. She played a "working girl" kind of real estate broker who falls in love with a man she's selling a house to or something like that. I wasn't paying that much attention to the plot.

It got me to thinking about Laurie Bateman again though.

For no particular reason, I went over to my computer and began looking up other movies she'd done. I hadn't seen a lot of them, and I hadn't missed much. They weren't exactly Oscar contenders. But I clicked on a couple of YouTube segments from them to get a feel for what they were about.

There was one where she was being stalked by a serial killer. Another where she and a group of other women were trapped in a haunted house. And even a few beach pictures—which had more soft porn shots than story line—where she frolicked around in a revealing string bikini.

I was just about to stop when I came across another movie she'd made. It was called *Victim of Love*. This one had hardly been seen by anyone. It was made a long time ago, and seemed to have gone directly to video. Laurie Bateman was very young; it must have been one of her first movies. I figured I'd give it a quick scan and be done with this. But then something on the screen suddenly caught my attention.

Laurie Bateman played the part of a young wife in an abusive marriage who fought back against her husband in self-defense during one of the attacks.

The climax of the movie featured an emotional scene where she was on trial for his murder. I watched as she delivered her lines from the witness stand.

"I couldn't fight back because he was so much stronger than me. Afterward, he would always apologize, tell me he loved me, and promise it would never happen again. But it did, over and over. Yes, I hated my husband and I hated everything he'd done to me. But I didn't kill him. I had plenty of reasons to want him dead. But so did a lot of other people. I'm innocent. I'm not a murderer! You have to believe me!"

I was stunned at what I was seeing and hearing.

I went back and watched it again.

And again a few more times after that.

It was almost word for word what she'd said in the courtroom during her real-life hearing that day. I found a few other instances where she had said something similar to what she'd said in the courtroom that day. Not exactly the same. But close enough so that it seemed extremely unlikely that it could be simply chance or coincidence.

I stared at the now frozen image of Laurie Bateman on my computer screen for a long time.

What the hell did this mean?

Did Laurie Bateman go back and take lines from one of her old, obscure movies in order to help make her case for freedom?

Or was she just playing a part that day too?

*   *   *

"What if she really did it?" I said to Jack Faron.

"Who?"

"Laurie Bateman. What if she did murder her husband to get her hands on his money?"

Faron was eating lunch in his office as we talked. He'd heated himself a Lean Cuisine spaghetti dish in the office microwave. Which would have been fine for his diet, except he had three of them on his desk in front of him. I wasn't exactly a rocket scientist when it came to calorie counting, but I figured that eating three portions kind of defeated the purpose of the diet meal.

"Wait a minute," Faron asked between bites of his lunch. "Weren't you on the other side of this before?"

"I was."

"You were the one who helped convince everyone Laurie Bateman was innocent."

"I'm not so sure I was right about that anymore."

"What changed your mind?"

I told him about the old movie I'd just seen. About how the dialogue from the courtroom scene in it was eerily similar to what Laurie Bateman had said in the real-life courtroom. About how it had made me wonder if she was really telling her own story that day or just playing another part.

"And no one else ever noticed this connection with the movie before?"

"Not that I can see. It's a very old, very obscure movie. Barely anyone saw it at the time and very few since then. I only came across it because I started looking into her past stuff."

Faron thought about it for a minute. He ate a few more mouthfuls of his meal, then pushed it aside. He didn't look happy with it. Or with me. I was bringing him a problem again, and he didn't like problems any more than the food he was eating these days.

"It doesn't prove anything," he said. "Maybe she was nervous about the upcoming courtroom appearance and wanted to prepare something. She remembered the part she played of an abused wife and it helped her to tell her own story. It could be as innocent as that."

"Except one of the biggest reasons she got out of jail and the charges were dropped were those emotional words she spoke about the domestic abuse in her marriage—first in the interview with me, then again in the courtroom. Everyone was overwhelmed by her sincerity. Including me. Now it doesn't seem so sincere if she was basically reading lines from an old movie."

Faron nodded.

"Do you want to go on the air with this then? Just raise the question. Show clips from the movie and then segments of her interview and the court appearance. It could be compelling."

I shook my head no.

"I don't want to tip my hand yet to let her know we found out about this. I'd like to do more digging first. See what else I can go back and find out about Laurie Bateman and the murder of Charles Hollister. There's one other thing—one other loose end— that's always bothered me. Why did the Hollister maid, Carmen Ortega, die? Of course, if it was just an accident—a coincidence— that a woman set to take part in a big murder trial fell in front of a subway train, then it's not relevant to anything else. But if it was murder, the murderer's motive must have been to prevent her from testifying at the trial. That meant the murderer was someone who didn't want Laurie Bateman to be convicted. Who could that be? Well, Laurie Bateman, of course, was the obvious possibility. Sure, she was in jail. But she had money, lots of money. She could have hired someone on the outside to get rid of Carmen Ortega for her and to make it look like an accident."

Faron shook his head in frustration. "I'm confused. Why are you asking this question now? Why are you asking any of these questions about Laurie Bateman now? Why not before? I mean the woman went free because of you, Clare."

"I know. That's what makes me so mad."

"Who exactly are you mad at? Laurie Bateman?"

"I'm mad at everybody, including myself. If Bateman killed her husband, then she subverted an important issue—the women's movement, which has accomplished so much for women, has righted so many wrongs for us, in recent years—to possibly gain false sympathy in order to beat the murder rap against her. If she lied about killing her husband, then maybe she lied about the domestic abuse against her too. That's an egregious affront to me as a woman. And it should be an egregious affront to any woman.

"But, even more than that, if she is lying—then I'm mad because I fell for it. I believed her. I trusted her. I fought for her. But now, if it turns out she really did it, that means she outsmarted me. I guess that's what bothers me the most.

"I did the same thing I accused the police and the DA's office of doing, Jack. They started off with the premise that Bateman was guilty and then looked only for evidence that could support that conclusion. They didn't pay any attention to evidence that might exonerate her. Well, I did the same thing—only I did it in reverse. I went looking for evidence that Laurie Bateman didn't murder her husband. And I found it. A lot of it. But, along the way, I ig-nored other leads I should have pursued.

"I hope Carmen Ortega's death turns out to be an accident after all. I hope the similarity in Bateman's words with the movie lines were a coincidence too—or, at worst, a misguided attempt by her to prove her innocence in court because she was so desperate to get out of jail for a crime she didn't commit.

"But I have to know the truth. I liked Laurie Bateman when this story started—and yes, I believed she was innocent right from the beginning. I still think she is innocent, at least until I find out more. But what if I'm wrong? What if Laurie Bateman is guilty—and she was responsible for the deaths of both her husband and Carmen Ortega?"

Faron realized the enormity of what I was telling him.

"Then that means . . ." he started to say.

"That means I helped her get away with murder."

PART III

THE FOG OF WAR

CHAPTER 32

By the time I got to work the next morning, Maggie had prepared a massive file on Laurie Bateman. I said I wanted to find out everything I could. Not only about the Laurie Bateman of today, as I had earlier. But everything about her past, too, all the way back to Vietnam when she came to the U.S. as a baby.

"Why do you care so much about the details of Bateman's background?" she asked. "I mean the Vietnam stuff was a long time ago."

"The past never dies, Maggie. It's not even past."

"Huh?"

"William Faulkner said that."

"Jeez . . ."

"You're not a fan of Faulkner?"

"Oh, I'm fine with Faulkner. I took English literature. I just never thought I'd hear you quoting him."

I told Maggie about the comparison I'd discovered with the old movie and my new questions about the story. If Maggie was surprised, she didn't show it. She went with the news flow pretty easily, understood that a story didn't always follow a straight line—there were often a lot of detours along the way. And I knew she trusted my news instincts, which was good to know when you worked with someone in a newsroom.

"I simply want to find out as much as I can about Laurie Bateman—or, more precisely, I want to find out what I don't know about her. I'm going to have to talk to her again about everything and this time it might not be as friendly as my previous meetings with her. I need to arm myself with as many facts as I can about her and her life before I take that step."

On the way into the office, I'd brought a large cup of black coffee at the deli downstairs and a poppyseed bagel smeared with scallion cream cheese. I figured it would be a long morning, so I wanted to fuel up. I took a bite of the bagel, a sip of the coffee, and then plunged into the Laurie Bateman file.

*   *   *

Even though I was too young to remember it, I knew enough about the last days of the South Vietnamese war to understand what a nightmare it must have been for the people there.

I'd seen those horrific images and video from April 1975, out of Saigon and elsewhere, of them desperately trying to flee the country before the Communists arrived: hanging from departing U.S. helicopters, swimming out into the ocean to try to get to any boat that might help them escape, storming the gates of the U.S. Embassy, and pleading for help as U.S. Marines pushed them back before abandoning the embassy themselves a short time later.

Most of the U.S. combat troops had pulled out of the country after a cease-fire agreement with North Vietnam in 1973, and two years later the entire South Vietnamese government was collapsing—with North Vietnamese and Viet Cong troops about to capture Saigon and the country.

Now it was total chaos as agonizing decisions had to be made about who got to leave—and who were forced to stay.

I thought about Laurie Bateman—who was then Pham Van Kieu—and her family and what they must have endured in order to escape. Did they manage to get on one of the helicopters? Did they get picked up by a ship? How did they get out when so many others didn't? Well, it was probably like everything else that happens in a war—the luck of the draw. Some people survived and some didn't.

There were only a few details available about them fleeing the war. Despite being asked about it in several interviews over the years, Laurie Bateman had never revealed what she'd been told about it.

All we knew was this: Only a few months old at the time, Laurie had come to America with her Vietnamese family. The family seemed to consist of her mother, father, an uncle, and a grandmother. Laurie and her mother had managed to get out of the country during those last days before the North Vietnamese and Viet Cong arrived in Saigon. They eventually made their way to California, where they were reunited with her father— who had been sent to college in Los Angeles earlier by the South Vietnamese government.

"Wait a minute," I said to Maggie. "If the father was alive, how did Marvin Bateman get into the picture?"

"That was a few years later. Her father died not long after the family arrived in America. A car accident. That's when the mother and Laurie met Bateman."

"What about the rest of the family? The grandmother is presumably long dead. But what happened to the uncle?"

"No one is sure. He was the brother of Laurie's mother. He just kind of disappeared after they came to the U.S."

"And the mother?"

"She's still alive. Marvin Bateman died a number of years ago. But she still lives in the same house. It's in La Jolla, a couple of hours south of LA near San Diego."

I wrote all this down as Maggie was talking. I wasn't sure why. Like I said, I didn't know what I was looking for in all this. But the same as I do with any story, I wanted to accumulate as much information as I could and hope it led me somewhere.

I already had questions that were bothering me though. About exactly how the family made it out of Vietnam. About the death of her father. And about the disappearance of her uncle earlier. None of it probably meant anything; it all happened so long ago. But I was still curious.

I was curious about something else, too.

"Bert Stovall, Hollister's CEO, told me they'd met when they were both in Vietnam during the war. Is there any possible connection between Hollister when he was there and Laurie's family? I have no idea how or why, but it does seem like an interesting fact that they were both there then. Maybe you could look into that . . ."

"I already did."

Of course. Maggie was always one step ahead of everyone.

"And?"

"Nothing."

"You're sure?"

"Here's what I found out about Charles Hollister and Vietnam: He was drafted into the Army in 1971. One of the last group of men that got drafted for the war. He wound up in Saigon working in an intelligence office at MACV headquarters. That was the major U.S. military center there. Not long before he rotated out of Vietnam and came back to the U.S., he encountered a Viet Cong soldier attempting to plant an explosive at the MACV building. The enemy soldier reached for his AK-47, but Hollister shot and killed him first—and before the explosive could be ignited. He probably saved a lot of lives that day. They gave him a medal for his heroic action."

That was the story Stovall had told me earlier.

Interesting, but didn't seem to have anything to do with what I was looking for.

"Is there any possibility at all that Hollister had any contact with the Pham family and his future wife while he was in Vietnam?"

"No way. He left Vietnam in 1973 when the U.S. pulled out its last combat troops. She wasn't born until 1975, two years later."

"Damn."

Maggie laughed. "What were you hoping for, Clare? That maybe Laurie Bateman was Hollister's secret daughter from the war? And he didn't know? Or she didn't know? And, one or both of them found out, which set off everything that happened later? Did you think this story was going to be that easy?"

I sighed. "One can only hope."

CHAPTER 33

THE LAST PERSON I ever wanted to see or talk to again was William—Wild Bill—Carstairs. I did not like Carstairs. I did not trust him. And, worst of all, every time I was around him reminded me of my moment of weakness when I'd slept with him. Nope, if I never saw Carstairs again in my entire life, it would be too soon.

I met Billy Carstairs that afternoon following my meeting with Maggie.

I had my reasons. The last few times I'd talked with Carstairs, we'd been on opposite sides. He was arrogantly predicting a conviction for Laurie Bateman, and I believed she was innocent. Now that I wasn't so sure anymore, I was more interested in finding out about what evidence he—and the DA's office and police—had accumulated against her before the charges were dropped. Which meant meeting with Carstairs. I've always said I'd do almost anything for a story. Well, this was going to be a real test of that.

When I called Carstairs, he said we should meet somewhere outside the DA's offices. He said he didn't want to be seen there with me.

"You're not very popular with the people there right now," he said.

"I can only imagine."

"Actually, I'm not very popular with them these days either."

"A lot of fallout from the collapse of the Bateman case?"

"That and other things."

He suggested we meet in the Foley Square area.

"Some place outside," I said, not wanting to find myself trapped in a restaurant or a bar with Carstairs.

"Isn't it a bit cold to be meeting outside?"

"I don't plan to stay that long."

He sighed. If he was insulted, he didn't say anything about it though. That was one of the good things about Billy Carstairs: it was pretty hard to insult him or hurt his feelings. He'd had it all said to him before.

"Remember that park near the courthouse, Clare?"

"The one where you tried to molest me?"

"Yeah, that's the one."

*   *   *

Even in December, there was still a guy selling hot dogs there. I wondered if these people ever went south for the winter. Carstairs and I both bought hot dogs and sodas—we went Dutch-treat by the way—and sat down on one of the park benches. It was a relatively nice day for the first month of winter. Temperature only down to the mid-forties. But I was still hoping this wouldn't take long.

"How bad are things for you at the DA's office?" I asked once we sat down and began munching on our hot dogs.

"I still have a job. But only barely. They're not giving me any work to do. And I've got a big meeting coming up with my bosses there that I don't think will go well. I'm going to have to start looking for a new job. Let's just say my star is falling. Or crashed and burned, I guess you could say. And it's all because of you."

"Uh, sorry about that," I said. I kind of meant it. I didn't really want to destroy the guy's career and his life.

"It wasn't just Laurie Bateman and the Hollister murder case. It was everything that came along with it. Once she opened it up to all the 'I'm a woman victim of an abusive man' stuff, people started zeroing in on me as the prosecutor and looking at my own sexual background. As you might expect, there was a lot of damaging stuff they came up with. Both in the office and out."

"In the office?"

"My assistant, Annette, you met her. She's now filed sexual harassment charges against me. Piling on, I guess, once all this stuff about me and other women came out. She claims I made her sleep with me to keep her job."

"Did you make her sleep with you to keep her job?"

"Hey, I had sex with her. But I never made it a quid pro quo. I've slept with a lot of women in the office, and that was never a problem before."

"Times have changed," I pointed out.

"Yeah, I guess I found that out."

He definitely seemed more subdued than I'd ever seen him before. I could tell how much all this had taken a toll on him, professionally and personally. I mean, I'd already been sitting with him for ten minutes so far and he hadn't made a pass at me yet. A tiger doesn't change his stripes though, and I figured the same old Billy Carstairs would return.

I asked him about the Laurie Bateman case.

"I want to know more about the evidence you had accumulated against her," I said.

"Why do you care now?"

I didn't want to tell him the truth. I didn't trust Billy Carstairs—even the new Billy Carstairs—that much. I said I was working on a follow-up story that we were doing on air soon about how she'd gone free.

"We thought we had a good, solid case against her at the beginning," Carstairs said. "But, as you well know, a lot of it began to fall apart. Once that interview with you aired, all this sentiment began building for her—and no one was interested in the actual evidence. The other big damaging blow though, even before that happened, was the death of the maid. I mean, the maid would have testified about finding Bateman trying to flee the crime scene with her husband's dead body behind her. But, once the maid was gone, all we could do is enter her testimony in the court record—and Bateman insisted that wasn't accurate. That she wasn't running away, she was simply in a state of shock after finding the body. We lost a lot when we lost that maid as a live witness against Bateman."

"Are there any new leads about what happened to the maid on the subway?"

"The police have a video from a transit security camera showing the scene on the platform. Begins while the maid is standing there waiting for the train and ends with her down on the tracks after being hit by the incoming train. I've watched it. It looks like someone might have shoved her as the train was approaching the station. But it's hard to tell if it was deliberate or accidental. And, even if it was deliberate, that doesn't mean it had anything to do with the Bateman case. There's a lot of crazy people on subway platforms. There've been other cases where people are shoved into the path of trains by a psycho or whatever for no reason at all. It happens."

Except this time it happened to a key witness in a sensational murder trial, I thought to myself.

"Anything else?" I asked.

"There is one other thing. I don't know what it means. But it always bothered me about this case. The detectives who arrived at the crime scene said Bateman was crying and very emotional and kept insisting she was innocent of the murder. The same way she was during the interview she did with you and then later in court."

"Isn't that what you'd expect?"

"Exactly."

"Then what's the problem?"

"She wasn't that way before the police arrived. That's what the maid, Carmen Ortega, told us in her statement. She said Bateman was composed, completely in control, and seemed—well, almost happy about her husband lying dead on the floor. It wasn't until a short time after, when the police arrived, that she became emotionally distraught the way you'd expect from a wife who just found her husband murdered."

He shook his head. "I don't know. The way she changed once the police were there, it's almost as if . . ."

"She was acting?"

"Yes, like she was acting," Carstairs said.

CHAPTER 34

MY NEXT STOP was to see another one of my exes. This time it was Sam Markham, the homicide cop on the Hollister case, who also had been my third husband. I wanted to ask him about the video that Carstairs had told me about, the one of the subway platform when Carmen Ortega died.

On my way uptown to the precinct, I thought about how strange it was that both of the men I needed information from happened to be ex-lovers of mine. But then again, maybe it wasn't so strange. I've been with a lot of men over the years.

My daughter had brought this up to me the last time we talked. "You're almost fifty now, Mom," she said. "You need to settle down. Stop sleeping with every man you find attractive, find one man—the right man—and start a life with him. It's time."

Yes, that came from my own damn daughter.

Sam and I got along though. At least as well as two divorced people can expect to get along with each other. I liked Sam. Hell, I liked all my ex-husbands. All three of them. I'm the first person to admit that the dissolution of my marriages was more my fault than theirs. Sam and I had gone through a rough period a year or two ago after the divorce when he came onto me while he was drunk, and I rebuffed him. He was angry at me about that for a while. But now he seemed happily married to a new woman and with a young child—and I was pretty sure I was just history to him. Like I was with a lot of men.

I found him in the squad room and asked about the video from Carmen Ortega's death on the subway track.

"Why do you want to see that?"

"I'm an investigative journalist. I'm investigating the Laurie Bateman case. The maid's death is part of that story."

"But you already made sure Bateman got off on the charges."

"I'm working on a follow-up story now."

"What kind of a follow-up?"

"To see if she was really innocent."

Unlike Carstairs, I trusted Sam enough to tell him the truth about what I was there for.

"You have doubts?" he asked.

"I have questions."

"Such as?"

"Well, here's one question for you, Sam: Do you think she did it?"

He shook his head. "I don't know for sure one way or another. But it doesn't matter anymore what I think, does it? She's never going to be charged with anything again now. Because of you. You played a big part in getting the charges dropped. Once you did that interview with Bateman and she played the woman card—claiming she was the victim of continual domestic abuse from her husband—it didn't matter whether she did it or not in the arena of public opinion. Laurie Bateman never paid any attention to women's groups or feminist causes until it helped her to paint herself as a battered woman. And it worked. To be honest, I find the whole idea of her claiming to be a victim because he might have slapped her around a bit pretty despicable."

"That's because you're not a woman," I said.

"Meaning?"

"Meaning a man can't relate to what Laurie Bateman might have endured the same way as a woman."

"Well, before you label me as a sexist male curmudgeon, I know one thing for a fact: I never hit you when we were married."

"No, you didn't."

He smiled. "But I did think about it a few times."

"I'll bet you did," I said.

*   *   *

We watched the video together on a computer screen at Sam's desk. It had been taken with a routine surveillance camera on the subway platform. There were cameras everywhere in the city now—Big Brother was always watching. But that didn't mean it would tell you much about a crime. Sometimes, like with the video Sam showed me, it just left you with more questions.

The screen was black at first, then I suddenly was watching a view of the subway platform that day. It was filled with people for the evening rush hour. Everyone was bustling around, and there was a lot of pushing and shoving by people trying to get in position for the trains.

Sam paused the video at one point, then pointed out the Ortega woman to me. She was standing near the edge of the platform. A middle-aged woman, dark hair, carrying a handbag—she looked just like anyone else waiting for a subway ride. Watching her like that was kind of eerie. Because I knew—and she didn't—that she only had seconds to live.

But I sat there transfixed at her on the screen—trying to find anything that could give me a clue about what happened to her.

Sam started playing the video again, but paused a few times more to show me some specific people. One was a homeless man panhandling from riders as they waited. Another was an apparently mentally disturbed woman gesturing wildly and yelling at people. Not an uncommon sight in the streets and subway stations these days.

"We thought it might have been someone like that who shoved her onto the tracks, either deliberately or accidentally," Sam said. "But there's no evidence of that. We talked to them both. At least as well as we could, because neither was very coherent. But neither one seemed to know anything about the woman or how she wound up on those tracks in front of the subway train. And there's nothing here that shows they were involved in any way. Or anyone else on that platform. It all looks pretty normal for an evening rush hour until the Ortega woman died."

He played the rest of the video now.

Sure enough, you could see the crowd pushing and shoving on the platform. Carmen Ortega was standing in the center of it, close to the edge of the platform. The train pulled into the station. After that, it was pure chaos as everyone realized that a woman, Carmen Ortega, was on the tracks in front of the oncoming train.

"I was hoping for more," I said. "What's the Ortega woman's death being called?"

"Accidental, for now."

"Even though she was scheduled to testify in a big murder trial?"

"We can't prove anything else at the moment. And Laurie Bateman was in jail when Ortega died so she sure couldn't have done it. Besides, it doesn't mean much now that Bateman has been cleared of the charges."

I nodded. That all made sense. I didn't like it, but I didn't have any other answers. I stood up to leave.

"Do you want to see the end?" Sam asked.

"There's more?"

"Just a guy who tried to save her."

I looked back at the video of the scene. There was a man down on the tracks now, attempting to get Carmen Ortega back up onto the platform. He finally did, and she was lying there when the first EMTs arrived. But it was too late. She'd apparently been killed instantly by the impact of the train.

"That was a pretty heroic thing to do," I said, looking at the man on the screen.

"Yep. Of course, she was already dead. But he didn't know that when he went down on the tracks to try to save her. Everyone else on the platform just watched. But this guy tried to help. Except he couldn't get her out of there in time."

"What did he say about it afterward?"

"Nothing. We never talked to him. He left before anyone could get to him. No one else knew who he was. Just a Good Samaritan. We put out the picture of him in hopes of finding him. But nothing. Of course, it's not a very good picture. All you can tell is he looks Chinese."

I looked at the picture of the man on the screen now. Sam was right. You never got a good look at his face. Just a glimpse from the side. Nothing else. He could be anybody out there.

"Asian American," I said.

"Huh?"

"The term is Asian American, not Chinese."

"Even if he's from China?"

"We don't know that. There's a lot of different types of Asian Americans living in New York City."

I looked at the paused picture of the man on the screen again.

"Do you think he could be Vietnamese?" I asked.

"I suppose so. Why?"

"Laurie Bateman is from Vietnam."

"I know, but . . ."

"I think he looks Vietnamese," I said.

CHAPTER 35

THERE WERE NOW three possible links to Vietnam in this story:
1) Laurie Bateman was born in Vietnam as Pham Van Kieu and
came to the U.S. as a baby after the war there ended; 2) Charles
Hollister served in Vietnam as a soldier during that war; and 3)
The man who had jumped onto the subway tracks in a heroic if
unsuccessful effort to save Carmen Ortega, the Hollister's maid
and a key witness in the murder case, was—or at least appeared to
be—Vietnamese.

I did not have the slightest idea what any of this all meant.

Probably nothing.

But I wanted to find out for sure.

I started back with Laurie Bateman again. I'd been trying to
reach her ever since I left the precinct where Sam worked. I'd left
a lot of messages, but gotten no response. So much for the personal stuff from her at her party about how she and I would be
inseparable now as "girlfriends."

Of course, maybe she was just busy or hadn't gotten my messages
yet. But I had a feeling she didn't want to talk to me again. Maybe I
was being cynical, but I couldn't help feeling that she'd gotten what
she wanted from me—and now she didn't need me in her life anymore. My job was over, as far as Laurie Bateman was concerned.

I was going to have to talk to someone else about the Vietnam angle. Who? Well, Bert Stovall was the person who first told me how Hollister had served there—they'd been in the same unit and become lifelong friends after meeting in Vietnam. So he seemed like my best choice.

I wondered if he might avoid my call like Laurie Bateman seemed to be doing.

But Stovall got on the phone right away. He thanked me for all I'd done for Laurie, talked about how Laurie had taken over now as the head of the Hollister business empire—and about all the changes that had happened in just a few days since then. But he said she'd assured him he would continue to be the CEO and she would rely on him in the same way that Charles Hollister had for so many years.

I let Stovall go on like that for quite a while, as if I'd only called him for a personal update rather than for any professional reason.

"Tell me about Vietnam," I said finally during a break in the conversation.

"What do you mean?"

"You talked last time in your office about how you and Hollister met there. Served together—and then you went to work for him when you got back to the U.S. and left the Army. I thought that might be interesting for a follow-up story. You know how we operate in the media: we're always trying to keep a big story like this alive for a bit longer, if we can."

It seemed like as good an excuse as any to explain my sudden interest about Vietnam.

"Charlie and I got drafted just before the U.S. was getting ready to pull out of the country altogether at the end of the war. Bad luck for both of us. They ended the draft after that. But not in time for us. Charlie and I were both assigned to MACV headquarters in

Saigon. We just kind of hit it off, I guess. We became inseparable for the rest of our time there. And we stayed friends for more than a half century afterward."

"What exactly was MACV?" I asked Stovall.

"MACV stood for Military Assistance Command, Vietnam. It was the headquarters for special operations and intelligence operations through the entire country. Not that there was much intelligence going on there, we used to laugh. Both of us were just counting the days until we could go home.

"I still remember how great it was when that finally happened. We were on this jet that took us back to the States at Fort Lewis, Oregon. When the plane touched down on U.S. soil, this huge cheer erupted from all of us. God, it was good to be out of Vietnam. Of course, neither of us ever had to go out into the field for real combat, thank God."

"Except there was that time Hollister shot the enemy soldier."

"Yeah, the Viet Cong sapper outside our MACV headquarters. Let me tell you, that was damn shocking—and why the Vietnam war was so scary. It turned out this kid with the explosive had been working for us at the base for a while. Pretending he was on our side, while he was working with the Viet Cong too. That was what happened a lot over there with that damn war. You never knew exactly whose side anyone was on. Damn, it was confusing to have to fight a war that way."

"The 'fog of war,'" I said.

"Huh?"

"That's what Robert McNamara called it years later. In a documentary movie about how both sides stumbled into a war they didn't want. He said neither side really understood it. There were no rules, no boundaries, no hard and fast allegiances like in previous wars we'd fought. No one could be sure who were the good guys and the bad guys. Everyone was always confused about Vietnam. And, in many ways, he said, they still are today. The documentary was called *The Fog of War.*"

"Yeah, that sums it up pretty well." Stovall sighed. "It was such a mess, the whole year we were over there."

"What happened after you and Hollister got back from the war?"

"I had gone to work as an accountant—I went back to school to get my MBA—and then one day I got a call from Charlie. He said he was starting this new business, with computers. He kept talking about the future of computers and how everyone would be using them one day soon. He asked me to join him in his business. I was young and it seemed like fun, so I said yes. And the rest is history. That's how we started the Hollister company."

"Did it take long for you and him to become successful?"

"Not at all. We hit it big right out of the gate. Charlie, he was really into computers, even back then when no one paid much attention to them. Anyway, he came up with this idea for a new super chip, which totally revolutionized the computer industry. Just like Steve Jobs and the iPhone would do later. Everything broke just right for us. And, after that, came the oil wells and the real estate and the media properties and the pharmaceutical companies and everything else."

I waited until the end to bring up Laurie Bateman again. I asked him if he was surprised, after their time together in Vietnam, that Hollister had wound up marrying a woman born in that country.

"Nah, like I told you, Charlie always liked the Asian American look."

"And there was no connection from the time you and he were in Vietnam?"

"What do you mean?"

"Well, her family was there, you were there . . ."

"She wasn't even alive when we were in Vietnam."

"Right," I said.

*   *   *

I finally managed to reach Laurie Bateman. Maybe she got tired of dodging my calls and figured it was easier to talk with me. Anyway, she called back after the latest message that I left for her.

"Sorry, Clare, but it's been pretty hectic around here. I'm in charge now, you know."

"Congratulations," I said.

I wasn't sure if that seemed inappropriate, given the circumstances under which she got the job. But it didn't seem to bother her.

"I wanted to ask you a few questions about Vietnam," I said.

"Why?"

"I found out that your husband had served in Vietnam back in the seventies."

"What does that have to do with anything?"

"You were born in Vietnam."

"I still don't understand what you're driving at. I've got a lot of work to do and I don't have time right now to talk about this with you. I'm sure you can understand that. So . . ."

"There's something else. One of the people at the scene of the subway accident that killed your maid, Carmen Ortega, appeared to be Vietnamese too. Do you have any idea . . . ?"

"I've got to go now, Clare. Let's talk some other time. Goodbye."

She hung up on me.

"Goodbye, girlfriend," I said into the empty line.

CHAPTER 36

"I WANT TO go to Los Angeles," I said to Jack Faron the next day.

"What's in Los Angeles?"

"Unanswered questions about Laurie Bateman and her past."

I told him everything I'd learned over the past few days. Including the vague—but still intriguing—Vietnam connections to Hollister. I said I wanted to interview Laurie Bateman's mother and track down other information about Laurie Bateman's early life in Southern California after coming to the U.S. I said I believed it was all part of the Bateman story, even if I wasn't exactly sure what the story was yet.

Under normal circumstances, I wouldn't have had much of a chance to pull off a cross-country road trip assignment like this. I was supposed to be the news director, which required me to be here to run the Channel 10 newscasts. Also, I didn't have any hard leads or evidence about the Los Angeles angle—merely speculation on my part at the moment. Finally, and this might be the biggest obstacle, the Laurie Bateman story was over as far as most people were concerned. The charges against her had been dropped, and the rest of the media had moved on to other stories. Everyone but me.

But I knew I had some things going for me with Faron too. I'd landed a couple of big scoops for Channel 10 by following my instincts like this over the past few years, and Faron knew that—so he was willing to give me a lot more leeway than with another journalist. Plus maybe, just maybe, Jack Faron—who showed good news instincts of his own in the past—wanted answers to the questions about Laurie Bateman, too.

"While you're in California, will you be talking to West Coast Media?" he asked.

That caught me off guard.

"Who?"

"Mitchell Lansburg?"

"Who?" I said again.

I couldn't think of anything else to say.

"Please don't say 'who' again."

"Okay," I said warily.

"Lansburg is the Vice President for talent at West Coast Media. I have a friend in Los Angeles. He told me how this Lansburg guy and West Coast Media were looking for a big new star to be part of a daytime talk show being broadcast from there. Apparently, they zeroed in on a choice they like for the job. A woman who's broken a lot of big stories and had a stellar career as a journalist—in print; also now on TV. Said this woman even won a Pulitzer once. Are you negotiating for a job with West Coast Media, Clare?"

I had been trying to figure out the best way to bring it up with Faron. But I wasn't planning on dealing with that right away. Except now it was out there.

"I had lunch with Lansburg," I said.

"Why didn't you tell me?"

"I have lunch with a lot of people."

"Did Lansburg offer you a job?"

"Not exactly."

"But he made it clear they were interested in you?"

I nodded.

"Is that what you want to do, Clare? Leave New York and move to Los Angeles? Leave behind everything we've built, you and I, here at Channel 10 News? Being an on-air personality on a TV talk show instead of running a newsroom?"

"I'm not sure. I wanted to think about it. But then everything else happened with the Laurie Bateman story, and I haven't had time to deal with it."

"Remember, Clare, that I was the one who brought you here. After your newspaper went out of business and you were out of a job, I was the one who gave you the opportunity to be in TV journalism. And I was the one who took a chance and made you my news director."

"Uh, is this the part where you make me feel guilty for all you've done for me so I'll stay?"

He smiled. "I thought I'd give it a shot."

I knew this was an uncomfortable subject for him. It was uncomfortable for me, too. I liked Jack Faron. Even more importantly, I respected him. That's pretty rare in the TV news business to have a boss like that. I wondered if I'd find anyone like Jack Faron if I moved to LA.

"Look, I'm going to go out to talk to them about the job sooner or later. At least this way it will all be out in the open between us. I promise you that I won't make any decisions about the talk show job before talking to you first. You know me well enough to know that, even though I do have some unscrupulous qualities, I always keep my word."

In the end, Faron agreed to let me go.

* * *

I told everyone at the news meeting later what I was doing and said that Maggie would be in charge while I was out of town on this assignment.

I was pretty blunt with them about what I was hoping to find out there—evidence that linked Laurie Bateman to her husband's murder again, even though I didn't have the slightest idea what that evidence might be.

"Wait a minute," Dani said when I was through. "Are you now saying you think Bateman really did murder her husband to make sure she got control of his money and his company?"

"I think it's a possibility."

"If that's true, then we—well, mostly you—were the ones who helped her go free and beat the rap," Dani pointed out. "Is that why you're doing this? Because you think you might have messed up—and now you want to make it right?"

"That is a motivating factor," I admitted.

Cassie O'Neal had a question.

"If she's already had the murder charges against her dropped, she can't be charged again even if we find out she did it, right? Isn't that what they call 'double jeopardy'? Like with O.J. Simpson. Even if he called a press conference today to confess he murdered Nicole Brown and Ron Goldman, he couldn't be tried again for murder. Because he's already been acquitted."

Normally, I would have made fun of Cassie—at least behind her back—for not understanding how the law worked.

But I'd wondered about the "double jeopardy" thing myself at first.

Except, as I found out, "double jeopardy" only applied to an actual murder trial where the defendant was acquitted. Not a pre-trial hearing like with Laurie Bateman. She could still have murder charges reinstated against her if substantial new evidence against her was uncovered. I explained that to everyone in the news meeting now.

I also told them I was going to go on air for the 6:00 p.m. newscast to tell viewers about the latest Laurie Bateman story developments I knew—and that I would drop a few hints there, too, that there might be more explosive stuff coming soon.

Then I sat back and listened as everyone talked about the stories we'd be running on the newscast that night. An out-of-control taxicab that jumped the curb and hit a group of tourists in Times Square. A new political squabble between the mayor and the city council president. Speculation from weather forecaster Wendy Jeffers about the possibility of a white Christmas this year.

But I wasn't listening that closely to any of it.

All I cared about right now was Laurie Bateman.

* * *

At least until I got back to my office after the newscast.

There was a phone message waiting for me from Nick Pollock, the Treasury Department guy who looked like Brad Pitt.

I called him back right away.

"I saw your broadcast tonight," Pollock said. "What you were talking about with Laurie Bateman and her taking over her dead husband's position at Hollister's businesses. I wondered if I could meet up with you to talk more about it?"

"Do you plan on picking me up off the street and bringing me to a government building to interrogate me like you did last time?"

"I was thinking about something less official. Are you free for a drink tonight?"

Was I free for a drink tonight? Hell, I had a lot to do. I had to make sure everything here was organized for the 11:00 p.m. newscast. Then I had to go home and start packing for my trip to California. Yep, my schedule was packed with all sorts of stuff I definitely needed to deal with.

"I'd love to have a drink with you," I said.

CHAPTER 37

WE MET AT the Old Town, a historic bar on East 18th Street not far from Union Square. Pollock was sitting at the bar when I came in. As soon as he saw me, he grabbed his drink and moved to one of the booths along the side. I sat down across from him.

"What are you drinking?" he asked.

"How about you?"

"Beer."

"Beer is good for me too."

I decided I'd let him do the talking at first. Until I figured out where this was headed.

"That was an interesting newscast you did tonight about Laurie Bateman and the Charles Hollister murder. It sounds like you know—or at least you suspect—more than you're telling at the moment. That's why I wanted to talk with you."

"Because you liked me so much on TV tonight?"

"Because I also know about you as an award-winning investigative reporter. I found out all about you. The Lucy Devlin kidnap case and everything that went along with that. The media sensation you became for breaking the story about that former Congressman, Bill Atwood, and all the people in the financial scandal a few years ago. Then last year the way you tracked down that serial killer who murdered so many women until you figured it out. You're smart, you're tough, and you're dogged and determined."

"Not to mention that I'm cute as a button too," I said brightly. He smiled.

"Anyway, I was thinking that maybe it was a good idea for you and me to keep in contact about this."

Keep in contact? Him and me? I liked that kind of thinking.

"I know this is a bit tricky. Government and the media, it's a slippery slope in terms of ethics."

This wasn't exactly what I was expecting, but I was interested. Damn interested.

I told him what I'd found out. My questions about the possible Vietnam connection. About my upcoming trip to California to check out more on Laurie Bateman's background and family connections there. About Laurie's sudden change in attitude toward me and refusal to answer my questions about her past. About how I'd been convinced in the beginning that she was innocent, but now I wasn't sure.

He gave me more details about the tax investigation into the Hollister business activities and the search for possibly large amounts of missing funds.

"We think there are serious irregularities going on with the Hollister finances—involving hiding money and assets in secret accounts in the Caribbean and Switzerland—but we can't prove it yet. We were just zeroing in on this full-time when Charles Hollister wound up getting murdered. Maybe it had to do with the financial stuff. Maybe someone killed him to shut him up so he couldn't reveal anything he knew if it all blew up on them."

"And the police know about this possible angle on Hollister's murder?"

"Of course they do. We filled them in on everything. But they weren't convinced. They believed Laurie Bateman murdered him in a rage that night. Now they're looking at everything all over again, but I don't think they're close to cracking anything about the murder."

We talked a lot more after that. It was good. I liked this guy. I'd had a few beers by that point and was starting to feel more relaxed after all the stress and effort of the long workday I'd put in. I decided to take our conversation in another direction.

"Tell me about yourself, Nick."

"What do you want to know?"

"How long have you been working for the Treasury Department?"

"Over twenty years. I joined right after I got out of college with a business degree. I never thought back then I'd make a career out of a government job like this. But it's good. I like it. It's a nice life."

"Do you live in the city?"

"Brooklyn. Got a two-bedroom apartment in Park Slope."

"Nice."

"Yeah, I got lucky. You know how it is with finding a good apartment in New York City these days."

"Are you married?" I asked him, throwing that last question out there as casually as I could.

"Not yet."

Uh-oh. I didn't like that answer. It sounded like there was more to come. And I was right. There was.

"But you're thinking about it?"

"A lot."

"So you're in a relationship?"

"Yes, I am. Neither of us have been ready for marriage until now. But we're definitely thinking about it. Maybe next year. That's what he and I are looking at right now."

There was a word I'd just heard from him that hung out there now like a flashing red light between us.

"He?" I asked.

"My partner. His name's Joe Trecker. He's on the faculty at NYU. Teaches American History. Good guy. You'd like him."

"So that means you're . . ." I said slowly.

"Right. I'm gay. Does that shock you?"

"Uh, no . . . I mean I didn't realize . . ."

"Nothing wrong with that, you know," he laughed, uttering the famous Seinfeld line.

"No, of course not."

*   *   *

"He's gay?" Janet said to me when I called her afterward.

"Oh, he's gay."

"Jeez, how come you didn't see that one coming?"

"Well, it's not like he was wearing a sign around his neck."

I told her how I planned to stay in touch with him on the Hollister stuff once I got back from California.

"I like him, Janet. He's smart, funny, and totally dedicated to his job. We had a good talk together about everything tonight. He's pretty much everything I would want if I drew up a design for the perfect man in my life."

"Except he's gay."

"Well, there is that," I said.

CHAPTER 38

THE TEMPERATURE WAS 75 degrees, the sun was shining brightly, and I was humming "California Dreamin'" when my plane landed in Los Angeles. It had been 22 degrees and sleeting when I left New York, and I slipped and fell on a patch of ice trying to hail a taxi on my way to the airport. I sure could get used to this Southern California weather if I did decide to move out here.

I rented a car at LAX, drove north up the I-405 Freeway, and headed toward LA. My hotel was in Beverly Hills, right off of trendy Rodeo Drive. In the end, Faron had chosen to go first class with my accommodations. But I wanted to play tourist for a while before I checked into the hotel.

So I went first to Hollywood and checked out famous spots there. Grauman's Chinese Theater. The Wax Museum. The Capitol Records building. Eventually, I got to Hollywood and Vine, the legendary cross street in the middle of Hollywood.

The Hollywood Walk of Fame ran through much of this area—more than 2,500 stars on the sidewalk that memorialized the great Hollywood names over the years. Cary Grant, Jimmy Stewart, Audrey Hepburn, Charlie Chaplin, Marilyn Monroe, Bette Davis, John Wayne, Elizabeth Taylor, and so many others. I'd visited Los Angeles in the past, even been in Hollywood a few times, but this was the first time I was here knowing I could be a part of this whole glamorous town soon. It was a sobering thought.

There was even a star for Laurie Bateman on the walk. She hadn't been as big in movies as a lot of the other big names, but she made it a few years ago because of her fame in TV advertising and the modeling world and for just being an A-List celebrity. Which counted for a lot in this town.

Standing next to Laurie Bateman's star now, I could see the iconic Hollywood sign off in the distance, proclaiming to all that this was the capital of the entertainment world, a magical place where dreams could come true for anyone. Like Laurie Bateman. Her dream had sure come true.

Hell, she had probably stood on this same spot in the past and looked at that sign from her own star. Maybe thinking about how far she'd come from the little girl born to a family 6,000 miles away in war-torn Vietnam and everything that had happened to her since then. Yes, the American Dream came true for Laurie Bateman in Hollywood.

*   *   *

I drove back to Beverly Hills and ate lunch at a café where I sat outside at a table overlooking Beverly Drive, around the corner from my hotel.

As I watched the people on the street walking past dressed in short-sleeve shirts and shorts and casual clothes, I thought about how much different December and the holiday season looked in LA compared to New York City. Sure, there was no snow and the Christmas trees and other decorations that festooned the streets here looked out of place in this setting. But, all in all, the weather sure was a big plus when it came to deciding whether to move here or not.

I was trying to watch for celebrities, of course. Everyone told me you saw movie stars and other celebrities on the streets of LA all the time. That was pretty cool. Except I hadn't found one yet. No Bradley Cooper. No Jennifer Lawrence. No Leonardo DiCaprio. I thought I might have seen Kurt Russell at one point. Or Jeff Bridges. The two of them always look sort of alike to me. Or maybe he was just some scruffy guy with long hair looking around for celebrities just like me.

I was excited to be here. Excited about the possibilities of the new job. And, most of all, excited about digging into Laurie Bateman's past. While I ate, I went over everything I hoped to accomplish in the next few days.

The first thing I planned to do was look into the death of Laurie Bateman's father. Sure, it had been more than half a century ago when he was killed in a traffic accident. But I was still intrigued by the timing of that—so soon after his family arrived from Vietnam—and figured it would be an interesting part of whatever Laurie Bateman background story I came up with. My ex-husband Sam had set me up for a meeting with an LA cop friend of his who said he would dig up the old file on the case for me.

The biggest thing, though, was getting an interview with Laurie Bateman's mother. She still lived in her dead husband Marvin Bateman's house located in La Jolla, a few hours south near San Diego. I wasn't sure she'd talk to me. I hadn't called ahead to try and set up an interview though. It's too easy for her to say no like that. I was going to just show up at her door and see what happened. Sometimes the surprise interview is the best way to go.

I'd discovered that Laurie Bateman's first agent—the one her mother had used to try and make her a child star in the beginning—

was still working in LA. His name was Stuart Gilmore, and I made an appointment to meet with him after I went to see Laurie's mother in La Jolla. I figured he might have good information for the story too.

There was also a Charles Hollister angle. His first wife, the one he married in the seventies, was still alive and living in Northern California. She wouldn't know anything about Laurie Bateman, but maybe she could tell me more about Charles Hollister back then in his early days after he first came back from Vietnam. I contacted her and made arrangements to fly up to see her before I went back to New York.

And no, I hadn't forgotten about the job offer. I'd notified Mitchell Lansburg that I planned to be here and could meet with anyone he wanted me to see. Turned out he was going to be in LA at the same time. So, we made plans to get together and he would introduce me to everyone I might be working with in LA.

Yep, I had a busy time ahead of me. A jam-packed schedule. But right now, I was tired from my long trip. So after lunch I drove to my hotel, checked in, fell onto the bed, and took a nap. When the going gets tough, the tough get some sleep. I woke up feeling refreshed, rejuvenated, and ready to go to work. There was a window in the hotel room where I could see another view of the beauty and enormity of Los Angeles.

Hollywood, the place where dreams come true.

That's what happened to a lot of people who've passed through this town, including Laurie Bateman.

And now I was here.

Clare Carlson, the hotshot TV chick.

Look out LA, here I come!

CHAPTER 39

I DROVE THE next morning over to Parker Center police head-quarters in downtown LA to meet with Sam's cop friend.

His name was Sergeant Dennis Lang. Lang looked to be at least fifty, with gray, thinning hair, and a paunch that suggested to me he hadn't been running around on the streets for a while. He confirmed that, telling me he'd worked in the records division at Parker Center for a number of years now.

He used to be on the NYPD, he said, which was where he worked with Sam. But he retired and left New York for the West Coast. When he got bored in retirement, he signed up with the LAPD and wound up in this desk job.

"Sam told me you were a good journalist and I could trust you," Lang said.

"Good to hear."

"He also said that you had a big mouth and could be a real pain in the ass."

"Hard to believe, huh?"

"Why do you think he would say something like that about you? Do you know him pretty well?

"Uh, we used to be married."

"Sam never mentioned that to me."

"It might have slipped his mind. It was over so quickly."

"And he's still your friend?"

"He used to be my enemy right after the divorce."

"And now?"

"I think he tolerates me."

Eventually he got around to the death of Pham Van Quong, the father of the little infant girl who would grow up to be Laurie Bateman. He had a file with a few records and documents he'd copied on the accident that killed Pham. It wasn't a big file. Not that I expected it to be for a traffic accident that happened nearly fifty years ago.

Lang said Pham had attended night classes at UCLA and also worked as a repairman in an electronics shop. He had come to America on a government grant program from the South Vietnamese regime a year or so earlier—then was joined by his family later after the collapse of the South Vietnam government.

Pham had been hit by a car at an intersection not far from the UCLA campus as he was heading home from classes there on September 23, 1975. The impact hurled him onto the hood of the car until he fell back onto the street. He was pronounced dead at the scene.

"And that's all there is to it?" I asked. "What's in this file?"

"Pretty much."

"What about the driver of the car that hit him?"

"No one ever found out what the driver's story was."

"What do you mean?"

"He left the scene without stopping or contacting anyone for help."

"It was a hit-and-run?"

"Yes. This man you're asking about was killed by a hit-and-run driver."

*   *   *

The file on Pham Van Quong contained the address of the electronics shop where he had worked and also the address of where he had lived back then. Presumably with his wife and the baby that would grow up to be Laurie Bateman. I went to both places. It was foolish, I knew—there was going to be nothing there after all this time that could help me. But I did it anyway. And, of course, I was right—both places were long gone. The electronics store was now a CVS pharmacy and the house where Pham Van Quong and his family lived had been torn down many years earlier to make room for a new apartment complex.

I went to UCLA, too. That took a long time because I first had to find someone who would be willing to help me on what was going to be a difficult—and probably fruitless—task. I eventually talked to a young woman named Cheryl who was impressed by the fact that I was a TV reporter working on a story. Cheryl said she would love to be a TV reporter one day. The fact that I told her I might be joining a TV show in LA soon didn't hurt my image in her eyes either. She agreed to do whatever she could to help.

"Everything's on computer now," she explained when I told her what I was looking for.

"That should make it easier, right?"

"The computer files only go back about twenty-five years or so."

"Right."

It's never easy.

"What about paper records? Would they still be around?"

"We never throw anything away." She smiled.

"So you could go look through them?"

"It would require a lot of work for something that long ago."

"Hey, that's what we reporters do, right, Cheryl?"

It did take a while, but she came back with records on Pham Van Quong. They showed he had attended UCLA until September of 1975 when he suddenly stopped showing up at classes. Which I now knew was because he was dead. I asked if there was anything in the records about the government program that had allowed him to come to America and enroll at the school.

"Yes, it does appear that he was here on a government grant program. That's where the money came from. I have records of his tuition payments here and they all are from the government."

"The South Vietnamese government, right?"

"No, the U.S. government."

"Excuse me?"

"Pham Van Quong's tuition was being paid for at UCLA by funds from the U.S. Government."

"What agency?"

"It looks like the Department of Defense."

"Why would the U.S. Department of Defense pay for his tuition?"

"I have no idea."

There was one other thing I wanted to know before I left.

"What was he studying at UCLA?"

She looked back through the records for the information.

"Well, it looks as if he was enrolled in several different kinds of courses. American History. English, learning how to speak it better. But most of all it looked like he was pursuing a course of study in computer sciences."

"They had computer sciences back then?'

"It was the beginning of the computer era, and I can see from the records that Pham Van Quong's goal was to work in this field."

*   *   *

The final thing I did was go to the location near the UCLA campus where he had been run down by a car on that long-ago night.

Again, I didn't expect to find anything out there that I didn't know. It was a busy intersection with lots of cars and people walking on the sidewalk or sitting in cafés and visiting stores nearby. No one knew anything or cared about an accident that happened there a half century ago. But standing there now, on the same spot where Pham Van Quong might have stood that night, I tried to put together all the pieces I knew about his life and his death.

There were an awful lot of coincidences in this story.

Charles Hollister had been in Vietnam, which was where Laurie Bateman's family came from.

Both Hollister and Laurie's father had been interested in computers, which were just starting to emerge as a force at the time.

Hollister went on to become a billionaire from his groundbreaking work with computers while Pham Van Quong—Laurie's father—died a lonely death right here.

I didn't know what any of this meant—or if it meant anything at all.

Neither did the police.

But maybe Pham Van Quong's wife—the mother of Laurie Bateman—would.

CHAPTER 40

IF I WAS looking for reasons to make the move to California, La Jolla sure would be a good one. The two-hour drive down there from LA was pretty spectacular. But the town of La Jolla itself was even better. Nestled against the coast with beautiful homes and beautiful views and the smell of the ocean everywhere you went. I even stopped off at a Starbucks in town when I got there, and the table where I sat overlooked the Pacific Ocean. Definitely a cool spot to drink your morning coffee.

Laurie Bateman's mother lived in a place about five minutes out of town. Her name was Gloria Bateman. As with her daughter, she'd changed her Vietnamese name to an American one when she came here. And she still used the name Gloria Bateman, even though her husband had died years earlier. She had been Gloria Bateman for a long time now.

The house was impressive, but not ostentatious. It was located on a slight hill, which gave it an unfettered view of the water and many of the other nearby houses. I'd read how Marvin Bateman had bought this house as a retreat from Hollywood and all the people and pressures there.

Gloria Bateman herself had to be close to seventy now, but she didn't look it. She was almost a mirror image of her daughter, albeit a more mature version. But still beautiful with striking features and an almost regal presence about her.

I hadn't been sure on the drive down to La Jolla whether or not she'd agree to talk to me. But that turned out to be no problem at all. When I knocked on her door and told her who I was and why I was there, she invited me in without any hesitation.

Sitting in the living room now and drinking tea, I asked her why she was so willing to meet with a strange reporter who unexpectedly knocked on her door. I was curious.

"I know exactly who you are," she said. "I know all about you. You're the woman who helped save my daughter from prison. I am so grateful to you. And happy to help you now in any way that I can."

I told her that I was putting together a piece about her daughter's background, coming here to America as a baby and finding fame and fortune. I said I wanted to find out everything I could about that time. Which was pretty much true. I asked what she could tell me about their flight from Vietnam to arrive in the U.S.

"I know it was a long time ago, and you probably don't remember . . ."

"Oh, I remember," she said. "I remember every second of it. You can never forget something so life-changing as that. They aren't pleasant memories, I'm afraid. Instead, it was a nightmare for a long time, a horrible nightmare that I thought I would never be able to wake up from."

There were pictures on the wall next to me. Many of them were of her and her young daughter in America. A distinguished-looking man was in a few of them. I assumed that was Marvin Bateman, the husband she had met here—after her first husband died—who became Laurie's stepfather. But there was one picture that showed her with a good-looking Vietnamese man and a baby. I asked her if that was the birth father of Laurie, Pham Van Quong. She said he

was. I couldn't tell from the picture whether it had been taken before they left Vietnam or after they arrived in America. Looking at
it now after all these years, I couldn't help but wonder if the people
in the picture had any idea about what the future held in store for
them. Or, in the case of Pham Van Quong, no future at all.

She talked then about those last days in Vietnam and the fall of
Saigon and the desperate efforts to get out of the war-torn country.

"Vietnam was our home, the only home we had ever known.
But now the war was lost and the Communists were coming. We
all knew the horrors that would mean to those of us who had
supported the South Vietnamese government and the U.S, so we
had to get out. I lived in a small town at the time, which was outside of Saigon.

"My husband had already left for America to attend classes in
college here. But we—me and my newborn baby—were left behind.
I knew we had to get to Saigon if we were to have any chance of es-
caping. That's where the American helicopters were evacuating
people to ships off the coast. It was terribly difficult to get to Saigon.

"And, when we finally did, even more difficult to get close to
the American embassy where the helicopters were taking off from.
Thousands of people were massed outside, storming the embassy
in hopes of being one of the people picked to leave. Marines had
to battle the crowds back. It seemed hopeless."

"But you did manage to get out of Vietnam," I pointed out.
"How did you do that?"

"I sold the most valuable thing I had to the U.S. Marines
guarding the embassy."

"What did you have that was so valuable?"

"My body."

I suddenly realized what she was telling me. I let that sink in for
a few seconds without saying anything. I didn't have to. She was

perfectly willing to keep telling the story without any prodding from me.

"Yes, I knew I was attractive to men. And so I used that to my advantage. I had to do something to get myself and my baby daughter on one of those evacuation helicopters. So that's what I did. I did whatever it took."

I sipped on my tea. This was a great story. One way or another, this was going to be great stuff on the background of Laurie Bateman. This wasn't the fairy tale we'd already heard about the American Dream and all that crap; it was the real deal.

I'd come without a video crew because I wasn't sure if she'd talk to me, and I figured it was best to meet one-on-one first. But my plan was to do a big on-air interview with her later, and to do the same with everyone else I talked to out here. Then, rather than just put the interviews on air immediately, I'd do a special exclusive report on all of it when I got back to New York. Right now though, I wanted to hear more of Gloria Bateman's story.

"I thought that was the worst part of my nightmare, but it wasn't over yet," she told me. "It took us a long time to get to America. First, they switched us to Guam, then to Hawaii, and finally to San Francisco before we wound up in Los Angeles. I was reunited with my husband then. But times were still hard as he tried to work to make enough money to support a family while going to college at the same time. And then he died."

I tried to find out more about how her husband managed to come to America before the rest of his family. But she didn't know, or at least wouldn't tell me if she did. She said he did some kind of work for the government in South Vietnam and they sent him to the U.S. for training in electronic sciences. She also told me she didn't know anything about any involvement by the U.S. government—or more specifically the Defense Department, as the clerk at UCLA had told me.

I asked her about the car accident that had killed her husband. She didn't give me many more details. But she did say: "I was devastated when he died. I was living in a strange country, along with my baby daughter, and I had no money and no way of knowing how we were going to survive here."

"Until you met Marvin Bateman," I said.

"Yes. Marvin was the solution to my problems. He married me, he gave me a home, and he later made my daughter a star. As a child actress in TV commercials at first, then modeling, and eventually TV and movies."

The American Dream. It had all come true for her. There was one other question I had though. The accounts I'd read in Maggie's file said she'd had a brother that lived with them in Vietnam. I'd wondered about the brother when she'd been talking, but I didn't want to interrupt the flow. Now I brought it up.

"You had a brother with you in Vietnam. Where was he when all this was happening?"

She shook her head sadly.

"My brother, Binh, never made it out of Vietnam. It was only Laurie and me."

"Why . . . ?"

"Binh died in Vietnam."

"Died how?"

"He was killed during the war."

"Killed in the fighting?"

She nodded.

"Was he with the South Vietnamese Army?"

"My brother died during the war," she said, and that was all.

It was clear that it still pained her to talk about her dead brother even after all this time.

"Have you talked to Laurie since she took over Charles Hollister's business?" I asked now, deciding to switch the subject.

"No."

"When is the last time you talked to her? When she was in jail and charged with murder?"

"No, I didn't talk to her then either. I haven't talked to my daughter in several years. We don't speak anymore."

That was another shocker I hadn't seen coming.

"Why is that?"

"I disagreed with my daughter's decision to marry that Hollister man. I pleaded with her not to do it. She ignored me and married him anyway. She got the wealth she wanted, I guess, but she and I no longer have a relationship."

"Why didn't you want her to marry Hollister?"

"I had my reasons."

"Have you met him?"

"Yes, I met him."

"When was that?"

"The last time? Not long ago. A few weeks before he died. He showed up at my door here. Just like you did today. He wanted to talk to me, too. But I wouldn't see him. I just slammed the door in his face. That made me feel good to do that."

"Why did you hate him so much?"

"I thought he was wrong for my daughter. He hurt her and did bad things to her. He was a bad person. That's why I was willing to talk to you. You helped my daughter. I still love my daughter. And I will do anything I can to protect her from people like Charles Hollister."

"Even though you haven't talked to her in years?"

"She's still my daughter."

CHAPTER 41

If the years had been kind to Laurie's mother, they weren't to Stuart Gilmore, her first agent.

His office was in a run-down-looking building near the old center of Hollywood at Hollywood and Vine. There were so many legends about that spot. Lana Turner being discovered at a soda fountain at a Schwab's drugstore and all the rest. Many of those colorful buildings from the old days were gone now, replaced by fast-food places, coffee shops, and convenience stores.

They hadn't gotten around to replacing Stuart Gilmore's building yet. But it didn't look like it would be there for long. There was a sign on the elevator in the lobby that said it was out of order. There was also a tattered directory with only a few names on it; all the other offices seemed to be empty.

Gilmore's office was listed on the sixth floor. I trudged up the steps, gingerly making my way through debris, garbage, and even a sleeping derelict.

"I've been here for a long, long time," Gilmore told me inside his office. It was small, but comfortable. There were pictures of celebrities on the wall behind his desk, many of them either dead or long forgotten. One of the pictures, though, was of Laurie Bateman.

Gilmore himself must have been near eighty now, and the suit and tie he was wearing looked almost as old. He was bald and frail, but he seemed to enjoy the opportunity to talk about the old days when he represented a young Laurie Bateman. I wondered if he had any clients now or if he just came to the office every day out of habit.

"Laurie was only probably four or five when I met her. That must have been back around 1980. She came to see me with her mother. Of course, her name wasn't Laurie Bateman then. It was still her Vietnamese name, Pham Van Kieu.

"She was cute and precocious, and I thought she could be special. But there are a lot of cute, pretty little girls in Hollywood. Hundreds of mothers seem to bring them in to agents like me thinking their daughter can be a big star. As you might suspect, most of them aren't. It's hard to get attention in this town.

"That's what happened to the little girl I knew as Pham Van Kieu at first. She didn't get much attention. She was just another face in the crowd when I was representing her. Those were tough years for her—and her mother. Her mother wanted to make her a star. Every rejection made her more and more desperate to try something else. Nothing worked. And then, suddenly, she exploded into this incredible celebrity superstar she became. It was pretty amazing."

"What changed to make all this success happen?"

"Pham Van Kieu became Laurie Bateman."

"You mean the name change did it?"

"Not just the name. Her mother married Marvin Bateman, the big Hollywood producer."

"And that's what made her a star?"

Gilmore nodded.

"Bateman was powerful enough to pull a lot of strings and get her the roles I couldn't. She went on to become the Laurie Bateman she is today. Me, I didn't get anything out of it. After Bateman came into the picture, her mother told me she didn't need me anymore. And I guess she was right. I mean, she had Marvin Bateman."

I thought about what he had just told me.

"What was the mother doing for a living when you first met her?"

"She had a couple of jobs. She cleaned houses for people in Hollywood. She worked as a waitress, too, at a restaurant out in the valley. Back then, she did anything she had to to support her and her daughter. Her husband had died, I believe, and they didn't have much money."

"Then how did she meet someone like Marvin Bateman?"

"I always wondered about that. At first, I thought it was just luck. But later I wasn't so sure. The mother was a beautiful woman. I think she realized that and used it to her advantage. She used her sexual attractiveness to get what she wanted—and what she wanted for her daughter."

I remembered her story now of using sex to help her get her and her baby daughter out of Vietnam.

"She slept with Bateman to get her daughter the big break that made her a star in Hollywood?" I asked.

"Something like that."

"Do you know that for a fact?"

He shook his head. "All I know is that I found out she had gotten herself a job as Bateman's housekeeper. He was married to another woman at the time. But shortly after she started working for him, he divorced his wife and married the housekeeper. She became Gloria Bateman and Kieu became Laurie Bateman. Everything exploded for her in Hollywood after that. You can connect the dots on that pretty easily, right?"

I sure could. And, having just met Gloria Bateman, I had no doubt that she was capable of using her beauty and sexual wiles to snare a big catch like Marvin Bateman. Damn, this was a woman who would do anything to get what she wanted. I wondered if her daughter was the same way.

"From what I've heard though, she and Bateman were pretty happy together," Gilmore said. "They seemed to be in love with each other. He was supposed to have been a good father to Laurie when she was growing up. No matter how the whole thing started, people say it turned out to be a good marriage."

"That's what they said about Laurie's marriage to Charles Hollister, too, before the real truth emerged," I pointed out.

Gilmore shrugged. "Anyway, then Marvin Bateman died."

"How did that happen?"

I realized I'd never checked into the details of Bateman's death. It didn't seem important at the time.

"Suicide."

"He killed himself?"

"Yes. They discovered him in the bedroom with a gunshot to his head. There was no suicide note, but he was holding the pistol in his hand. And there was no sign of any kind of break-in or other criminal activity in the house. It was declared a suicide. I'm told Laurie was devastated by his death. That it took her a long time to get over what happened to her stepfather. It was horrible for her."

"Because they were so close?"

"Because she was the one who found the body."

CHAPTER 42

I WAS SUPPOSED to take a meeting with Mitchell Lansburg at West Coast Media Studios. That's the way people in Hollywood talked, you "took a meeting" with someone. Or you "do lunch." I'd done my research on this. I wanted to fit into the Southern California lifestyle. And my knowledge of that lifestyle up to this point had pretty much consisted of watching reruns of *Baywatch* and *Melrose Place*.

The West Coast Media studios were located in Burbank, like many of the other big TV studios for shows that were produced in LA. I drove there in my rental convertible with the top down, singing "It Never Rains in Southern California." Except it did. Well, it wasn't actually raining at the moment, but it was cloudy and the temperature was barely above sixty. Still, it was better than the sub-freezing weather back in New York.

I wondered if I'd see any celebrities at West Coast Media. I wasn't doing that well on the celebrity sighting front. The only one I'd encountered so far was Pat Sajak, who was eating dinner in a restaurant at the hotel where I was staying. I wasn't sure if Pat Sajak qualified as a bona fide celebrity or not, but he was the best I had so far. I resisted the urge to go over and get his autograph. If I had, I planned to ask him if he would "sell me a vowel" in his name. But then he's probably heard that joke a lot. So I let him eat in peace. Now if it was Vanna White, that would have been a whole different story. I would have been all over Vanna doing autographs and selfies and anything else until they threw me out of the place.

There were a lot of people lined up in the lobby of the West Coast Media studio building. Not celebrities though, just tourists and sightseers on one of the tours or with tickets for a show. I talked to one of the security people and told him who I was and why I was there. He checked with Mitchell Lansburg's office, then escorted me to the front, past the waiting crowd and toward the elevator. Everyone in the crowd looked at me with curiosity as I walked by them. Probably figured I was a celebrity. I waved at them and tried to smile like a star. Some of them waved back. They'd seen a Hollywood star, even if they weren't sure who it was. Something to tell the folks back home.

Lansburg was waiting for me when I got off the elevator. He was dressed more casually than he'd been in New York—no suit, just slacks and an open-collared sports shirt. He was still wearing the wedding ring though, not that it really mattered to me. He led me to an office with a long window wrapped around with a view of Hollywood and the hills in the distance. It was a pretty terrific view.

"So how are you enjoying Southern California so far?" he asked. "Is it everything you hoped it would be? Does it look like a place where you'd be comfortable working and living?"

"I like it, Mr. Lansburg," I said. "I like it a lot."

"Call me Mitchell," he said, like he had the first time we met.

"Mitchell seems awfully formal for a first name."

"That's my name."

"Can I call you Mitch?"

"Not if you want this job." He smiled.

"Then I guess Mitchie would be out of the question."

He smiled again. "That's what we like about you. The snappy comebacks, the quips, the repartee. Imagine yourself doing that on the air, not just sitting here with me. Just being yourself. That's all we'd be asking you to do, Clare. Be yourself on the air. Just be Clare Carlson for the audience."

"And you'd pay me a lot of money to do that?"

"We would."

"That sounds like a pretty good deal."

He took me then on a tour of the place. Showed me the studio where the show would likely be broadcast from. It was empty now. But I tried to imagine it filled with people and me onstage in front of them. Like Ellen or Dr. Phil or the people from *The View* or *The Talk*. It was an exciting image. He said that I'd have my own big office like the one we'd been sitting in, my own assistant—and they'd rent me a car and also pay for my rent in a condo to live out here.

"Can I have a convertible?" I asked.

"If that's what you want."

"What make?"

"What make do you want?"

"Something more expensive than Ellen drives."

I did have a serious question for him. "You haven't made me a specific offer yet. Is that coming soon? I still haven't decided what I'm going to do, but I can't do anything until you actually offer me the job."

"These things take time." He sighed. "We have to get approval from the West Coast Media board of directors and set up the advertising and talk about marketing options and a lot of other things like making sure all the local outlets are on board. It's not a simple process. But I have every confidence that we'll get a green light for your show, Clare. Then it will be up to you to decide what you want to do."

He asked me about the Laurie Bateman story. I told him what I'd been doing. He was excited about it all. Said that was the exact kind of story he hoped I'd be doing on the air soon for them. Digging into a big murder, exploring the past, looking for answers even if I wasn't sure what the questions were.

"Would you like to have dinner with me tomorrow night?" he asked me then out of the blue.

"Dinner?"

"Yes, I thought we could talk more about all these ideas—in a less formal setting. I've got a business conference I need to attend tonight. But I thought maybe tomorrow night you and I could hang out and go over all this."

"Dinner," I repeated, thinking about my options here.

I looked down at the wedding ring on his hand. Yep, the wedding ring was still there on his finger.

"I'm going up to Sacramento tomorrow to talk to Charles Hollister's ex-wife," I said finally.

I'd already made an appointment to see Susan Daily, Hollister's first wife, and I didn't want to take any chance of her backing out on that.

"Okay, then let's say we do it when you get back to New York."

"That would be nice," I said.

*   *   *

After I left his office, I spent time making phone calls.

First to Janet.

"He asked me out on a date," I told her.

"The guy who's interviewing you for this big job?"

"Uh-huh."

I told her about our conversation.

"That's not necessarily an invitation for a date," she pointed out.

"I know, but it sure sounded like a date invitation."

"Okay, this is potentially a real dangerous area, professionally speaking. He's in charge of hiring you. If he comes on to you, that's a real mess depending on what happens after that. For both of you. He comes across as a guy flaunting his power and authority to get sex. And you run the risk of being accused of using sex to climb the career ladder."

"Good point."

"And, from what you say, he's also married."

"Even better point."

"What are you going to do?"

"Probably have dinner with him when I get back to New York."

"Are you that desperate for a man, Clare?"

"I think my actions speak for themselves," I told her.

*   *   *

Later, I called my daughter. She asked me if I'd decided yet whether or not I could come to Virginia to spend Christmas with her and my granddaughter, Audrey, and her husband and family. I said I still wasn't sure about that. She said it would be wonderful if I could figure out a way for us all to be together for the holidays.

Then she brought up the business about the breast cancer gene again. I'd been trying to avoid that topic, but I assured her that I had gone to see a doctor and taken the tests to determine if I was carrying the gene.

"You're telling me the truth about this, right?"

"Why would I lie?"

"Because I know you well enough now to know that you put off things that you don't want to deal with."

"I promise you I will let you know as soon as I find out the test results."

"Why don't you call the doctor again and check?"

I did do that after I got off the phone with her. But the people that were in the office then didn't know anything. They asked if I wanted to leave a message for someone to get back to me. But I said I'd call back later on.

The truth was I didn't want to deal with this right now.

I had a big story to do.

The Laurie Bateman/Charles Hollister story.

I'd deal with everything else later . . .

CHAPTER 43

I saw Susan Daily in Sacramento the next day. The wife Hollister left—and eventually divorced—in a psychiatric hospital. I wasn't sure what I'd find when I met her, but it turned out to be a lot different than what I expected.

She was a psychiatrist herself now.

After getting treated for depression, she decided she wanted to devote her life to helping other people with the same problems. After her marriage to Hollister ended, she used the money from the divorce settlement to go to medical school, get her degree in psychiatry, and open up a practice in Sacramento.

I sat in her office in a medical complex and listened to her as she told me about how she'd managed to turn her life around.

"Doctor, heal thyself," I said when she was finished.

"Something like that."

"Hey, that's great, Dr. Daily."

But what I really wanted to talk about, of course, was her ex-husband. She'd been stunned by the news of his murder, she said. Especially, she said, because she had just reconnected with him again before that happened. He had come to see her again after all this time, she told me.

"When was that?"

"A few weeks ago, I guess."

About the same time he'd gone to see Laurie Bateman's mother.

"To say that I was surprised to see him after all this time would be an understatement. I was floored when he walked in. I mean this was the Charles Hollister who had gone on to become so rich and so famous. But he didn't act that way when he was here that day. He was just . . . well, just Charles. The good Charles. The one I knew a long time ago and married.

"I told him that I was mostly responsible for the failure of our marriage, not him. I mean, it wasn't deliberate. But I was sick, and I had no idea how or why I did many of the things I did. It turned out that I was living with a chemical imbalance. I had a disease. I didn't understand all of the ramifications of depression then. I do now.

"The doctors I saw back then diagnosed me with clinical depression. The first doctor gave me drugs to deal with the depression. The second put me in psychiatric analysis five times a week. The third tried both at the same time and suggested electroshock therapy. None of it worked. My problems, my depression, just got worse.

"By the fifth year of our marriage, I wasn't even able to leave the house. I refused to go to the store or go out to eat or even walk out to get the paper or the mail. At the end, I covered the windows, locked the door, and sat there in the dark struggling with my undefinable demons.

"It was tough on Charles. He tried to help me for as long as he could. But, in the end, I think he needed to get away from me for his own sanity. I was eventually committed to an institution, and I didn't even realize our divorce had gone through until later. But I never blamed Charles. I blamed myself for why our marriage failed. I told him that the day he was here."

I asked her what Hollister had talked about with her—and if he explained why he had come to see her.

"He talked about a lot of things," she said slowly. "Almost like he came to me for professional advice. But I can't discuss much of it. Even though he's dead now. Patient-doctor confidentially, I guess I'd call it. Even though I wasn't really his doctor. So maybe just respect for his privacy. But I can tell you a few things. Mostly, I'd say Charles was here searching for answers."

"Answers about what?"

"His life."

"Something in his life now? His marriage to Laurie Bateman?"

"His entire life. All the way back to when he was a young man."

"Give me an example."

"Well, he talked a lot about Vietnam. That time he spent there seemed to have a dramatic impact on his life. More than I realized when I was married to him. Maybe even more of an impact than he realized back then. But now he said he thought about Vietnam a lot. He seemed to have a lot of regrets about what he did in Vietnam."

She said that Hollister also seemed to have a lot of regrets about his children. That his son, Charles, had not turned out to be the man he'd hoped for in a son. And that his daughter, Elaine, and he no longer had a relationship.

"He didn't tell me what happened with him and the two of them. But he seemed sad about it. He always wanted children when we were together, but all my issues kept getting in the way of that. I knew having a family—having children to carry on for him when he got older—was important to him. I'm sorry the way it worked out."

"Did you ever know Karen Hollister, the mother of the children?"

"No, they met after our divorce. Charles was faithful to me while we were together. At least as far as I know. She died, right?"

"Yes, a few years ago."

"And then he married Laurie Bateman."

"Did that surprise you?"

"Nothing surprised me about Charles after everything he accomplished in his life. He was rich, he was powerful, he was famous. So I guess it made sense for him to acquire a trophy wife. Like Laurie Bateman. Just like another one of his oil wells or big companies."

"Did he talk about Laurie at all when he was here?"

"No, he never mentioned her. I thought that was a bit strange. I assumed that things weren't going well in their marriage. But he never brought her up at all. Mostly kept talking about us and a lot of other things from the old days. He kept saying he was looking for answers about his past. I was never sure exactly what answers he was looking for. Or why he had come to see me because it had been so long since we were married. But then he said he went back to talk to the woman before me too so . . ."

At first, I didn't understand what she was talking about.

"What woman?" I asked.

"Janice Novak."

It hit me then. Janice Novak was the woman I'd read about in the Hollister background file who he'd been married to briefly after he got back from Vietnam. They ran off to Las Vegas to get hitched, then had the marriage annulled the next day. They must have barely known each other. Why did Charles Hollister go back looking for her in those last days of his life?

Susan Daily shook her head sadly.

"I hope Charles found out the answers he was looking for before he died," she said.

"Me too."

I didn't tell her though that I was beginning to suspect one of those answers might have been what got him killed.

CHAPTER 44

JANICE NOVAK LIVED in Atlanta. Her husband was a lawyer and a lobbyist there for the Georgia State Legislature. I found all this out about her pretty quickly after I left Susan Daily's office, along with an address and a phone number in Georgia.

I called the number and asked Janice Novak if she'd be willing to meet with me to talk about Charles Hollister for the TV report I was doing.

It was a long way to go for a single interview, especially one I didn't need to do for the Laurie Bateman story. But that's the thing about being a reporter. You never really know what you need—or don't need—on a story until you track down all of the information. And I was curious.

So once Janice Novak agreed to talk with me, I booked a flight to Atlanta.

Even after all these years, she was still an attractive woman. Gray hair by now, but striking features and well-proportioned body that looked like she spent a lot of time in the gym to keep it that way. Damn, all of Hollister's ex-wives looked good. He must have had good taste in picking women, ultimately landing the prize of Laurie Bateman. At least he was lucky as far as the looks were concerned.

"Yes, I was married to Charles," she said to me as we sat on the patio of her house in Atlanta. "Briefly. Very briefly back in 1975. Less than twenty-four hours later, we had the marriage annulled. We were young then and obviously didn't think it through very well."

She took out a picture and showed it to me. It was a wedding picture, taken at a chapel in Las Vegas where'd said her vows with Hollister, she said. She had long, straight dark brown hair then and was wearing a T-shirt that said "Impeach Gerald Ford." He had on a pair of shorts with no top and was wearing sandals.

"They gave us this picture along with the vows." She smiled.

"I guess the wedding wasn't formal, huh?"

"All they cared about was that you gave them the $25 for the ceremony."

"And what about the annulment afterward?"

"That cost us another $25 to undo the vows."

"No picture that time, I guess," I said with a smile.

She smiled back. She seemed like a nice lady. Not the kind of person who would wind up with a man like Charles Hollister, no matter how young she was.

"Had you known Hollister long?" I asked.

"I met him less than twenty-four hours before."

"Wait a minute . . . you met him twenty-four hours earlier, you were married to him for only twenty-four hours, and then you went your separate ways? How did that happen?"

She explained how she'd met him at a party in Santa Monica in 1975. She'd been attending school at USC and it was a party thrown by one of the guys in a fraternity there. Hollister had told people that night how he'd just gotten out of the Army after serving in Vietnam and was eager to have fun.

"I was anti-war, and outspoken about the Vietnam War—as you might expect. When he told me he'd just come back from

Vietnam and the Army, I called him a 'baby killer.' He called me a 'left-wing peacenik.' We argued about it for a while and then we jumped into bed together.

"There were a lot of drugs at the party. Drugs were everywhere back then in the seventies. We smoked a lot of weed and took a bunch of pills. Somewhere along the line, we met someone who told us about a guy who lived out in the desert and had amazing grass for sale.

"We got in my car and drove out there to try and find him. We did, and it was great grass, that's for sure. We got really, really high and we had sex—mind-blowing sex, like I'd never experienced before. I lost count how many times we made love that night. All I remember is that we decided it would be a great idea to get married right then. Crazy, huh? But that's what we did.

"The next day we came down off our drug high and realized what we'd done. I had big plans for the future, and so did he. I wanted to go into the Peace Corps and save the world back then. He was talking about a company he planned to start. And so, we annulled the marriage and both of us went our separate ways. Just like two ships passing in the night."

She told me she hadn't gotten married for a long time after that, then was with her first real husband for only a few years—until she met the man she was with today. She told me about their children; how they'd just had their first grandchild the year before and were looking forward to more; and about how they planned to travel around the world in a few more years once her husband retired.

She never got around to joining the Peace Corps. Instead, she'd become a schoolteacher. But she still dreamed about saving the world and making it a better place.

"I guess I've always been an idealist at heart," she said. "A romantic, too. That's why I did what I did that time with Charles

Hollister. It seemed . . . romantic. Look—and this is totally off the record, just between you and me—I love my husband very much, but I've never forgotten about that short time I spent with Charles. The passion, the intensity, the feeling that he and I were the only two people in the world at that point. When I was a young woman with the whole world ahead of me . . ."

She shook her head sadly.

"Maybe that's why I cared so much when I heard about his death. Even after all this time, I felt bad. Bad for him, of course. But I think I really felt bad for myself. It brought back all those memories. Memories of what might have been—but never was . . ."

"Were you surprised when you saw how rich and successful he became?"

"Of course, I was. I never thought he would wind up like that. That wasn't the Charles Hollister I knew. But then I guess I never really knew him at all. We never had the time."

"Did you ever try to contact him after you got the annulment?"

"No, why would I? I never saw him again until a few weeks ago. When he came to see me here."

Of course. Just like he'd shown up unexpectedly to see his ex-wife and Laurie Bateman's mother.

"I couldn't believe it when I opened my door. Charles Hollister was standing there, after all these years. He never told me exactly why he came to see me. Just said he was getting old. He didn't know how much longer he had to live, and he wanted to 'clean the slate' before he died. That was the expression he used: 'clean the slate.' I remember that clearly."

I asked Novak what they talked about. She said the party where they met, the drug- and sex-filled drive out into the desert, the crazy marriage, and the rest. He seemed sad when he talked about that time, she told me. She said the memories made her sad too.

"We had the whole world in front of us then, Charles and me," she said when I asked her to explain her feelings. "I was so passionate against things like war and politicians like Nixon and Ford. He kept talking about Vietnam the whole time, which made sense, I guess, because he had been risking his life in that crazy war. We talked so much about Vietnam during that brief period we were together. Vietnam. Now hardly anyone even remembers Vietnam. But it was all we cared about back in those days."

Vietnam.

Wherever I turned in this story, the Vietnam conversation kept coming up.

There was something bothering me though about what she'd told me.

"You said earlier that all this—you meeting him, the quickie annulment, and the rest—happened in 1975?"

"Yes."

"Not 1973?"

"No. I was still in high school in 1973. I remember clearly that it was 1975. Nixon had been forced out of office the previous year, and now we had Gerald Ford for another year until the '76 election. That's why I was wearing the 'Impeach Gerald Ford' T-shirt. I desperately didn't want to live in this country for another year under Ford, because I knew he had been appointed by Nixon. It definitely had to be '75. That makes sense, right?"

It did except for one thing.

Hollister had been discharged from the Army following a year in Vietnam in 1973.

Why would he tell Janice Novak in 1975 that he had just gotten back from Vietnam and been discharged from the Army then?

And what was he doing during those two missing years?

CHAPTER 45

"I NEED YOU to do something for me," I said to Maggie on the phone after I left Janice Novak.

"I'm a little busy right here at the moment, Clare."

"Doing what?"

"Your job."

"Oh, right . . ."

I told her I wanted another crew to meet up with me in Atlanta to film me interviewing Novak. "It's not directly related to Laurie Bateman, but its fantastic background stuff about Hollister. I think it will fit in well with what I'm doing."

I then asked Maggie—and this was the most important thing to me right now—to confirm information about Charles Hollister's military background with the Army during the Vietnam War. Mainly, I said, I wanted to get a specific date for when he left Vietnam.

There was no response from Maggie. I had a feeling she was mad at me, and it wasn't only that I'd left her with all sorts of extra work to do. It turned out I was right.

"When were you going to tell us, Clare?" she asked.

"Tell you what?'

"That you're up for a new job in LA."

Uh-oh.

I'd hoped to keep that a secret until I nailed it down.

I should have known better.

"How did you find out?" I asked her.

"This is a newsroom filled with journalists. We hear gossip. We gossip ourselves a lot. I just never expected the gossip to be about you. You're supposed to be our leader. And you're leaving us."

"Nothing's definite yet. They haven't even made me a formal offer yet. At some point soon, I'm going to have to make a difficult decision. When that time comes, and I do that, you'll be one of the first people I tell, Maggie. I promise you that."

That seemed to placate her a bit.

"Just for the record," she said, "and since I have to do all this work for you, what's so interesting about Charles Hollister's Vietnam service?"

"The facts I know about it aren't consistent."

I told her about my conversation with Janice Novak and her insistence that she met Hollister when he was first coming back from Vietnam in 1975.

"All the U.S. troops—or most of them anyway—were pulled out of Vietnam at the beginning of 1973. Hollister was supposed to be one of them."

"So you want to know why he would have been coming back from Vietnam two years later in 1975?"

"Yes."

"But why is that important?"

"Because that's the same time when Laurie Bateman left Vietnam with her mother and came to the U.S. as a baby."

I heard a gasp from her on the other end of the line. I definitely had her attention now.

"Jeez, Clare . . . are you saying what I think you're saying?"

"There never was any connection in Vietnam between Hollister and Laurie Bateman or her family, but now there could be. Laurie was a newborn baby, and Vietnam was about to be overrun by the Communists. I found out that Laurie's mother was connected to U.S. servicemen—she even slept with them to help get her and her family out of the country during the evacuation. What if one of the men she slept with back then was Charles Hollister?"

"Which means Laurie could have been . . ."

"Hollister's own daughter."

"My God, do you think that's possible?"

"It's a theory," I said.

There were a lot of problems with the theory. It wasn't even a theory. Just speculation on my part. Pretty far-fetched, of course. I mean why would Charles Hollister marry her if she was his own daughter? Apart from all the obvious answers, the scandal—if ever discovered—could have destroyed him and his businesses in the public eye. And, for that matter, why would Laurie Bateman marry a man she knew to be her father?

Well, there was a possible answer: What if they—or at least one of them—never knew? And found out just recently. Maybe by Charles Hollister. He'd been looking into his past for some reason, trying to make sense of his life—as he told his ex-wives. What if one of the secrets he discovered was that he had fathered a daughter in Vietnam? And that daughter was now his wife? That could have triggered a lot of repercussions if it turned out to be true. Maybe even murder.

But this was all speculation.

Unsubstantiated speculation.

And pointless speculation, as it turned out.

Because the facts Maggie came up with didn't support it at all.

I found that out when she called with what she knew about Charles Hollister and Vietnam.

"Everything in the military record conforms with the original story about him. He arrived in Vietnam in April of 1972, was stationed in Saigon for nearly a year, working as an intelligence analyst at MACV headquarters. He was discharged from the Army at Fort Lewis, Washington, in early 1973 following the pullout of U.S. combat troops from South Vietnam. That's it. End of story."

So where did that leave me?

All I had was this woman's story—her insistence, for whatever it was worth—that Hollister had told her he'd just returned from Vietnam and gotten out of the Army in 1975.

Maybe she got mixed up with the dates and the year after all this time.

"There is one more thing, Clare."

"What?"

"I did check the Nevada Bureau of Statistics. They keep marriage records that go back a long time. It took a bit of digging, but I finally talked to someone who looked up Charles Hollister and Janice Novak. Found out they did get married—and then had the marriage annulled. All within a twenty-four-hour period. Same as she told you. And guess what year that happened in."

"1975?" I asked.

"1975," she repeated. "There's something else. I did a background check to see what else I could find out about Hollister at that time. I found the Army drafted him in 1972, discharged from the military in 1973, the marriage in 1975, and his first efforts to launch his business career by incorporating a computer company here in New York after that in 1976. All that activity is pretty well chronicled in official records. So we know a lot about what he was doing back then. Except I can't find anything from his Army discharge in '73 until he pops up marrying the Novak woman in '75. There's two missing years there, Clare. It's as if Hollister just disappeared off the face of the earth from 1973 to 1975."

1973 to 1975.

The two years after the U.S. pulled out of Vietnam—leading up to the final collapse of the South Vietnamese government.

And the same time as Laurie Bateman—then Pham Van Kieu—was born in Vietnam.

CHAPTER 46

As soon as I got back to New York, I began calling everyone I could think of who might know about those missing two years in Charles Hollister's life after Vietnam. First, Susan Daily again in Sacramento. Then Bert Stovall, the CEO in Hollister's company and his lifelong friend. But neither of them did.

Daily said Hollister never talked about that period of his life while they were together. Stovall said he'd lost touch for a while with Hollister after they got back from Vietnam, and they didn't hook up again until the mid-'70s when Hollister contacted Stovall about starting his first computer company.

I tried Laurie Bateman again, but she didn't return my calls. Neither did Charles Jr., which didn't surprise me. I was pretty much persona non grata with the Hollister family these days, I decided.

Except maybe not.

Not with all of them.

Elaine Hollister had seemed different than the rest of them that day we talked after the funeral. Friendly and forthcoming. She'd even told that story about her and her brother and about the long-ago falling-out with her father.

I did some checking and found out she was still in New York. She had an apartment in Tribeca where she stayed when she was in town. She agreed to meet me there.

It turned out to be a fancy apartment with a lot of fancy furniture in a fancy neighborhood. I wondered if she lived this well when she was in Europe helping battered women. I guess it's easier to be a noble do-gooder when you have a lot of money to spend on it. I didn't say that to her, but she must have heard the same thing before.

"Yeah, I know, I'm a hypocrite, right?" she said when I did compliment her about how nice the apartment looked. "I live like this, while I'm out there trying to save the rest of the world, huh? I'm not apologizing for being wealthy, Ms. Carlson. And I have tried to use my money to do good in this world. That's what matters to me."

"What's the situation with your father's will and all his money now that he's gone?" I asked.

"It appears that his most recent will remains in effect. There's nothing anyone can do about that. Yes, he was planning to write a new will, which would cut Laurie Bateman out of a lot of things. But he died before that happened. I'm not that concerned—there's still plenty of money for me and Charles. Charles is furious though because she gets control of the company. He hates her, and she hates him. So now that she's in charge, he'll be out very soon. That's pretty difficult for him to handle, I'm sure."

"What do you think of Laurie Bateman?"

She shrugged. "My father loved her. Then he didn't love her. That's about all I know. My mother was the only Mrs. Hollister I could relate to. Once she died, I didn't care who my father was with—Laurie Bateman or his mistress or anyone else."

"Did your mother ever tell you anything about your father's past life? Especially the period right around when he left Vietnam in 1973?"

"That was before my mother knew him. He was with his first wife then, wasn't he?"

"No, she came after that."

"What exactly are you trying to find out?"

I told her about the missing time gap in Charles Hollister's life between 1973 and 1975. "Long before your time, of course," I said. "I was just hoping you might know something."

But she didn't. I kept asking her questions. Because you never know for sure where the answers you get are going to take you.

"Tell me again about that last phone conversation you had with your father," I asked at one point. "When he called you up out of the blue in Paris. What did he talk about?"

"A lot of things. About him and my mother. About him and me and how much he loved me. More than anything, he talked about his regrets over his life. He talked about being in his seventies and facing his own mortality. And not liking what he saw when he looked back at his life in the mirror. He assured me he wasn't dying or anything like that. He had a few health problems, but they weren't serious at the moment. He said something had happened recently though—something he'd found out—that gave him a real wake-up call about his own life. He said he was trying to deal with that—to make things right, if he could—now with the people he had hurt over the years."

Of course. Hollister seemed to be following a pattern during those last weeks of his life. Going back to see a lot of people from his past. People he had hurt in some way and he seemed to want to make amends. Why not his own daughter, too?

"I had so many emotions and mixed feelings about everything that had happened between us, I wasn't sure exactly what to say to him right then. I wanted to think about it all and then talk to him again, when I came back to the U.S. Before I could do anything though, I heard about his death. I'm not sure what I would have said to him. But I would have liked the chance to try and make things right between us again before he was gone."

I had one more question for Elaine Hollister before I left. Something else that had occurred to me.

"How did your mother die?"

"Oh, she drowned."

"An accident?"

"Yes, she fell overboard during a cruise on Charles' boat."

CHAPTER 47

"Charles Hollister's last wife drowned—she fell overboard during a cruise on her son's boat," I said to Jack Faron.

"Okay."

"Laura Bateman's father was killed by a hit-and-run driver in Los Angeles not long after she came to the U.S. from Vietnam as a baby in 1975."

"So you told me."

"The maid for Hollister and Bateman died when she was hit by a subway train."

"I already know that."

"And Laurie Bateman's stepfather died from a gunshot wound. It was ruled a suicide, but she was alone with him in the house that day."

Faron stared at me.

"Don't you see where I'm going with this?" I asked him.

"Not a clue."

"All of them suspicious deaths. All connected in some way to Charles Hollister or Laurie Bateman. Individually, they might not seem that significant. But put them together and you begin to see a pattern. A pattern of murder."

"No, it's not. First off, not all of those deaths are suspicious, Clare. Authorities ruled the Hollister wife's death accidental; she'd had too much to drink, fell off the boat during a storm with heavy waves. And the police said the death of the maid could have been an accident—there's no proof she was pushed deliberately by anyone. The first death, Bateman's father, happened when she was a little baby, for God's sakes. Her stepfather was a suicide. And she was in jail and Hollister was dead when their maid went in front of that subway. What's the point? Exactly where are you going with all this?"

"I'm not sure yet," I said.

It was my first day back in the office working as news director, and I had a news meeting coming up next. But I'd wanted to meet with Faron first to tell him what I'd found out on my trip and about the story I planned to do on air about it all. So far, the meeting was not going well.

Faron was eating while we talked. Either a late breakfast or an early lunch, I couldn't be sure. It consisted of a container of cottage cheese and a kind of health bread toast. Whatever it was, Faron didn't look happy about eating it. I also didn't notice any weight loss on him since I left for LA. I wondered if there'd been more of those late-night visits to McDonald's or the Baskin-Robbins store. Maybe that's why he was in such a bad mood. Maybe it wasn't just about me and this story. I decided to say something about his dieting to cheer him up.

"Glad to see you're sticking to your diet," I said. "How's it going?"

"I want to throw up every time I see cottage cheese."

"Well, that bread looks like it might be good though. What is it?"

"I don't know, and I don't care. All I know is it tastes like friggin' cardboard."

"Have you seen any results on the scale from all this yet?"

"I only lost one pound—one pound!—after eating all this damn horrible stuff."

"As they say, a journey of 1000 miles—or 1000 pounds—begins with a single step," I said brightly.

Faron glared at me. I didn't think I'd cheered him up much.

I talked to him then about all the stuff I'd done and found out. The interviews with Hollister's ex-wives. The one with Laurie Bateman's mother about the trauma and tragedy of their journey from Vietnam to the U.S. And Hollister reaching out to his estranged daughter to question many of the things he'd done and decisions he'd made in his life. I told him it would make a terrific profile of the background on Hollister and Bateman leading right up to his murder.

"The tragic story of a fairy tale gone wrong," I said. "A Channel 10 Exclusive Report. We could call it 'Behind the Headlines—the real Laurie Bateman Story.' What do you think? It could be really good."

Faron agreed. "But what about the deaths? The father, the ex-wife, and the maid? Like we said, there's no real connection to any of them. How are you going to handle that on the air?"

"I'll say there are all these unanswered questions. And I'll go through each of the deaths we talked about. No links, no obvious answers to them. But it will add to the drama and color of our story. Just ask the question of what happened to all these people. Who knows what might come of it?"

Faron finally agreed to let me do it that way. I'm not sure if he did so because he thought it was a good idea or because he wanted to keep me happy so I wouldn't leave for the new job.

Before I left, he asked me about that. "Did you meet with the West Coast Media people while you out there in LA?"

"I did. No change. Everything is still up in the air."

"Let me know when there's a decision because I'm going to have go looking for a new news director if you're leaving."

"I'll let you know more details as soon as I hear," I answered.

*   *   *

When I got to the news meeting, I found out that everyone else had heard about my possible new job. Like I said, this is a newsroom. Gossip travels fast.

I wanted to talk about the stories. Particularly my story. But everyone wanted to discuss my future first. They acted upset about me leaving. I told them, like I did with Faron, that no decision had been made. I like to think their concern was a genuine respect and affection for me as their boss, but a lot of it was really about themselves and their future too. I understood that.

"I'm not sure Dani and I can deal with a new news director right now," Brett said. "We have so much going on between my divorce and our marriage and the baby on the way. Damn, we don't need anything else to be worried about now. You couldn't have picked a worse time to do this, Clare."

"I'll try to coordinate my career with your lives better in the future," I said.

A lot of them wanted to know if I planned to take anybody with me from Channel 10 to the new job. One of them was Maggie. She said she'd be willing to come along as my producer or whatever if I was interested. I was uncomfortable talking about this in a public meeting with the staff, but I didn't have a choice. The elephant was in the room, and no way I was going to get rid of the damn thing now.

The most surprising response came from Cassie O'Neal. She said she wanted to come with me.

"I could help you there, Clare. I could be your sidekick so you don't have to do all the work. I could do a lot of the soft feature celebrity stuff, while you concentrate on all that hard news you like. And I'd be a big help to you for your on-screen appearance. You know I look good on TV; everyone says so. I could give you fashion and makeup tips. Because you . . . well, sometimes you could use work on your style if you know what I mean. No offense."

I nodded.

"Thank you, Cassie. You'll be the first person I call if I get the job."

CHAPTER 48

BEFORE I WENT on the air with this Laurie Bateman story, I wanted to do one more thing. Talk to Laurie Bateman again. Ask her about all these new questions I'd uncovered about her past. Maybe she'd have some answers. The only problem was she wouldn't talk to me.

I'd tried repeatedly to reach her again. Before, during, and after my trip to the West Coast and Georgia. At first, I got polite responses about her being busy and promising to get back to me. But after a while, even those stopped. There were no responses at all to my phone messages, emails, or texts.

How did I go from her best girlfriend to this so quickly? I assumed it had to do with the fact that I was still covering—and putting stories on the air—about her and her husband's murder. She clearly didn't like that; she wanted the story to go away. But why? What was she hiding?

I needed to confront her and force her to talk to me. I thought about stalking her at her offices in the Hollister building as I did with Charles. But I didn't think that would work with her. She was smart, a lot smarter than Charles. She'd have security throw me out of the building before I asked my first question.

No, I had to do this in a public setting where she couldn't afford to make a scene like that with me. Not Laurie Bateman, America's sweetheart. I found the perfect spot when I read about an upcoming appearance by her at a charity event.

It was a dinner at the National Arts Club in Gramercy Park to benefit young Asian women who had come to this country as refugees just like she had a long time ago. There was money being raised for housing, education, and job opportunities for them. All the guests would pay big bucks for tables there. And why not? It was for a good cause, and there was star power in Laurie Bateman as the speaker.

I didn't pay big bucks to get in; I waved my press credentials and did some fast talking instead. And so I was sitting there in the back of the ballroom when Laurie Bateman delivered an emotional speech about the importance of what they were doing for the young Asian women present.

"When I look at the faces of these women on this stage, I see myself in them," she said. "Like them, I came to this country with hopes and inspirations and dreams that came true far beyond anything I could have imagined. That is why it is so important to me to help other women like myself to lead the American Dream that I have been so fortunate to achieve. Thank you for your support to enrich the lives of these women, and for your support to me. I thank you all from the bottom of my heart."

They were nice-sounding words. She came across as caring and sincere. But I wondered how much of it was true. I wasn't sure about anything involving Laurie Bateman anymore. It was like there were two of her. The one the public knew and the real one without all the celebrity hype. That was the Laurie Bateman I needed to find out about to get the answers I needed.

At one point during her speech, Bateman saw me in the audience. If that rattled her at all, she didn't show it. She simply kept talking about the young women there and herself—and then she even included something about me.

"Many of you know I went through a horrible experience involving my husband, who was killed in a violent crime. Amazingly enough, the authorities at first even believed I had something to do with it. Fortunately, the truth about my innocence came out—thanks in large part to a woman here in the audience tonight. Clare Carlson, the news director of Channel 10 television. I want you all to join me in thanking Clare for getting my story out and my name cleared. Let's have a hand for Clare Carlson . . ."

Everyone turned to look at me. Then they all started to clap. I wasn't sure what to do. Should I stand up from where I was sitting? Should I wave to acknowledge their applause? I wound up standing up partially from my chair and giving a half of a wave. Bateman had surprised me with that. But now it was my turn to surprise her.

I followed her as she left the podium and started to walk away. There were security guards around her, but I managed to push myself close enough to shout out to her.

"I have some questions for you," I yelled. "I've been trying to reach you."

"Clare, I'm sorry I haven't had a chance to talk with you again. I've just been so busy. I'm sure you understand. But I'll catch up with you soon. We'll have a nice long conversation then."

She turned and began walking away from me.

"That's not good enough," I said.

"What?" she said over her shoulder."

"I have a lot of questions for you."

"Well, I don't have time to answer them all now."

"Okay, let's try one then. What was your husband doing in those last days before his murder when he started looking into his own past? Why was he doing that? And how did it involve you?"

"I don't know anything about it."

"Was there a connection between him and your mother and your family in Vietnam?"

That one stopped her. She turned around and faced me now. She moved close to me. Close enough that no one else but me could hear what she began saying to me in a low whisper.

"Clare, I really am grateful to you for what you did for me. But now it's over. Your story is over. And your part in my life is over. It's time for you to stop all this, including the stories you're putting on the air. I'm asking you nice just this one time to stop what you're doing, Clare. Because if you don't stop, I'll make you stop. I have the power to do that now. I have the power to do anything I want. I can even talk to Brendan Kaiser, who owns your station, and tell him to make you stop. Do you want me to do that? Do you want me to ruin your career for you? Or do you just want to go away quietly and we'll both move on with our lives?"

Wow! She was threatening me. I must have really gotten to her. And she was even threatening me that she would be able to get Brendan Kaiser to keep a lid on this story. I wondered if she could pull that off. Not that it mattered. I wasn't going to stop doing this story. Not until I got all of the answers that I was looking for.

"I was watching an old movie of yours the other night, Laurie," I said. "One of those movies that hardly anyone remembers. But I recognized some of the lines you used in it. Because they were the same lines you used when you talked about living in fear of your husband and playing your brilliant act to get you out of jail. That's what it was, right? An act. Was any of it true? Were you telling the truth about anything up there onstage tonight? Or is it all just part of the public act of being Laurie Bateman?"

She smiled now. Like she knew exactly what I was talking about. Even though she'd never admit it.

"Let me tell you something I learned about being an actress, Clare," she said. "A director taught me this a long time ago. Don't stay on the stage, don't stay on the screen too long. Know when to make your grand exit. Deliver your big line—and then get off. Know when it's time to go. That's what I'm telling you now. It's time to go. It's time to make your grand exit. The story is over."

Not for me it wasn't, I thought.

Not by a long shot.

*   *   *

At 6:00 p.m., the red light went on and the intro for the evening newscast began to roll:

ANNOUNCER: This is Channel 10 News.

With Brett Wolff and Dani Blaine on the anchor desk, Steve Stratton with Sports and Wendy Jeffers at the Accu 10 Weather Center.

If you want to stay up-to-date in this fast-paced city, you need to keep on the go with Channel 10 News.

And now, here's Brett and Dani . . .

BRETT: Good evening. Here's what's happening: A shooting at a Times Square restaurant has left two people dead and five injured; the mayor has a new plan to try and help the homeless on the street during the holiday season; the Yankees just signed another big name free agent; and we'll hear the latest from Wendy Jeffers at the Channel 10 AccuWeather Center.

DANI: But first, we start with an update on a story that's been in the headlines recently—about slain billionaire Charles Hollister and his celebrity wife, Laurie Bateman. Our Clare Carlson, the award-winning news director of this station, has an exclusive report:

I was on camera now:

ME: More than a half century ago, in the spring of 1975, Laurie Bateman came to the U.S. as a months-old baby fleeing with her family from war-torn Vietnam as it fell to the Communists.

Earlier this month, her husband, Charles Hollister, was found murdered in their posh Fifth Avenue townhouse—and Bateman was first arrested, and then released on murder charges.

The slaying of Charles Hollister remains a mystery, but then so is much else about the whole story of both Hollister and Bateman.

Channel 10 News went looking for answers in the past of both of them and came up with some surprising information—and a lot more questions.

Here is what we found . . .

CHAPTER 49

THE DAY AFTER my broadcast aired, we got a call in the newsroom from the security desk downstairs. They said a man there wanted to talk to me about the story. Did I want to see him?

"He says he has information about the Laurie Bateman story," Maggie told me.

"I'm busy catching up on all the paperwork I missed when I was out of town. How about you or one of the reporters out in the newsroom talk to him for me and find out whatever it is?"

"He said he'll only talk to you."

I sighed. But I learned a long time ago in this business to never turn down a tip on a story. Sure, you get a lot of crazy news tips from a lot of crazy people. But, every once in a while, one of them pays off. You don't want to be the kind of journalist who missed out on a good one.

I told Maggie to have someone bring him to my office.

A few minutes later, a man walked in accompanied by two security guards. I could tell he was older, even though he didn't look as old as he probably was. He was slightly built, he had gray hair, and he walked with a limp. The most noticeable thing to me though was his nationality. He was Asian. In fact, I was pretty sure he was Vietnamese.

I was pretty sure I'd seen him before.

Not in person.

But on a video.

The video of the subway station where Carmen Ortega, the Hollisters' maid, had died after being pushed or else fallen in front of a subway train.

He was the Vietnamese man I'd seen in the video trying to save Carmen Ortega after she was hit by the train.

"I'm Clare Carlson," I said, glancing over at the two security guards and glad they were there in my office with me and this man at the moment. "You said you had something important to tell me?"

"My name is Pham Van Quong," he said now.

The name sounded familiar. At first, I didn't realize why. Then it hit me. The name Pham. That was Laurie Bateman's birth name. The name of her family in Vietnam before they came to the U.S. and the mother changed it to Laurie Bateman.

I realized, too, now that I'd seen a picture of him once before.

Besides on that subway video.

It was the picture I'd seen at Gloria Bateman's house in La Jolla.

"Are you . . ." I started to say.

"I'm the man you were talking about on the air as Laurie Bateman's father," he told me.

PART IV

BEYOND THE HEADLINES

CHAPTER 50

"You're supposed to be dead," I said.

It was a stupid thing to say, but it was the only thing I could think of at the moment. I had played through a lot of scenarios in my mind about Laurie Bateman's life and past all the way back to her birth in Vietnam. But this never was one of them.

"Obviously I'm not dead. I watched your broadcast last night, Ms. Carlson. I've seen some of the other things you'd said and done. You've clearly talked to a lot of people and gathered a great deal of information about my family and many other things I care about. That's why I decided to come see you. I want to tell you the truth. The truth about everything that I know."

Pham Van Quong sat down in front of my desk. Looking at him up close now, I could see some of the age in his face. But he still looked remarkably good for a person who had to be in his seventies, just as his wife had when I met her in La Jolla. Good-looking genes sure ran in Laurie's family, which I guess helped explain why she was so attractive.

He was a short man, no more than five-foot-seven or five-foot-eight, thin but seemed to be in good athletic shape. He was dressed in what appeared to be an expensive suit, with a dress white shirt and a red tie. He looked like a man who had done well in America, the same as his wife and daughter did. He spoke perfect English, so I assumed he'd lived in this country for a long time.

"I imagine you must have a lot of questions for me," he said.

"I sure do."

"Okay, I'll try to give you as many answers as I can."

"Let's start with this question: How come you didn't die in that traffic accident?"

"It wasn't a traffic 'accident,' Ms. Carlson. What happened that night was deliberate. The driver of the car meant to hit me. Hit me and kill me."

"Why did someone want to kill you?"

"Because I knew too much."

"About what?"

"We'll get to that later."

I was confused. None of his answers were helping me much so far. There was also another real concern I had right now. If this man was Laurie Bateman's father, if his story about surviving that long-ago traffic incident was true—then he could logically be a suspect in the murder of the man who married his daughter.

I had no idea what his motive might be, but for some reason, he was coming out of the shadows now so maybe he wanted a share of the fortune his daughter was inheriting after Hollister's death. And I was sitting face-to-face with a potential murderer in my office.

Except he didn't act like a murderer. He acted like a man with a story to tell. I had to find out what that story was.

"Tell me about the car that didn't kill you outside the UCLA campus," I said. "If you didn't die that night, then who did?"

"A classmate of mine. His name was Nguyen Hau. He was Vietnamese too. We'd met when I started attending classes at

UCLA. And we bonded there—and became friends—because we were both from Vietnam. It was nice to have someone I felt comfortable with in a strange country.

"We'd both had a class in the same building that night. We left together, but he was walking a bit ahead of me. When he stepped off the curb as the light changed to green for him, the car barreled through the red light and aimed directly at him. I watched it all happen from a few feet behind.

"It was deliberate, there was no accident that night. The driver of the car meant to hit him. But I was convinced I was supposed to be the target, not him. I think the driver found out I would be leaving class, waited for me, and then tried to run me over. Except he mistook Nguyen Hau for me. He looked a lot like me, he was Vietnamese, and it was dark outside. So Hau died that night, instead of me."

I still had no idea why anyone would want a Vietnamese refugee—either Pham Van Quong or Nguyen Hau—dead, but I asked him the next most obvious question first.

"Why did the police think the dead man was you?"

"That's how he was identified. And I never corrected anyone. I decided it was best if whoever wanted me dead thought I was already dead."

"But how did the authorities mistakenly identify you? Wasn't there ID on him?"

"I switched our IDs before the police arrived."

"What about fingerprints? Dental records?"

"They didn't need any of that. They had a confirmation from a family member. A family member who identified the body as me."

"Who?"

"My wife."

I tried to take that information in now. It didn't make sense to me. This was all getting really crazy.

"Your wife knew you were alive?"

"Yes."

"But you never went back to live with her and your baby daughter."

"No, I left Southern California right after that and relocated in another part of the country. I changed my name. My name is James Dawson now. It has been for a long time. I became a completely different person. Pham Van Quong was dead as far as anyone knew, and I decided to keep him dead."

"Didn't you want to be with your family? Your wife and your little daughter? Why didn't you take your wife with you?"

"That was her decision. Not mine. She did not want to be a part of my new life—or a part of my life at all anymore. When I told her what I had to do after the attempt on my life, she saw it as an opportunity for her. She made that clear to me. That was her price for identifying me to authorities so that I could be officially dead. I had to disappear from her life. She had other plans, other aspirations she wanted to pursue—and she said she couldn't do that with me as her husband."

"She wasn't in love with you?"

"My wife was—and still is, from what I saw during her TV appearance with you—a very beautiful woman. She's always attracted men in her life. Many men. I was only one of them."

"She was seeing other men while you were married?"

"Yes, there were always other men in her life."

I thought about Gloria Bateman telling me how she'd slept with men to get out of Saigon.

I thought about how she'd gone after Marvin Bateman here in the U.S. who made her rich and her daughter famous.

I thought, too, about her marriage to Bateman—and realized it had probably been illegal because she was still married to her husband, whom she knew was alive.

"Does your wife know you're still alive today?" I asked him.

"I'm not sure. I haven't been in contact with her in years."

"What about your daughter?"

He sighed.

"I told you I wanted to tell the truth. So let me tell the truth now about that. I came to this country after the U.S. troops pulled out of South Vietnam in 1973 and the peace accords were signed in Paris that ended the American war involvement. I began taking courses at UCLA in 1973. I never returned to Vietnam after that. Laurie was born in September of 1974. You do the math . . ."

"Do you mean . . . ?"

"She's not my daughter. Someone else is her father."

CHAPTER 51

IT WAS THE question that had been hovering around this story right from the beginning.

Had there been a previous connection between Charles Hollister and Laurie Bateman and her family that dated back to the days when Hollister was a soldier in Vietnam?

And, if there was a connection, what was it?

Now that Pham had revealed he could not be the father of the little girl who grew up to be Laurie Bateman, could the father have been Hollister? Did Hollister father a baby in Vietnam a half century ago, then marry her years later when she became a famous celebrity? If so, did he know who she was when he married her or did he find out later? Did Laurie Bateman know that the man she married might have been her biological father?

"Who was the father if it wasn't you?" I asked.

"I don't know."

"Your wife never told you?"

"All she ever said was that he was an American GI. She told me she did what she had to do to survive in Vietnam without me. She brought the baby with her to America when she arrived, and she told me that she was going to find a different husband to raise her. I still remember her telling me: 'I can do better than you—and I will.' And that's what she did. She married Marvin Bateman after my 'death' that night on the UCLA campus. I was already dead to my wife."

Damn. Gloria Bateman was a real piece of work. I remembered her telling me how she had sex at the end of the war with U.S. soldiers to get on one of the helicopters leaving from the U.S. Embassy. But this sexual encounter with a military man would have taken place more than a year before that. With an American who must have helped her in some way then. She was a woman who would do and say whatever it took with a man to get her way. Just like her daughter seemed to be.

Could that man in Vietnam she had sex with that produced a daughter been Charles Hollister? Except he left Vietnam when the U.S. combat troops pulled out in early 1973—months before the baby would have been conceived.

Or did he?

I wanted to ask Pham a lot more about this. But he kept going on about everything else that had happened to him in Vietnam before he left and came here to the U.S.

So I let him talk . . .

* * *

"I grew up in Saigon," he said. "My father was a professor of physics at the college there, and we were pretty well-to-do. Which was important in those years of the war. If you had money and influence, you got benefits other people in Vietnam didn't. Vietnam was extremely class conscious back then.

"The biggest thing was the war, of course. A lot of people don't realize this, but not all young men then got drafted into the South Vietnamese Army. There were college deferments, just like in the

U.S., that could keep you out of the military. The key was a test that high school students had to take if you wanted to continue your education. If you scored high on that, you got to go to college and receive a deferment from Army service. There was a lot of pressure in taking that test. Fortunately, I did extremely well and got into a college in Saigon.

"For a time, I wasn't even that aware of the war because I was so involved in what I was doing at school. That all changed when the war started going badly. And, toward the end, when it became clear the war was coming closer to Saigon, it affected us all. We had to make decisions then. Did we switch allegiance to the Communists once it appeared that it was only a matter of time before they took over the country? Or did we depend on the U.S. to keep us safe? I did the latter.

"At college, I loved courses with math and science and technology. I was always good at that kind of stuff. Gifted, the instructors called me. While I was there, I became friendly with another student who was even smarter than I was in these courses. He was what I guess you would call a genius when it came to technology.

"Anyway, we spent a lot of time together, not just in the class but also working on our own ideas. I mean, at one point. we even came up with our video game—sort of like a version of *Pong*, the first one back then in the seventies.

"But the biggest idea we had, the big thing we developed, was an idea for a computer. A different kind of computer. Back then, the only computers were the big ones that were used at places like NASA. But we came up with a device—a microchip—that we believed might make the computer accessible to everyone."

Which is what Charles Hollister did a few years later. I was pretty sure I could see where this was going.

"By this point, we'd told other people about our idea for the computer microchip. We had to do that. Because we needed help, we needed support—financially and otherwise—to keep working beyond what we were doing at the school.

"We got that from the government. First the South Vietnamese government, but then—when that began falling apart—from the U.S. people still there. Because even after the U.S. troops pulled out in 1973, there were still members of the U.S. intelligence community based secretly in Saigon who wanted us to keep working on the idea.

"That's why I went to the U.S. They wanted me there, in an American college, and I agreed to do that. I didn't think I had much of a choice. And so, I said goodbye to my wife and went to America. She would meet me there soon, or so they promised me. My friend refused to go along with them though. He told them it was his idea, and he would keep working on it there without their help if necessary. He told me he feared the Americans would steal the microchip from us. He said he would give it to the Communists before the Americans, if necessary, to prevent that."

"What happened to your friend?"

"Le Binh. Le Binh was more than just my friend. He was my wife's brother. That's how I met her. Through her brother, Binh. I'd hoped all three of us could go to America and be together. But he never made it to America. He died before the war was over."

Gloria Bateman's brother!

She'd said he died during the war, but wouldn't give me any details.

I'd been listening to all this, taking a few notes as I did, but reluctant to break up his flow of words because he was telling me so much.

Now, though, I had to ask him more about his brother-in-law's death.

"Was he killed by the Communists?"

"No, by the Americans."

"Why?"

"They said he was working for the enemy."

"Was he?"

"He was not working for anyone. All he cared about was his project. He was a scholar, not a soldier. There's no way I could ever believe he was trying to blow up a U.S. facility. Yet they said he did. And they killed him."

"Do you mean . . . ?"

"Hollister shot and killed him. He got a medal for it."

"The man who was planting the explosive in the bunker was your partner and friend—and your wife's brother?"

"He wasn't killed because he was trying to plant an explosive. He was killed by Hollister to keep him quiet and to steal his ideas from him. The same way Hollister must have tried to kill me later in America. He didn't succeed in that, but I knew it was only a matter of time before I met the same fate. So I walked away back in 1975 when he thought I was dead. I just let Hollister become rich and famous with the microchip. The idea we had come up with, but he had then stolen."

There was no proof for any of this, of course.

No proof that Hollister had been guilty of going to any length—even murder—to get control of the idea that started his financial empire.

But, even without proof from Pham Van Quong, I believed him.

"I let Hollister take the idea for himself, which I imagine is what he planned to do all along—from the first moment he found out about it. He let us develop it, then he took credit—and all the profits—from it. But at least I was alive. And I knew I had to disappear if I wanted to stay alive in a strange country for me at the time like America.

"I've had a good life since then. I wound up starting several technology companies of my own. I didn't get as rich as Hollister, but I've made good money with them. I've also used my computer skills to win big in the casinos down there. Did you know that you can almost make as much money in legalized gambling with the right technology as you can in the computer industry? I've used my computer skills to make millions. I'm married now to a wonderful woman; I have a wonderful family. Yep, I've done all right. I even almost forgot about everything that happened back in Vietnam and afterwards a half century ago. Until everything happening now. So, when I heard your broadcast last night, I decided it was time to come forward and tell my story."

"And you never saw or talked to Hollister again in all those years?"

"Not until a few weeks ago."

"A few weeks ago? What happened then?"

"He came to see me."

"On the Gulf Shore?"

"That's right. He just showed up at my door. I have no idea how he knew I was there or how he even found out I was alive. But there he was. Charles Hollister, in person."

Of course.

Hollister had gone back to see a lot of other people from his past.

Why not the man whose idea had made him so rich?

"What did Hollister say to you after all this time?"

"He told me he was sorry. He told me he was sorry about everything. And then . . . he asked me to forgive him."

CHAPTER 52

"CHARLES HOLLISTER WAS clearing the decks," I said to Faron. "Going through all the excess baggage of his life. He went back to his ex-wives. To the mother of his current wife. And even to this man Pham who claims he was the one who invented the microchip that made Hollister rich—and that Hollister tried to kill him to keep that secret a half century ago. Why was Hollister doing this? What did he hope to accomplish? And, most importantly of all, what did he find out? If we can determine the answer to that, we might be able to figure out who killed him."

"Was Hollister sick?" Faron asked. "Maybe he was dying and wanted to make amends for the bad things he'd done before he met his Maker or whatever. People do strange things when they know they're dying."

I shook my head no.

"No indication of it. From what I've been able to find out, he had some early signs of Parkinson's disease. But nothing that would significantly affect him for some time. Other than a slightly elevated blood pressure and cholesterol level, Hollister was in pretty good physical health for a man his age."

"What's your best guess then, Clare?" Faron said, sipping from a can of SlimFast as he we talked.

I assumed that was his lunch.

Another day, another diet.

"I think maybe Charles Hollister suddenly got an attack of conscience."

"He developed a conscience at seventy-plus years old?"

"Better late than never," I said. "Or maybe he discovered something that started him looking through his own past like this."

We were sitting in Faron's office where I'd finished going through all the details of my conversation with the man who identified himself as Pham Van Quong.

"What do you make of this guy?" Faron asked me. "Do you think he's for real? Do you believe everything he told you?"

"There's no proof of any of it. Nothing that shows he invented the Hollister microchip or that he played any role in it whatever. Nothing to indicate Hollister even knew him in Vietnam. Nothing placing Hollister anywhere around the scene of that hit-and-run outside the UCLA campus. Nothing to even confirm that this person I met with is the same man who used to be called Pham Van Quong. But yes . . . I do believe him. Everything he told me checks out so far. He is a businessman in Mississippi, runs a group of technological companies there. The rest of the details of his life since 1975 were accurate too. And there seems to be no history of him in this country until 1975."

"If all that is true, it means he could be a suspect in the Hollister murder. He certainly had a motive for wanting Hollister dead."

"I think there's something else going on here, Jack. I'm not sure what it is yet. But I believe it all revolves around Laurie Bateman. She's the key to this whole story."

"Are you planning on putting him on the air tonight?"

"Not yet. Like we said, there's no real proof he's who he says he is or that he's telling the truth. I have to check him out—and his story—a lot more first. But he did say other intriguing stuff."

I told Faron first how I'd asked Pham why he was in the subway station when Carmen Ortega, the Hollister maid, was hit by the subway train.

"He said he went there to meet the Ortega woman. He got a message that she wanted to talk to him. That she had information about Charles Hollister that could be extremely important to him."

"So, someone else besides Hollister knew Pham was alive?"

"Apparently."

"What kind of message was it?"

"A phone call. An anonymous phone call that gave him a time and place to be. It was the subway platform where Ortega was standing when she died. He said he'd just arrived on the platform when something—or somebody—pushed them both from behind into the path of the incoming train. He managed to keep his balance and stay on the platform. But she didn't. He said he jumped down to try to help her, but then left before authorities could ask him any questions. He wanted to stay dead, especially after this new attempt on his life. Or at least he wanted to stay dead until he saw my report on the air last night. Now he thinks his best choice is to go public with everything."

"That is weird," Faron said.

"It gets weirder."

Then I told him why Pham said he had originally come to New York City.

"He was supposed to meet with Hollister again. Hollister had said to him during that first meeting on the Gulf Shore that he

wanted to do right by Pham, financially and otherwise. He promised they'd talk later in New York and work out all the details so
Pham could get his fair share of what he deserved for helping to
invent the original microchip that had made Hollister so rich. So
Pham traveled to New York for this meeting. Hollister was supposed to come to Pham's hotel to see him on the night before he
was found dead. That was the plan they had worked out. But
Hollister never showed up."

"Maybe Hollister changed his mind about seeing the man,"
Faron said.

"I don't think so. He said Hollister called him earlier that night
from the charity event he was at. He said he'd be at the hotel later.
First, he had to go back to his apartment to deal with some business, Hollister said. He said he'd arrive at the hotel to see Pham
around ten thirty. Except he never did."

"And we have no idea why Charles Hollister cancelled out of
that late-night meeting?" Faron asked.

"Pham never knew why."

"I can't think of any reason either," Faron said.

I could.

"What if Charles Hollister was already dead at ten thirty?" I
said.

CHAPTER 53

THE ONE HARD fact about the timeline of Charles Hollister's death—the thing that provided everyone with the window of time within which he must have been killed—was that last phone call he made.

He left a message on his secretary's phone at the Hollister headquarters. The time of that message was 6:38 a.m. on the morning that he was found murdered. Carmen Ortega, the maid, arrived and found him dead around 9:00 a.m. So we knew he must have been killed between 6:38 a.m. and 9:00 a.m. Yep, that much was a basic fact. Or was it?

I had a copy of that phone message from Hollister that we'd played on the air at Channel 10 after the murder, and I sat in my office listening to it now.

"I'm heading directly over to the *Chronicle* this morning to meet with that goddamned editor there as soon as he gets in," he said to his secretary on the message. "He screwed up the front-page story today. I had to order them to rewrite the front-page headline. I want to deal with him right away this morning. I'll see you after that."

I played the message over and over again, trying to find a clue there—something that I and everyone else might have missed.

Maggie was there with me, and we both listened intently to the voice of Charles Hollister uttering his last words shortly before he would be murdered.

But who killed him?

Was it his wife, Laurie Bateman?

Any of the other potential suspects—a long list of them, including his own son—that I'd identified as people who had a reason to want Hollister dead?

Or was there someone else out there that no one had thought of yet?

The emergence of Pham Van Quong had made this story even more confusing for me than it had been before. If you believed his story—and, for whatever reason, I did believe his story—then Charles Hollister planned to meet him at the hotel the night before Hollister was found dead. Hollister even called to give a specific time he'd be there. At ten thirty p.m., after he'd finished meeting with someone else at his apartment. Except Hollister never showed up for the meeting with Pham Van Quong. Why not? And who was the person he met with on that last night of his life?

I picked up the phone and called Sam Markham, my ex-husband, at the Manhattan East Precinct.

"You said there was a security video of the entrance to Hollister's building, Sam. And that Laurie Bateman and then the maid, Carmen Ortega, were the only ones on it from that morning. But what about the night before? Did you look at the security video for that?"

"No," he said slowly.

"Why not?"

"Because we couldn't find it."

"The security video from the night before was missing?"

"I'm not sure it was missing. We just couldn't find it."

"Didn't that make you suspicious?"

"Suspicious of what? We know Hollister was alive the night before because he made the phone call the next morning. So whatever was on that security video from the night before doesn't really matter."

"Right," I said.

"Do you know something you're not telling me, Clare?"

"Not really."

"Because if you—"

"You'll be the first person I tell, Sam. I promise."

*   *   *

Maggie and I listened to the phone message one more time. It could have been the 10th time or the 100th time, I'd lost count. But when you're desperate on a story, you cling to any possible angle. I was desperate. And the last message from Charles Hollister was the only thing I had at the moment.

It was Maggie who finally noticed something.

"Listen to Hollister's voice," she said.

"I am listening to it, Maggie. I've been listening to it over and over again. What's your point?"

"It sounds different."

"Different than what?"

"Different than other times I've heard him speak."

She picked up her laptop, then clicked on a Hollister interview she found on YouTube. First one with TMZ. Then another when he appeared on the *Today Show*. Finally, one from a speech he'd made a few weeks earlier at an awards dinner. We listened to them all. Then we listened to the phone message to his secretary again.

Maggie was right. Hollister did sound different on the phone message. Yes, the same voice. It was Hollister's voice. But it sounded . . . well, artificial. "He sounds so impersonal here," Maggie said. "It sounds almost . . . almost mechanical."

"Mechanical," I repeated.

We went back and played Hollister's phone message one more time.

"I'm heading directly over to the *Chronicle* this morning to meet with that goddamned editor there as soon as he gets in. He screwed up the front-page story today. I had to order them to re-write the front-page headline. I want to deal with him right away this morning. I'll see you after that."

I was listening differently to all his words now after what Maggie had said.

"Did you notice he called it the front-page headline?" I said.

"Yeah."

"Not *the wood* or *the splash*."

"Like they do at a newspaper," Maggie said.

"Right. No one at a newspaper like the *Chronicle* calls it the *front-page headline*, it's always *the wood* or *the splash*. I remember that well from my own days in newspapers. And people told me Hollister prided himself on learning all the newspaper terms and jargon. He fancied himself as becoming a media baron. I don't think he would have called it the *front-page headline*."

"So what does that mean?"

I shrugged. "I'm not sure what it means either. But I think it means something."

Maggie thought for a second.

"Clare, do you remember the Alphabet Kidnapping case?"

"Sure. That was a pretty famous one a few years back. The kid-nappers sent notes by cutting letters out of newspaper headlines."

I saw where she was going with this.

"What if someone did the same thing with a phone call?"

I nodded. "Someone who wanted to make it look like Hollister was alive at 6:38 a.m. with the message he left on his secretary's phone. Someone who wanted to camouflage the timetable of the murder. Someone who wanted to make sure no one knew they were in Hollister's apartment the night before—and maybe killed him."

"But who?" Maggie asked. "Who could put together a phone tape of Hollister's voice like that?"

"Someone who already had a lot of samples of Hollister's voice," I said.

CHAPTER 54

THERE WAS NO sign of Victor Endicott, the private investigator hired by both Hollister and Laurie Bateman at different times, when I went back to his office on Park Avenue South.

The glass front doors were locked. The secretary in the lobby was nowhere to be seen. And there was no indication of any other people or activity inside the suite of offices that had seemed so professional and busy when I was there the first time to see Endicott.

I thought about trying to break in myself to search the place for clues or evidence. There were a few problems with that idea though. First, it was illegal for me to break into an office. I could get myself and Channel 10 into big trouble. Second, I didn't know exactly what I was looking for if I did get inside. Third, and this was the biggest problem of all, I had no idea how to break into a locked office.

I made a few calls instead. First, I called Sam and told him where I was and why—and that Endicott appeared to be gone. Then I called Nick Pollock, the Treasury agent who was investigating Hollister's finances for fraud—I figured he'd want to be in on this. Then I called Maggie and told her to send a video crew over to get footage of whatever this all turned out to be.

And so, a short time later, I was standing inside Endicott's abandoned offices with Sam, Pollock, and a lot of other police and crime forensic people all looking for answers about what happened to the private investigator.

It was quite a scene for me. Sexually speaking, as well as professionally. I mean, there was my ex-husband, who on various occasions had indicated that he would still like to have sex with me again—even though he was now married. And the Treasury agent I'd hoped to have a sexual relationship with until I discovered that he wasn't interested in me . . . well, at least he wasn't interested in that way. Damn, all I needed was to call Scott Manning, the FBI agent I'd had the affair with last year. Maybe throw in Wild Bill Carstairs from the DA's office. Then it would be a real trip down memory lane for me and my romantic hits and misses.

All around us, everything in the offices of Victor Endicott was in disarray—papers strewn everywhere, drawers open, filing cabinets turned over.

It sure looked like someone had made a hasty exit from this place.

Not everything was gone though.

One of the cops came over with a package in his hand.

"I think I've got something," he said to Sam.

The package had a label on it, which said: "CHARLES HOLLISTER—SURVEILLANCE."

Inside it were hours and hours of tapes and transcripts from Endicott's surveillance of Charles Hollister for Laurie Bateman.

We skimmed through the transcripts of what was on the tapes. Lots of it was tedious and boring, of course. Chronicling endless conversations between Hollister and Melissa Hunt. A little bit of it in bed that was titillating, but most of it was pretty routine stuff—the kind of conversations everyone has day to day and night to night, even if you are with a sexy young mistress as Charles Hollister was.

I explained to Sam and Pollock my theory about how Endicott had used the tapes.

"You're saying Charles Hollister never made the phone call to his office that morning?" Sam asked.

"It was his voice. But I think you'll find some of these surveillance tapes of him with his girlfriend—containing all these hours of conversation—were spliced together to make it seem like he was actually talking on the message."

"How can you be sure of that?"

"Hollister complained on the call that he didn't like the front-page headline. But newspaper people at a place like the *Chronicle* don't call it *the front-page headline*. They call it either *the splash* or *the wood*. Hollister prided himself on using newspaper jargon. Whoever put the tape together—presumably that was Endicott— didn't know that about newspaper jargon."

Sam looked over at Pollock now. "Can you explain to me why you're here? Why does the Treasury Department care about Endicott?"

"Because of the millions of dollars we've found missing from the Hollister business money funds."

"I thought you were looking at Hollister for that."

"We were."

"Then what does Endicott have to do with it."

"He might have been involved too—he knew a lot of secrets about Hollister and his business. Professionally and personally. He could have been playing both sides of the fence. Using this information for his own personal gain. We've been gathering more information about him ever since Hollister's murder. It looks like he found out about that. And that's why he's gone."

"Where do you think this guy Endicott is now?"

"Probably in Rio de Janeiro or Europe," Pollock said. "Living off money taken from the Hollister funds."

"So this is about stolen money?"

"And maybe murder, too . . . the murder of Charles Hollister."

"You think Endicott murdered Hollister because of the money—and then fled the country with a fortune in stolen funds?"

"That's certainly a possibility."

Sam shook his head.

"I should have listened to my horoscope this morning."

"What did it say?" Pollock asked.

"That I should have stayed in bed."

I hadn't said anything yet. It didn't seem like anyone particularly wanted me to say anything. I mean, I wasn't a hotshot homicide detective or Treasury agent or anything. I was just a nosy TV reporter. But I was the one who had led the law to Endicott's office and alerted them to everything he had probably done.

So I figured my opinion counted for something.

"I don't think it was Victor Endicott who killed Hollister," I told everyone. "I think he just got scared and ran. I think he was working for someone else."

"Well, we know he was working for both Charles Hollister and Laurie Bateman at different times."

"But who else besides them?"

"Huh?"

"Maybe there's another player here. Someone we're missing. Someone who hired Victor Endicott to do his dirty work for him. Someone with a better motive for murdering Hollister than Endicott had. We need to figure out who that is. And the answer could be right here in whatever he left behind."

And, in the end, the answer we were looking for was there.

It was a video. A security video. It turned out to be the missing security video from Charles Hollister's house on the night before his body was found. And why not? Endicott was all about security. He probably even installed the video security system there. So he'd have had no trouble removing a security video he—or, more specifically, whoever he was working for—didn't want found.

We plugged it into a machine in Endicott's office and played it.

Sure enough, it showed the front of Hollister's building. The time stamp on the video put the date as the night before his death and the time as 9:30 p.m., between the time he'd come home from the charity event he'd attended with Laurie Bateman and the 10:30 date he'd set with Pham Van Quong at the hotel.

The video itself wasn't long. Someone had deleted the beginning and the end. The rest was all blank.

All that was left was several seconds of footage from outside the Hollister townhouse that night.

But it was enough.

Enough to see who had been there.

I looked at the figure on the screen in front of me.

The last person to probably see Charles Hollister alive.

It was Hollister's son.

Charles Blaine Hollister Jr.

CHAPTER 55

BETWEEN COVERING THE Laurie Bateman story and running the newsroom, the last thing I needed was another thing on my plate to deal with right now. But I got just that when I went back to Channel 10 after leaving Endicott's office.

There was a message for me to call a Dr. Polis. He was the doctor I'd gone to for the test on the breast cancer gene. He must have gotten the results. I thought maybe his office would want me to make an appointment to come back to see him again. But when I called the number, I wound up talking to Dr. Polis himself.

"I have good news," he said to me. "Your test came back negative."

"Meaning I don't have the gene?"

"No sign whatsoever of the BRCA1 gene in your tests, Ms. Carlson, I'm happy to say."

I sure was happy about it, too. But good news like that is rarely perfect. And this wasn't. There was more. And I should have seen it coming.

"The BRCA1 gene—if it was detected in your daughter—must have been transmitted to her by your husband."

I hadn't given him any details about my daughter or the circumstances of her birth.

"I wasn't married when I had her," I told him now.

"Okay, the father—the man you were with when you conceived her—must have the gene. Do you understand what I'm saying?"

Oh, I understood.

"Can you contact this man?"

"That would be pretty difficult without a séance."

"Excuse me?"

"He's dead."

"I see. Can you contact his relatives? Are you still in touch with them?"

"Look, Dr. Polis, he was a one-night stand. We had sex together when I was nineteen years old, and I never saw him again. That's all that happened between us. Except for me getting pregnant and having his baby."

Dr. Polis didn't respond right away. I wasn't sure if it was because he was shocked or because he was trying to figure out what to say.

"Do you know if this person went on to have other children?" he asked me finally.

I thought about what I'd read on Cowell's death and background the time I'd looked up the information.

"Yes, I believe he did."

"You need to try and contact the family. If your daughter carries the gene and it didn't come from you, but from him—then his children are at risk for carrying the gene just like your daughter. You should reach out to them, if you can."

I wanted to tell him I didn't know how to do that. And whatever happened between Doug Crowell and me a quarter century ago during a brief one-night encounter had nothing to do with me now. Let his family deal with their own medical problems, like I was doing now. I didn't have time to worry about all this. But I knew none of this was true. I was a reporter; I could track down Crowell's family if I tried. And I couldn't live with myself if I didn't do the right thing for his children, whoever they were.

"I'll do that," I told Dr. Polis. "I'll reach out to them, transmit this information to them, and even put them in contact with you."

After I hung up, I thought again about that night I had with Doug Crowell. There I was, just nineteen, a sophomore in college, who had too much to drink at a campus fraternity party. Crowell was the president of the fraternity, a good-looking guy who was a big man on campus. So I was flattered when he started paying attention to me. Flattered enough that I slept with him that night.

It's always a temptation to look back on your life and do the "what if?" thing. I try to avoid doing that most of the time because it never accomplishes anything. But I did it now. I played the "what if" game to myself. What if I hadn't gone to that fraternity party? What if I hadn't gotten so drunk that night? What if I had never met Doug Crowell there? And, most importantly of all, what if I had never slept with Crowell that night and gotten pregnant with his baby?

My life sure would have turned out a lot differently.

But instead, those brief moments of passion when I was so young have defined my life ever since.

And continued to do so, because I was still dealing with the aftereffects.

* * *

Doug Crowell's wife was named Sheryl. She lived in Dallas, Texas. She had been a flight attendant at the same airline where Crowell flew as a pilot, and they'd been married for more than twenty years before he died. They had three children—two daughters and a son—all in their late teens or early twenties. I was able to find out all this information pretty easily online. I had no idea if she might have remarried or if the children still lived with her or anything else about Sheryl Crowell. But I did track down a phone number for her.

That was the easy part—finding all this about Sheryl Crowell.

The hard part was what I had to do next.

I tried to play out in my mind how a conversation between me and this woman might go:

"Hello, Mrs. Crowell. You don't know me, but I used to have sex with your husband. Well, we only had sex once. And, in our defense, he was drunk—and so was I. But there were significant repercussions from that. A lot of them. For me and now for your family. Apparently, your husband carried a potentially deadly cancer gene called BRCA1 that can get passed down to his children. I know that because we had a child. Yeah, I know, that's a shocker, and he never knew about it—but I got pregnant from that night we had together. I recently discovered that my child from that, who's now a twenty-nine-year-old woman, has tested positive for the gene. I've tested negative. Which means it must have come from him. The bottom line here is you need to see if your children are carrying the gene, too, which could put them at great risk for potential cancer. Uh, I think that about covers it all. Nice talking to you, Mrs. Crowell. Oh, and have a nice day."

Okay, I know it wasn't going to go exactly like that.

But no matter what I said to this woman, that was the basic message I was going to have to deliver.

Damn.

On the positive side, once I made the call, I could go back to concentrating on something easier—like figuring out who killed Charles Hollister and why.

I picked up the phone in my office and punched in the number for Sheryl Crowell . . .

CHAPTER 56

THINGS BEGAN TO happen very quickly after the discovery of the security video that showed Charles Blaine Hollister at his father's apartment that night.

The cops talked to Charles for hours—first informally in his office at the Hollister building, then later in an interrogation room at police headquarters with the battery of lawyers representing him.

Initially, Charles denied everything. He stuck to his story that he'd argued with his father earlier in the day at the office, but he'd gone straight home afterward and never saw him again before his death.

That's when they showed him the security video—the one we'd found in Endicott's office—which showed him outside the Fifth Avenue townhouse later that night, shortly before his father was supposed to leave for a meeting with Pham. Enough time for him to have killed his father and then left his body for Laurie Bateman and the maid to find the next morning. Especially if he paid Endicott to send the doctored phone call at 6:38 a.m. to make it seem like Hollister was still alive then and also got Endicott to remove the security video showing him there the night before. It all made sense. Endicott had worked for both Hollister and Laurie Bateman. Why not hire out to Charles Blaine Hollister, too?

Things began to fall apart in a hurry for Charles after that.

The police talked to people in a bar where Charles had been seen drinking for much of the night before showing up at his father's place, and they all said he was drunk, angry, and making threats against his father and Laurie Bateman and everyone else he believed was plotting against him.

They talked to his ex-wife who said he'd nearly beaten her to death one night in a drunken rage. While he was doing it, she said, he bragged about how he'd done the same thing to other people. One of them was his own sister. Charles said he'd beaten up his sister, Elaine, so badly that he'd scared her all the way out of the country, leaving the path open for him to claim all his father's wealth and power for himself. At least until Laurie Bateman came along.

When the police went to see Elaine, she confirmed it. She told them the same story she'd told me that day in the coffee shop.

All of it looked bad for Charles—it was clear that he had a violent temper, especially when drinking, that could well have led to an explosion with his father that night.

But the real damage came when police searched his office and then his home for evidence.

They found a bloodied handkerchief in his office with his father's blood on it—which he must have used to wipe himself off after the killing.

They also found his father's cell phone in there, which had been missing since the murder. There was a voice mail on it of Charles Jr. yelling at his father, and even threatening him at one point. Which must have been why he took it with him when he left his father's house that night.

Worst of all for Charles, though, police found a document. A damning document. A real motive for murder that pointed directly at him.

It was a copy of Charles Hollister's will. A new will that he'd just drawn up. He must have planned to give it to his lawyers, but never got the chance before he was killed.

The new will definitely removed Laurie Bateman from power and kept her inheritance at the original prenup levels they'd had when they were married. But it was even worse for Charles. Charles was written out completely. His father had left him with nothing—no income, no position within the company. His only hope to inherit now was if the new will never got filed, his father died—and Laurie Bateman got convicted of the murder. The authorities believed that was what Charles Jr. did and then framed Bateman as the prime suspect.

Hollister had written in the draft that his son had been "the greatest disappointment in my life"—and that he was through protecting him. Charles would be on his own. Instead, all his money and control of the company went to his daughter, Elaine. "Elaine is a good person," Hollister had written in the draft for the new will. "I've never done right by her. But I want to do that now. She's the person I want to carry on for me when I'm gone."

Charles insisted he had no idea how the bloodied handkerchief or the cell phone had gotten into his office. He admitted that he and his father had argued earlier in the day after his father told him about the new will he was preparing. And he admitted getting drunk and angry and going back to his father's house later that night to confront him about what he was going to do. But he said his father never answered the door—and that he left without even seeing him.

That was a hard story to believe.

Meanwhile, the Medical Examiner's Office now said that although it had originally estimated the time of death as shortly before Hollister's body was found, it could have been longer than that. They even speculated that Hollister could have been attacked with the lamp and shot the night before, but then lay mortally injured on the floor before finally dying several hours later. The ME declared it was possible he had been murdered around the time Charles was at the building, rather than the next morning when the maid and Laurie Bateman arrived.

The evidence was all pretty overwhelming against Charles Hollister Jr.

Just as it had once been with Laurie Bateman.

But the police were convinced that this time they had the right person.

And so, Charles Hollister was arrested for the murder of his father.

*   *   *

A video of Charles being led through a perp walk in handcuffs by police was at the top of the newscast for Channel 10 and every other station; it went viral on social media; and the picture was on the front page of every newspaper in town.

The appearance by Charles in court afterward was a media circus. TV cameras everywhere, hundreds of reporters. We broke into our daytime programming to cover it live. They brought Charles into the courtroom wearing a red prison jumpsuit, refusing to even allow him the dignity of putting on a suit and tie. He looked scared but still arrogant at the same time—if that's possible. He kept looking around the courtroom, like he was hoping someone would help him.

His father had always been there to help him out of jams like this in the past. But now his father was gone. And he was facing murder charges for being the one who killed him.

I saw Laurie Bateman in the court, viewing the proceedings from the other side of the defendant's bench this time. Elaine Hollister was there, too, staring silently at her brother. And Bert Stovall, who had lost his lifelong friend and now had to watch his friend's son being accused of the murder. He looked ashen and shaken by what had happened. This had clearly been a traumatic experience for him.

The lawyer for Charles Hollister pleaded with the judge to grant him bail.

"This is a leading citizen," the lawyer said. "He is an officer in one of the most prestigious businesses in the world. A man who has just suffered the trauma of losing his father to a violent act . . ."

That wasn't much of an argument. He lost his father because he murdered him, the prosecutor pointed out. Sort of like the son who kills his parents and then asks for sympathy because he's an orphan.

"Your client is charged with murder," the judge said, cutting off the lawyer in mid-sentence. "Bail is denied. The defendant is re-manded back into custody."

They put handcuffs on Charles again and began leading him out of the courtroom. As he walked past Laurie Bateman, his sister, and Bert Stovall, he looked over at them and said something that seemed to be some sort of a plea. For help, I presume. I couldn't make out what it was. But it didn't matter. They all just sat there stone-faced until Charles Hollister was led back to jail.

For us at Channel 10, it was another ratings bonanza.

The arrest of Charles Blaine Hollister for his father's murder was the biggest story in town.

And I was the one who broke it.

Damn, it sure felt good to be Clare Carlson right at this moment.

CHAPTER 57

MITCHELL LANSBURG CALLED me. I figured it was because he'd been impressed by all my latest exclusives on the Charles Hollister/Laurie Bateman story. Maybe he wanted to give me more money. Or a bigger car. Or something else that would make me an even bigger star than I was at the moment.

Lansburg asked if I was free for dinner that night. I remembered our conversation when I was in LA and wondered if this was another business meeting or a date. Either way, I was interested. I said yes.

The last time we'd met here, he'd taken me to the 21 Club, one of the most expensive restaurants in the city.

I wondered what fancy place we'd be going to this time.

He suggested we meet at Pete's Tavern. Pete's Tavern is a neighborhood place in Gramercy Park, where you get cheap drinks and decent affordable food. There was nothing wrong with it, but it didn't come close to matching the glamor of a place like 21. I guess that's when I should have realized this evening wasn't going to go the way I expected.

Lansburg looked as good as the last time I'd seen him. Wearing jeans, an open-collared sports shirt, and a corduroy sports jacket.

"There've been some developments," he said when we sat down in a booth.

"There sure have! Did you see all the great stuff I've been putting on the air?"

"Not those kind of developments. Developments at West Coast Media."

"What kind of developments?"

"It doesn't look like we're going to be able to go ahead with you on this show."

I sat there stunned. The last time we'd talked, I was going to be the biggest TV star in Hollywood. Now I was out?

"Are you telling me I got fired from this job before I even started it?"

"You're not fired."

"But I'm not going to be working for you, right?"

"It's not about you. It's about the show and the money we can raise for it and the advertising support we can count on and a lot of other things like that. That's the bottom line here. We thought we could make it work, but we can't. These things happen in the business. I'm sorry. I thought you would have been really good at it."

I tried to make sense out of all this. But it was impossible to do. I mean it didn't matter at all that I'd broken another big story. This was about business. About the business of TV. Things didn't always make sense in the TV business.

"What about another show? You said the money and advertising didn't work out for this one. Is it possible you could come up with another program idea for me?"

"Possible," he said.

"But not likely?"

"These things move quickly, Clare. You were the flavor of the month when we first talked about doing this. But once that idea fell through, even though that had nothing to do with you, you're kind of damaged goods in the eyes of many of the people I deal with."

"But I'm still breaking big stories on Laurie Bateman and all the rest."

"I understand that."

"Then why am I not a hot commodity in Hollywood for a talk show anymore?"

"That's the way it works, I'm afraid. There's a moment for everything, and sometimes that moment just passes—and then the ship has sailed."

I stood up. Our dinner hadn't come yet, but I didn't care. There didn't seem to be much reason to stay around and keep talking to this guy. I told him that.

"There is another thing I wanted to discuss with you," Lansburg said.

"About the job?"

"About you and me."

I sat back down.

"I'm sorry the way this worked out," he told me. "I like you, Clare. I like you a lot. Professionally. And personally, too. I couldn't do anything about my personal feelings while I was negotiating with you about the job. That would have been inappropriate, as I'm sure you understand. But now, since it looks like we won't be working together, I'm hoping we can still . . . well, spend time together."

Okay, I'd figured he might be coming on to me in LA when he'd talked about having dinner when he came back to New York. Now I was sure. But what I wasn't sure about was how I was going to react.

"There's no real reason we couldn't see each other on a personal basis going forward now," he said.

"Oh, I can think of a pretty good reason."

"What's that?"

"You're married."

"I used to be married."

"Used to be?"

"I'm divorced."

I looked down at his hand. The wedding ring was still there. He saw me staring at it.

"Well, I'm not divorced yet."

I didn't say anything.

"But I'm in the process of getting divorced."

"And you keep on wearing the wedding ring to remind you of all the swell times you had in your marriage?"

I thought about conversations I'd had with Dani Blaine about this, when she was waiting for Brett to leave his wife for her. Oh, he eventually did. And maybe Mitchell Lansburg would too. But I didn't feel like being the "other woman" in his life while this all played out.

"She understands that I'm going to be seeing other women," he said to me now. "We have an understanding. She's fine with it so you don't have to worry that we're doing anything behind her back. She wants me to be happy with someone else."

"Good for her."

"So what do you think?"

"I think we should call her."

"Who?"

"Your wife. Tell her about you and me. See how happy she'll be for you."

"Uh, that's not a good idea."

"You're not really getting divorced, are you? You just want to have an affair with me."

"Is there anything wrong with that? I like you. I know that you like me. I can sense it from the way you look at me. Is there anything that wrong about getting involved in an affair—simply having fun—with a married man?"

No, there wasn't. I'd done it before. More than once, including my affair with the married Scott Manning a year earlier. But I didn't want to do it again. Maybe it was because of something my daughter had said to me: "Mom, you need to stop sleeping around with every man you meet. You need to establish a relationship with a man, a good man, and make that work. Like I have." My friend Janet had said that to me many times in the past. But it was a lot more meaningful coming from my own daughter. Out of the mouths of babes, and all that. Whatever the reason, I knew what I had to do.

"Goodbye," I said to Lansburg. "Call me if anything ever changes on the job front."

Then I walked out of the restaurant.

* * *

Except I didn't want to go home. For one thing, I hadn't eaten anything yet. But more importantly I didn't want to be alone right now. I wanted to be with someone. I wanted to be with a man.

Mitchell Lansburg wasn't going to be that man. Neither was Scott Manning. Or Sam Markham, the homicide cop who was my ex-husband. They were all married. Billy Carstairs wasn't married, but I didn't want to talk with him again. That left only one person—one man I knew—that I could think of.

And so, a short time later, I was sitting back in Pete's Tavern again—this time with a different man than Lansburg.

It was Nick Pollock.

"I was surprised to get your call," he said.

"I was lonely and wanted a man to talk to."

"How did you pick me?"

"I wanted to make sure it was someone I wouldn't have sex with. Someone who wouldn't be attracted to me in that way. A man who I liked and thought I'd enjoy talking to without any possibility he was going to try to get me to go to bed with him— like the guy I was with here earlier tonight."

"And you decided on me," he said with a smile.

"You checked all the right boxes."

It turned out to be a nice meal. We talked about a lot of things. The Laurie Batman story, of course. His tax investigation into the Hollister businesses. But personal stuff too. At one point, after a few drinks, I told him how I'd slept with a lot of men over the years, but never could seem to find the right one.

"It's funny," he said, "but I had the same problem for a long time. I was with a lot of men. But until I met Joe, I never had a relationship that worked. I guess it doesn't matter whether you're heterosexual or not. This business of finding good relationships is still difficult for all of us."

"I guess that means experimenting with being a lesbian wouldn't make much difference for me, huh?"

He smiled.

"You're an interesting woman, Clare. You'll find the right man. Give it more time."

"I'm kinda running out of time at this point in my life."

I asked him more about the investigation into Hollister Enterprises. I wondered if the ascent of Laurie Bateman into the top role there had changed anything. He said they were still trying to figure that out. How much Hollister had been directly involved in the fraud and what, if anything, had changed since his murder.

"There was something weird with Hollister about that," he said. "When we talked to him and confronted him about the funneling of funds to secret accounts, he didn't react the way we thought he would. He didn't deny it or get belligerent or any of the other things you'd expect him to do once he found out we knew. He was more . . . well, he seemed shocked. He almost promised to help us in getting answers. And then he got murdered."

"And that was just about the same time Hollister started delving into his own past," I said as I sipped my beer and thought about it. "Reaching out to his ex-wives, his estranged daughter, and lots of other things. He even went back to the man who may have come up with the original idea for the computer microchip that made Hollister a fortune."

I told him the story about Pham Van Quong, aka James Dawson, which I hadn't put on the air yet. I still had no hard proof for everything Pham had told me. I also wasn't exactly sure how it fit into everything at this point.

"That is strange," Pollock said when I was finished.

"I keep wondering why Hollister did all those things at the end," I said. "Did he suddenly get a conscience? Or was there something else going on here that we don't know about? Something that led to his murder?"

"But we know who murdered him—it was his son, Charles Jr. And he did it because he was angry about being cut out of the will."

"Right."

"So all this other stuff about Hollister's past you uncovered doesn't mean much now, does it?"

"I suppose."

CHAPTER 58

JACK FARON WAS examining a box full of Dunkin' Donuts when I walked into his office the next morning.

It was a twelve-donut-sized box. From what I could see, there was a variety of sugar, glazed, chocolate-covered, and assorted other varieties inside.

"So many choices, so little time," I said.

Faron glared at me, picked up one of the chocolate-covered ones, and bit into it.

"What happened to the cottage cheese?" I asked.

"I got sick of eating it."

"But you're still on your diet?"

"Yes, of course."

"And how exactly do the donuts fit into it?"

"I'm moderating the dieting. I read where you can over-diet. Eat too much of the same thing. It's not healthy."

I glanced over at the waste can behind his desk. There was a pizza box in there.

"Pizza and donuts for breakfast sure sounds like a healthy combination to me."

"The pizza was from last night."

"Dinner?"

"I had to work late here."

"Hey, those extra pounds should start rolling right off you, Jack."

"I'm hungry," he said, finishing off his donut and reaching for another. "I'm hungry all the time since I started this stupid diet. And I'm sick of eating cottage cheese and fruit. Okay? You satisfied? Now did you just come in here to bust my balls or do you have something to tell me?"

"I have something to tell you. Actually, two things to tell you."

"So tell me."

"First, I'm not going to be leaving here to do the TV talk show in Los Angeles."

"You turned them down?"

"Uh, they turned me down."

I told him about my meeting with Lansburg. I figured I might as well just give him the truth. He'd probably find out anyway about what happened. He seemed happy to hear that I was staying at Channel 10. At least, I hoped he was happy. Sometimes with Faron it's hard to tell. But yeah, I'm pretty sure he was happy.

"What's the second thing you wanted to tell me?" he asked.

"I'm not sure the Laurie Bateman story is over."

I ran through all the questions I had about it, including the biggest question I'd been thinking about since my conversation with Nick Pollock the night before.

"Was Charles Blaine Hollister Jr. responsible for it all?" I asked Faron. "The murder. The stolen money. The cover-up. Everything. Was that all Charles Jr.? It's kind of hard to believe. Especially if you've met Charles Jr. He's not that smart . . . not smart enough to pull off all that."

"Let me make sure I've got this all straight," he said, clearly sounding exasperated with me now. "First, you go on this journalistic crusade to convince everyone that Laurie Bateman is innocent of murder. Then you decide she is guilty, and you spend all your time and effort trying to prove that. Finally, it turns out that

Charles Jr. is the one who did it, and you make sure he gets arrested and charged with his father's murder. Only now, you're not sure about that either. You think maybe—just maybe—someone else is the killer. Did I get that all right, Clare?"

"Yep, but thanks for the recap."

Faron put down the donut he was holding in his hand and pushed the box away. I'd apparently accomplished the impossible. I'd gotten him so upset with me that I killed his appetite.

"You know, Clare, there are times I think I would have been happier if you had gotten that other job. You do a lot of great things, but you're always causing me big problems like this along the way. There are days when I think you're more trouble than you're worth. And this is one of those days. Can't we just move on to another story?"

"Not until this one is finished," I said.

"What will it take to convince you that the story is finished?"

"Once I find out what Charles Hollister was thinking those last few weeks of his life. Why he was digging through his past. I think the answer to that will give us the answers to a lot of other questions. And I think that may have been what got Charles Hollister killed. There was something going on in Hollister's life in those weeks before he died. It started when the feds first approached him about the investigation into his company's finances. He suddenly went back and reached out to all of these people from his past. Apologizing to people. It was like Hollister was re-examining his whole life. I sure wish I could figure out what he was thinking about at the end."

"How do you find out what a man who's now dead was thinking?"

"I have an idea about that . . ."

CHAPTER 59

IF YOU WANT to find out what a man is really thinking, the best way is to talk to the woman he's been sleeping with. Laurie Bateman wasn't talking to me anymore. But it didn't appear as if Charles Hollister had been sleeping with her much before he died. He was sleeping with Melissa Hunt though. So I went to visit her again.

She seemed happy to see me. The story I'd aired about her had made her a star. Well, sort of a star. She told me how the interview had gotten her a bunch of offers to appear in movies, TV, and commercials. None of them seemed to me to be particularly desirable roles, more to take advantage of her sudden celebrity instead of her acting. I thought about how Laurie Bateman had made a career out of the same sort of celebrity status. It was kind of ironic that Hollister had been attracted to both of them. But then I suppose it wasn't their acting ability that attracted him.

"I imagine you must think I'm a terrible person to be so happy about all this while poor Charles is dead," she said to me when she was finished running through all those offers. "But, like I told you before, I don't get anything from Charles' will. Not a cent. It goes to his wife. Most of it does anyway, and the rest to his kids. I've got to take care of myself. So don't judge me."

I wasn't judging her, and I didn't think she was a terrible person. I didn't think much of anything about her. All I wanted from Melissa Hunt was information—anything I could pry out of her—about Charles Hollister in the days and weeks before his death.

I told her about Hollister visiting a lot of the people from his past including his ex-wives and Laura Bateman's mother.

I asked her if he'd ever talked about that with her—or if she remembered anything else like that he'd told her.

"Oh, my God, yes, he talked about it constantly," she said. "All about taking a hard look at his past and all the things he'd done wrong over the years. I didn't understand a lot of it. But he was on a wacky self-analysis trip, all right. Did you know he even went back to Vietnam?"

"I did not."

"He flew over there for a few days. Said he wanted to revisit the places he'd been there, see that country again."

"Did he tell you any more about the trip to Vietnam?"

"He said he had a lot of regrets about his life. Vietnam was a part of it. I wasn't sure what he was talking about. But he did tell me he'd done something really bad over there. And how that haunted him now. It didn't make sense to me that he'd be so upset now over whatever happened that long ago. I mean, it was a war. People do bad things in a war, right? But I just let him talk. He didn't even seem to be talking to me anyway. More like he was talking to himself. I did ask him what was the point of traveling all that way back there now. I said it just didn't make sense to me. He said a strange thing then. He told me:

"'I had to go back to Vietnam in an effort to understand myself better. What I was like back then. What influence everything that happened to me there in the past had on me. And how I got to be the person I am today.' That's what Charles said. Weird, huh?"

During my conversation with Melissa Hunt, she got a phone call. It was from Wayne Kanieski, her estranged husband who had threatened Charles Hollister over her. The one she said she did not need once she met Hollister.

She was friendly to him now. After she got off the phone, she told me they'd gotten back together since Hollister's death. That they were talking about living together again. I guess it was like she'd said to me earlier: "A woman's gotta look out for herself, she has to move on."

Yep, Melissa Hunt had moved on from Hollister now that he was dead. I felt sorry for her. I didn't think her marriage to Wayne Kanieski would survive. Or that she'd ever be a star in movies or TV. But none of that had anything to do with me.

I did have one more question I wanted to ask her before I left.

"You told me last time Hollister was obsessed with his newspaper at the end. That he talked about it all the time. Was there anything else besides the newspaper—and the stuff about his past—that you remember him talking about before his death?"

She laughed now.

"Well, there was the cheese . . ."

"Pardon me?"

"I happened to overhear one of his calls. It was actually the last time I saw him. He was talking about cheese."

"Cheese?"

"I think the conversation was about cheese. Swiss cheese. It must have been. He was talking to someone on the phone and he kept saying the word 'Swiss.' Didn't make sense to me—and he wouldn't answer when I asked him about it. But what else could he have been referring to? What else is Swiss besides Swiss cheese?"

"Lots of things. Swiss clocks. Swiss Army knives. Swiss Alps."

"I guess it might have been one of them. The only thing I thought of was Swiss cheese. But yes, I suppose Charles could have been talking about something else that was Swiss."

He sure could have been, I thought to myself.

Because I just remembered something else that was Swiss.

Swiss bank accounts.

Charles Hollister must have been talking to someone on the phone that last day about the missing money from the company funds.

But who?

"Do you have any idea at all who was on the phone with him?" I asked Melissa Hunt

"He never told me. But Charles sounded very agitated. Very upset. Very angry with the person on the other end of the line."

"You don't know who that was?"

"No."

"Is there anything else you remember at all about that last phone call?"

"Just that Charles said a strange thing to the person on the phone before he hung up. It didn't make sense to me. At the end of their conversation, he said: 'Don't call me *Charlie* anymore.'"

CHAPTER 60

BERT STOVALL WASN'T at his office in the Hollister Towers building when I tried to reach him there. Or, if he was, he wasn't letting me know about it. Maybe he figured out that sooner or later I would be back with more questions about his longtime friend Charles Hollister. I mean, Stovall *was* the only person that Hollister ever let call him "Charlie."

Just to be sure, I left Stovall a voice mail message that said:

"I want to talk to you about Charles Hollister. And about Swiss bank accounts. I understand you had a big argument with him about that right before he died. I also want to talk to you about Victor Endicott, the private investigator. Specifically, about that security video from outside Hollister's townhouse on the night before he was found dead. The one where everything else was deleted except the footage of Charles Jr. I'm betting Endicott might have had more footage of that beyond what we found in his office that showed someone else—maybe someone like you—there that night."

I thought that would get Stovall's attention, one way or another.

I was able to track down a home address for Stovall, a posh high-rise on Sutton Place, and checked that out, but he wasn't there.

I even went back to the Hollister townhouse on Fifth Avenue in case he was there meeting with Laurie Bateman, his new boss, about business matters. No luck.

Finally, I wandered back to the office on Park Avenue South of Victor Endicott, the private investigator. I wasn't exactly sure why I did that, but I couldn't think of anywhere else to look for Stovall. Besides, Endicott had worked for a lot of people involved in the Hollister company. Charles Hollister. Laurie Bateman. Charles Jr. So why not work for someone else, too? Someone like Bert Stovall?

I didn't think I'd be able to get into Endicott's office this time without the police. But it was open. That should have been my first clue something was wrong. It certainly wasn't very smart to go in there without knowing who was inside. But, from long practice of not doing smart things, I pushed the door open and walked into Endicott's office.

I heard sounds coming from one of the rooms. I pushed open the door and saw a shadowy figure in there, holding a flashlight. A man was at a filing cabinet, going through files. He suddenly realized I was there, whirled around, and turned on the lights.

It was Bert Stovall.

"Find anything you're looking for?" I said.

"What are you doing here?"

"I could ask you the same question."

"That's none of your business."

"You're the one who murdered Charles Hollister, aren't you? That's the real story here. The story I've been missing for the whole time."

Stovall reached into his pocket now, took out a gun, and pointed it at me.

The gun was a surprise.

He hadn't brought a gun the time he murdered Charles Hollister; he'd used Laurie Bateman's, which was already there.

"I'm afraid I can't let you tell that story on the air," he said.

Suddenly, my cell phone started ringing. I'd had it in my hand when I walked into the Endicott office and so I was able to look down and see who was calling me. It was Nick Pollock. We'd talked about getting together after I finished work for another conversation about the case.

"Don't answer that!" Stovall snapped.

"It's the Treasury agent working on your case."

"Even more reason not to answer."

I tried to think of some reason to make up that would convince him to let me answer Nick Pollock's call.

"I told Pollock I was coming here to search Endicott's offices again," I blurted out. "If I don't answer, he's going to come here looking for me. I don't want him hurt, too. At least let me convince him not to come."

It worked. Stovall hesitated for a second, then nodded. "Okay, take the call. But don't tell him anything. Just say you can't meet him right now."

I answered the phone. Stovall kept the gun pointed at me as I talked with Nick Pollock.

"Don't come over to Endicott's office like we talked about," I said. "There's nothing here. It's a waste of time."

"What are you talking about?" he said.

I tried to think of how I could send him a message that I was in trouble. I'd already let him know where I was. But I needed to convince him something was terribly wrong about the situation.

Something that wouldn't tip off Stovall to what I was doing.

"Look, how about you come over to my place later and we can spend the night together. Just the two of us in bed. That was amazing what we did last time. My body is still tingling all over from the way you touched me. Honey, I want to screw your brains out. I'm going to give you the best sex you ever had. Doesn't that make you hot, Nick?"

I hung up before he could answer.

Now I could only hope that it worked to tip him off I was in trouble. And, if it did, I had to buy enough time for Nick Pollock to come and save me. The only way to do that was to keep talking with Bert Stovall. Which is what I did. Stovall didn't say a lot at first, just a few words here and there or nodding to acknowledge that I was right about everything.

But I think he wanted to tell his story to someone.

Even to a woman he was planning to kill.

He'd held onto his secrets for a long time.

"You found out that Charles Hollister had been in contact with federal Treasury investigators," I said. "Hollister had discovered that it was you who'd been stealing money for years from the company account. He was ready to make a deal with the feds.

"You couldn't allow that to happen. You argued with him, first over the phone and then you went back to his house that night. And you killed him. Then you probably paid Endicott to remove that security video from the townhouse—and delete you from it too—so no one would ever know you were there that night.

"Even more importantly, you got Endicott to put together that phony phone message from Hollister, made up of previous audio he'd collected during his surveillance. Then you or he called his office and left the message with that audio so it sounded as if he was still alive in the morning. Which pointed the finger of guilt at Laurie Bateman—instead of you—when she showed up at the apartment the next morning.

"You must have had to pay Endicott a lot of money to do all that dirty work for you. But it was worth it, right? I mean look at the results . . .

"Hollister was dead and unable to talk to the feds; Laurie Bateman was in jail and couldn't claim any inheritance or position in the company once she was convicted; Charles had already been written out of the will and his mother was dead and his sister ostracized from the family. That left you to take over the entire Hollister business, which was probably your dream for a long time as you watched your old friend Hollister get richer and more famous and more powerful. Yep, this would have been the perfect crime for you. Until I came along and messed everything up."

Stovall still had the gun in his hand, but he was holding it casually now, not pointing it at me anymore. He didn't say anything. He seemed lost in thought.

"Did I get it all right?" I asked him now.

"Not everything. You see, I never wanted Laurie to be blamed for the murder. That was a mistake—it wasn't supposed to happen that way. That's why I even testified in her defense at the murder hearing. I'm glad it was Laurie who wound up taking over the company. I would never do anything to hurt Laurie Bateman. My God, Laurie is the most important thing in the world to me."

"Why?"

"Because I'm her father."

CHAPTER 61

I'D BEEN LOOKING for the Vietnam connection between Laurie Bateman and Charles Hollister since the beginning of this story. I'd suspected that Hollister might actually have been her birth father, as crazy as that sounded. But it wasn't Hollister who was Laurie Bateman's father. It was Bert Stovall, his lifelong friend and business partner. Which seemed even crazier.

"Charlie and I spent two more years in South Vietnam after the U.S. combat forces pulled out in '73," he said. "No one was supposed to know we were there or what we were doing. It was all top-secret. We were both in Army intelligence, and the idea was that we'd work with the South Vietnamese government as long as we could to get information—military, scientific, technological—that we could take with us when the last remnants of the U.S forces left the country. That's why you—or anyone else—never found out we were still there until the end of the South Vietnamese government in 1975."

The missing two years in Charles Hollister's life, I thought to myself.

"One of the things we found out about early on while we were there was the work in colleges being done by Pham Van Quong and his friend Le Binh. They were studying at one of the universities in

Saigon, and their idea about computers was so exciting that we didn't tell anyone else about it. We knew how valuable it could be.

"We decided we would try to team up with them and be a part of it. But, in order to keep it secret, we needed to get them out of Vietnam so no one else could find out about the microchip. That's why we arranged to have Pham sent to college in America. To get him out of the picture and make him dependent on us. But Le Binh said he was going to stay in Saigon until the war came to an end—and even deal with the Communists, if it came to that.'"

"Except he died before he could do that," I said. "Charles Hollister killed him."

Stovall shook his head no.

"Charlie didn't kill him. I did. Oh, I know he got all the awards and hero stuff for it, but it was me. I shot Binh, created the story about him trying to bomb the U.S. facility—and let Charlie take all the credit. He was happy to be the hero, even if he never knew the real story of what happened."

"Why would he do that?"

"That's the way things always worked between Charlie and me. He liked to be famous, he liked the notoriety, he always wanted to be in the spotlight. It was like that back in Vietnam and it's been like that for us all these years ever since. He has always been the face of the Hollister business, the ultimate celebrity tycoon— while I remained in the background. I preferred it that way."

"What about the little girl who grew up to be Laurie Bateman?" I asked. "Tell me about her."

"After Pham Van Quong went to the U.S., his wife was left alone in Vietnam. She was a beautiful woman. And, when it became clear the Communists were going to take over soon, she was willing to do anything to get someone to help her—someone like me—make plans to get to America.

"I took advantage of that. I slept with her after her husband was gone. She became pregnant and gave birth to a little girl. It was mine, she told me that—and I know she was telling the truth. So, at the end of the war just before I left for good, I made good on my promise to her. I got both of them out of the country and relocated to Los Angeles.

"I thought that was the end of it. But after she came to America with a baby that her husband knew could not have been his, Pham started asking a lot of questions. About the identity of the father, about the death of his friend in Vietnam—and demanding answers about how we were going to split up the big profits we all believed were coming with their microchip idea."

"So you ran him down in front of the college one night," I said. "You killed him. Or thought you killed him. It didn't matter though, did it? Because, one way or the other, he was out of the picture now. You and Hollister were free to make yourself rich on Pham's idea. Just out of curiosity, how much did Hollister know about all this?"

"I never told him much. Not until the end. Until then, I let him think whatever he wanted to think, while I did the dirty work. I even managed to convince him that the microchip really had been our idea, not that I had stolen it from Pham Van Quong and Le Binh. He didn't know about the Los Angeles hit-and-run either. And especially not about Laurie Bateman. That he was married to the 'daughter'—or at least she was supposed to be the daughter—of the man he stole his billion-dollar idea from."

"But how did the marriage happen?"

"I never talked to Laurie's mother after they settled in America. But I followed her and my baby over the years. It was hard not to once Laurie Bateman became so famous. One night a few years ago, Charlie and I were at that event in LA with a lot of celebrities that I told you about, and one of them was Laurie Bateman. There she was, my baby—all grown up. I made a point of making sure Charlie and she got introduced. I remembered how much Charlie loved beautiful Vietnamese women back when we were in Saigon—hell, I was lucky I got to sleep with her mother instead of Charlie. I guess I was hoping something would happen between him and Laurie that night. And it sure did. I'm not sure why I set their romance all in motion like that. At first, I guess I just thought it was funny. He wound up married to my daughter. Even though he didn't know that. It gave me an edge on him, I guess—just in case I ever needed it."

"Did she know?"

"No, Laurie had no idea."

"And Hollister?"

"He never knew either."

Stovall waved the gun in his hand around now, but not like he was going to use it. It was almost as if he'd forgotten it was there. He was lost in his own thoughts, his own memories.

"Anyway a few weeks ago, Charlie came to me to say the feds were asking him questions about secret overseas money funds. He said he wanted to cooperate with them. I couldn't let him do that. So I told him. I told him everything. About the stolen money. But also the real story of how we'd gotten the microchip formula and all the rest of it. I threatened that if I went down for it all, I'd bring him down with me.

"I expected that he'd understand that. But he didn't. Instead, he went on a crazy trip—reaching out to people from his past, our past, to try to make amends or something. That was the trouble with Charlie—he had a conscience. Everybody thought he was

this hard-hearted prick, and he could be. But he had a damn conscience that got in the way every once in a while. And that's what
happened.

"We didn't talk about it again, and I thought maybe he had
seen the light and was going to keep his mouth shut. But then,
that last day, he told me he was going to cooperate fully with the
authorities and tell them everything. He said he had to do it in
order to live with himself. There it was again, that damn
conscience."

"But you couldn't let him do that, could you?"

"I went to his place that night. I hoped Laurie would be there,
too. I was going to tell them both the entire truth. About how I
was really her father. I hoped the shock of that might get Charlie
to realize he was better off just leaving everything the way it was.
But Laurie was gone. And Charlie told me that he was going to
reach out to the Treasury people the next day and tell them
everything.

"We argued, and then—I'm still not sure exactly what happened—I got so mad that I picked up the lamp and smashed him
in the head with it. I didn't mean to kill him. Yes, I've killed people
before, but not Charlie. He was my friend. My best friend in the
world. But, when I saw him lying there on the floor, I realized
what I had done."

He looked down at the gun in his hand.

"Just like I realize what I have to do now," he said, pointing it
at me. "I'm sorry. I don't want to kill you either. But it's the only
way."

I heard a noise outside. Was it Pollock? Had he understood
what I was trying to tell him over the phone? It was my only hope.

"Don't do it," I said. "The police are outside right now. You
don't want another murder."

He smiled sadly. "That's an old ruse, Ms. Carlson. It never works."

"Only when it's true," I said.

The noise was louder now. A door opening, followed by the sound of footsteps. And then Nick Pollock burst into the room with his gun pointed at Stovall.

"Drop the weapon," he yelled.

But he didn't. Stovall just stood there with a shocked look on his face.

"Drop the gun," Pollock said again. "This is your last chance. If you don't, I'll shoot you right now. Do the smart thing, Stovall. Give it up. Drop the gun."

But Bert Stovall didn't drop the gun.

He pointed it instead.

Not at me.

Not at Pollock either.

But at himself.

"Fifty years," he said. "That's how long Charlie and I were together. We accomplished a whole lot in that time. We were a great team, Charlie and I. It was a fun ride. But nothing lasts forever. And I'm too old to go to jail . . ."

Stovall put the gun to his head, pulled the trigger, and killed himself.

CHAPTER 62

LAURIE BATEMAN LOOKED like America's sweetheart again. Her hair was perfectly coiffured, her makeup impeccable. She was wearing a pink pants suit with a white silk blouse that made her look beautiful and also like a big-time corporate executive. Which she was, of course, now that her husband was dead and his will had never been changed.

Funny how things had worked out so well for her in the end. But then things always worked out well for Laurie Bateman. They had all of her life ever since she came to America.

It had been a few days since Stovall's death, and now I wanted to finish the story with the perfect ending: one last TV interview with Laurie Bateman.

She was happy to talk to me on air again this time.

I guess we were back to best friend status now.

We were doing the interview in her office at the Hollister building. The office had a spectacular view of the Manhattan skyline from the big window next to her desk. It was like the offices there that her husband, Bert Stovall, and Charles Hollister Jr. had all once had. But now it was Laurie Bateman who was in charge.

The interview was being done live. Normally, we'd have taped it in advance, then played it on the newscast. But I wanted to do this one in real time for a lot of reasons. I convinced everyone—Laurie Bateman, Jack Faron, and other people at the station—that it would be more dramatic to do it on live TV.

But the truth was, I had other reasons I wanted to do it this way.

We'd done a big promo campaign for it in advance so I expected we'd have a lot of viewers for this show. That was good for our ratings, but also good for Laurie Bateman—who loved being in the spotlight. I figured that's why she agreed to be interviewed like this by me on live TV.

"This has been such a traumatic experience for me, as I'm sure you can understand," she said now as the cameras rolled. "To find out all this horrific information about what Bert Stovall did, the money he stole, and the lives that he took . . . it's almost too much to bear. It goes to show you that you never really know who someone is.

"I still can't believe that Bert Stovall was my biological father. And that the man I always thought had been my father from Vietnam is still alive. It's like I've been lied to all my life. Well, the lies are over now. I'm glad I finally found out the truth. And grateful to you, Clare, for helping to make all this happen."

She reached over, took my hand, and squeezed it. It was a very moving moment. I didn't respond. I just let her keep talking. Because it was good TV. But I had a plan, too. I waited until she was finished with her own emotional words before I segued into the topic of her dead husband.

"Laurie, how do you feel about Charles Hollister now that you have found all these new things about him and his life?"

"That's so complicated," she said. "I mean, I hated Charles because of the things he did to me. But now I feel that maybe there were some good things about him too. Yes, we had bad times at the end. But I'm sorry he's dead. He didn't deserve to die the way that he did. I'm glad that we finally found out who killed him. That it was Bert Stovall. Finding out the truth, no matter how painful, does give me a little bit of closure though to all the horrible experiences I've been through since Charles died."

She reached up and wiped a tear from her eye. At least I thought it was a real tear. I couldn't be sure though. She was an actress. Actresses know how to cry for the camera. And that's what she was doing now: playing a part for the camera.

And it was up to me to stop her performance.

Which is what I wanted to do right now on live TV, as risky as that was to pull off.

I hadn't talked with anyone about my plan. Not Maggie. Not the people on my news team. Certainly not Jack Faron. I knew they would all tell me the idea was reckless and irresponsible and dangerous. But I was determined to go ahead anyway. And I knew that if I did it like this on live TV, no one could stop me. No matter what happened afterward.

Okay, here we go, I thought to myself.

"Actually, I'm not sure Bert Stovall did kill your husband," I said.

That startled her.

"Of course, he did," she said. "He admitted murdering Charles. He hit him with the lamp and he shot him. You said he told you that before he died."

"No, he admitted that he hit Charles with that lamp. But he never said anything about shooting him with the gun. I think maybe the blow from the lamp wasn't enough to kill your husband. It just injured him and probably knocked him unconscious. But he wasn't dead yet. He wasn't dead until someone put three bullets into him."

"Bert Stovall."

"Or maybe someone else."

"Who?"

"It could have been anyone, Laurie—even you."

She glared at me now and I knew—just from the look in her eye—that I was right. The mask of her Laurie Bateman public persona had disappeared for just a few seconds. This was the real Laurie Bateman. A woman who would do whatever she had to do to get what she wanted. Even murder. But then it was over, and the Laurie Bateman we all knew and loved was back. She laughed, as if I'd made a joke.

"That's absolutely ridiculous," she said.

"Is it?"

"Bert Stovall killed my husband. That's what the police believe, and they're right."

"Not really. The investigation is still open. There's a lot of things that haven't been explained yet. But I have a theory. Just a theory. We're only talking hypothetically here, Laurie. I mean, no one knows exactly what happened to your husband. But, hypothetically speaking, let me throw this possible scenario out. Tell me what you think of it:

"You show up at your apartment that morning and you find your bloodied husband on the floor. He's still alive, but badly hurt. You know he hasn't had time yet to change the will. So you decide to take advantage of the opportunity you had right then. You go into the bedroom, grab your gun, and fire three shots into him.

"You assumed you'd be gone when the body was found. You knew the maid usually arrived for work at ten a.m. That gave you time to get out of there before she showed up. Except you didn't know that the maid, Carmen Ortega, had made a last-minute decision to come in an hour earlier that day. So she walked in on you before you could get away—and you got arrested.

"But then you came up with this story about how Hollister had abused you. Maybe he did, maybe he didn't. But, one way or another, you delivered a terrific acting performance—in front of the camera and later in court—that let you get away with murder. Hey, I even helped you to do just that."

I thought she might storm off camera at this point and maybe have me and the TV crew with me thrown out. That would have been all right with me. Because I'd accomplished what I set out to do. Make the accusation against her—planted the seed in the public's mind—on live TV. Lots of people would see this, and later I knew it was going to explode on social media. Everyone would be talking about it.

But she didn't leave. She sat there and smiled. It was a scary smile. She still thought she could get away with it. She'd gotten away with a lot over the years.

"Why are you doing this, Clare? Is this a cheap ratings ploy by you and your station? I thought you were better than that."

"No, it's just a hypothetical scenario. That's all."

"You have no evidence or proof for anything you're saying."

"Of course, I don't."

"I should point out that you are libeling me on live television—calling me a murder."

"I didn't call you a murderer. Like I said, I simply threw out a theory—a hypothetical scenario—of how it might have happened."

"Don't play word games. I could sue you and your station for that if I wanted."

"Only if it's not true," I said.

"But you have to prove what you're claiming is true. And you can't do that, can you?"

"Who knows? I'm going to keep investigating. And so are the police; they've told me that. I'm not sure how much you know about me, but I'm a pretty dogged reporter. I've broken a lot of pretty big stories in my time. And I don't give up on a story until I have all the answers. The police are going to do the same thing. You beat a murder charge once, Laurie. But I think it's going to be harder now. I don't think your tricks are going work again. I don't think there's going to be a happy ending for you this time."

She stopped looking at me now. Instead, she looked directly into the camera. That's who she was playing to—her audience out there on the other side of the screen.

"I'm a survivor," she said, her voice almost seeming to break with emotion as she said the words. "I've been a survivor all my life since the day I was born. And I'll keep on being a survivor. No matter what it takes to survive the lies and untruths that are said about me. I know people will believe me. I know they will believe my story. Because it's the truth. All I can do is tell the truth."

It was a nice speech. I imagine she hoped it would win public sentiment for her as America's sweetheart again—just like it did when she made that emotional plea in the courtroom to win her freedom.

Except the words didn't work for me this time.

Because I'd heard them from her before.

It was another line from one of her movies.

CHAPTER 63

LAURIE BATEMAN HASN'T been indicted for the murder of her husband yet. I'm not sure if she ever will be.

There's no hard evidence, only circumstantial, that she was the one who pulled the trigger of the gun that ultimately killed Charles Hollister. Especially now that Bert Stovall wasn't around to testify about what he did or didn't do to his lifelong friend and business partner.

And the District Attorney's office, after being burned so badly the first time they tried to indict her, seems reluctant to make that move again unless something more substantial shows up in the police investigation.

But an amazing thing happened to Laurie Bateman after that televised interview she did with me.

She *was* found guilty. Guilty in the eyes of public opinion. Everyone pretty much was convinced after the interview that she had murdered her husband, and she became a public pariah—sort of like O.J. Simpson. Found not guilty by the law, but a disgraced former celebrity that no one wanted to be around anymore.

She was eventually ousted as CEO by the board of Hollister Enterprises because of the unfavorable publicity she brought to the company. Her endorsements, media deals, and celebrity appearances all dried up. Everyone suddenly tried to distance themselves from—or, even worse, ignore—Laurie Bateman, the woman they had all once adored.

Which might have been the worst punishment of all for her.

* * *

Victor Endicott was tracked down to Rio de Janeiro where he was living in a villa on the beach with stolen money from the Hollister company.

It took a while for the extradition to happen. But eventually, the fact that he was a possible co-conspirator in murder broke the diplomatic logjam of red tape—and he was returned to New York. Endicott admitted embezzling money with Stovall and also putting together the false phone tape of Hollister on the night he died. After hours of intense questioning, he also broke down and confessed he had arranged the murder of Carmen Ortega and lured Pham Van Quong to the site hoping to kill him, too. He said Bert Stovall had paid him to do it because Stovall had found out that last night from Hollister that Quong was still alive. He said Stovall paid him to plant evidence from the murder in Charles Jr.'s office—and to leave the edited security tape with Charles Jr. on it for police to find—in order to make him look guilty. But Endicott insisted he had nothing to do with Hollister's murder. He also denied knowing anything about the deaths of Marvin Bateman or Hollister's former wife. It didn't make much difference though; he was going to jail for a long time.

I'm not sure we'll ever find out the answers about the deaths of Marvin Bateman or Hollister's ex-wife. Maybe they both happened the way it seemed. Bateman committed suicide, and Karen

Hollister accidentally fell off her son's boat. Or maybe Laurie Bateman had somehow been involved in both of the deaths. Because it helped her get what she wanted if they were out of the way. There are always unanswered questions to every big story, and this one was no exception.

*   *   *

The one good thing was that Elaine Hollister was now the head of her father's company. After Laurie Bateman was removed from power, the board members turned to her—instead of Charles, who had alienated so many people over the years—to carry on the business that her father had built up.

I met her for coffee not long after she started the job, and she was full of exciting ideas about what she planned to do with the company. Not just to make money, she said, but to make the world a better place.

She wanted the Hollister business, with all its resources, to carry on the kind of work she'd been doing all her life with battered women and sick children and other needy people. I didn't think it was very realistic. Big companies aren't usually altruistic if they want to keep on making money. This sounded too impractical to succeed for her. But I love people who want to do the impossible like that, so I wished her well.

I liked Elaine Hollister.

I thought she was a good person.

And sometimes good things do happen to good people.

Charles Hollister? He no longer worked for the company. He would still get a substantial amount of money from his father's estate, and, of course, he was freed from jail on all the charges. I'm not sure what's going to happen to him, and I don't care. Strange how two different children from Charles Hollister could turn out so differently like that. It was like Elaine got the good genes; Charles the bad ones. As for the elder Hollister himself, I wasn't sure what to think of him. Yes, he'd done bad stuff in his life. But, in the end, it seemed like Charles Hollister had tried to do the right thing. It was just too little, too late.

*   *   *

Pham Van Quong, or James Dawson, went back to the Gulf Shore of Mississippi to run his businesses.

I thought he might have a bit of a messy problem to deal with on his marriage, since he was still legally married to the woman who was now Gloria Bateman. But he'd been declared legally dead after the hit-and-run so no one expected many repercussions. Overall, he'd come out of this okay.

No, he hadn't made a fortune on his microchip idea that he and his friend had come up with in Vietnam all those years ago. Charles Hollister—with the help of Bert Stovall—had gotten rich with it, instead. But Pham had done all right for himself. He achieved the American Dream, even if it took him a few detours along the way to do it.

Gloria Bateman never did talk any more about what she knew and what she didn't know.

Why should she? She had never cared about anyone else but herself in the past, and she didn't want to do anything to mess up the sweet deal she had here in America. She'd always done whatever it took to survive. Starting back in Vietnam when she sold herself to get out of the country and then again in the U.S. when she snared a rich husband—and someone who could help her daughter—in Marvin Bateman.

I wondered if Gloria Bateman ever thought about what her life might have been like if that hit-and-run had never happened and she'd stayed together with Pham Van Quong in that little apartment and they'd raised her daughter to be different from the greedy person that she turned out to be.

Probably not.

But I thought about it.

*   *   *

Things in the newsroom are pretty much back to normal, whatever that is in TV news.

Brett and Dani talk a lot about hiring the right nanny and other stuff like that now as they get ready for the baby. I had come up with an idea to take advantage of all that. We now had a regular segment of the show a couple times a week aimed at expectant parents, with Brett and Dani talking all about the joys of her being pregnant.

It turned out to be a wildly popular idea, with more people than ever tuning in to it. Brett and Dani were good at it, relating to the audience and the issues on a personal level. Both of them seemed happy that they were about to become parents. So maybe I'd really accomplished something here. Pulled off a new version of Happy News!

No one has said much to me about losing out on the big talk show job. Normally, I get a lot of kidding about everything from the staff—about my age, my unsuccessful romances, and other stuff like that—but I guess everyone realized this was a tough one for me.

I'm still not sure whether or not I would have taken the job and moved to Los Angeles and left Channel 10 behind. But I'm glad now that I'm still here. I love my job, most of the time anyway. Jack Faron gave me a raise when he found out I was staying, and the station owner, Brendan Kaiser, praised me for all the big news I'd made for the station.

Hey, careers don't always last long in TV news, especially for a woman approaching fifty.

But I'm still here.

Fighting the good fight.

*   *   *

I've become friends with Nick Pollock, which isn't a big surprise after what we went through together on this story. We've hung out together a few times since then, just like I do with my friend Janet.

"He's like you, only male," I told her.

"Is that possible for you?"

"What?"

"Being friends—just friends—with a man like that."

"It's a problem if there's sexual tension in the relationship. But there's nothing like that here. It's great! He's not interested in me at all. At least he's not interested in me . . . well, that way."

"And you're sure about that?"

"He's getting married. I met his partner. Nice guy, I like him. If I ever do find a man to go out with again, we can all double date together. Is that still cool to say these days? I've kinda lost track about what you're supposed to do and what you're not supposed to do in terms of sexual etiquette these days. But then I had trouble in the old days, too, when it was all so much simpler."

"Anything else going on in your personal life? What about that TV guy from LA? Did you ever hear from him again?"

"Yes, he actually called me. Was upset I left our dinner so early and wanted to meet up with me again. I told him what he had told me when he said the job had fallen through: 'There's a moment for everything, and sometimes that moment just passes—and then the ship has sailed.' I said that's how I felt about him and me too."

"What about Scott Manning, the guy you always seem to be in love with—more than any other man you've ever met since I've known you? I figured the two of you were going to wind up together."

"He's still married last time I checked. That kind of puts a crimp in the living happily ever after fantasy."

"And your ex-husband, the homicide cop who worked on this case with you?"

"Also married."

"Which leaves you . . ."

"Unmarried."

* * *

But I've kind of buried the lead here.

About me, that is.

Me and Christmas.

I went home from work on Christmas Eve through crowded streets. There was Christmas spirit everywhere. Stores brightly lit. Christmas carols reverberating through the air. Holiday decorations all around. Except at my place. No sign of any Christmas spirit at my apartment. I let myself into my darkened living room, poured myself some scotch, and sat on the couch contemplating the four walls.

I had almost wound up going down to Virginia to spend Christmas with my daughter and granddaughter. They were so insistent about it that I agreed to try and make it. I even bought presents to take with me. It would have been our first Christmas together. But, in the end, the Laurie Bateman story broke wide open and—as has happened to me so many times in the past—my professional life took precedence over my personal one. I decided to cancel the trip. I said I'd send the presents to them in the mail and we'd have to wait for another Christmas.

And so there I was sitting by myself in my apartment on Christmas Eve. Drinking alone and watching *Miracle on 34th Street* on one of the cable channels. *It's a Wonderful Life* was coming on after that so I could watch again how an angel earns his wings by saving George Bailey on Christmas. Holiday miracles like that always seemed to happen on-screen, but not so much in real life. At least not for me.

I stood up now from the couch where I was sitting, poured myself another drink, and looked out my window at the lights of Manhattan. Outside, I could hear Christmas bells ringing a holiday tune.

Silver bells, silver bells,
It's Christmas time in the city
Ding-a-ling
Hear them ring
Soon it'll be Christmas Day

*   *   *

Suddenly I heard another bell ringing. But not from outside. This was my doorbell. When I opened the door, my daughter was there. My Lucy. And my granddaughter, Audrey. Along with Gregory Nesbitt, the man my daughter had married. They were carrying bundles of brightly gift-wrapped packages.

"We decided if you couldn't come to see us, then we'd come spend Christmas with you," Lucy said. "Merry Christmas, Mom!"

When I recovered from my shock at seeing them there, I hugged her as tightly as I could. I hugged Audrey tightly too. And I hugged Nesbitt as well. I didn't know him very well, we'd only met a few times—but I figured if my daughter loved him, he must be a good man.

"I have presents too!" I told them.

"For me?" Audrey asked, her eyes wide with excitement.

"Especially for you, honey."

Pretty soon, we were ripping open presents and eating and drinking and celebrating Christmas like a happy family.

Which is what we were.

I guess I was wrong after all.

Sometimes Christmas miracles do come true.

EPILOGUE

DEATH CAN BE a funny business sometimes.

I've spent my life covering death and making jokes about death in newsrooms, never thinking much about how one day death could become real for me.

Then a year ago I nearly died at the hands of a serial killer who had murdered twenty other women.

Now I've cheated death again with Bert Stovall.

But it was a different kind of life-and-death situation that scared me the most right now.

A long time ago as a young college student in Ohio, I'd had a spontaneous sexual encounter with a man I would never see again.

But that seemingly casual encounter had led to a series of memorable events in my life—and the consequences of that night weren't over for me yet.

Because I'd found out that the stakes had gotten a lot higher.

I look over at Lucy now and I see the daughter that I never knew for too many years until she became the woman she is today.

I look at my granddaughter, Audrey, and see the little girl I still have a chance to be there for while she's growing up.

Which is what makes me so afraid.

We all face death at some point, and—no matter how much we try not to think about it or make jokes about it—we're always aware that one day death will come knocking at our own door.

And we have no idea how or when that might happen.

I do not know if my daughter will be a victim of the deadly cancer gene from Doug Crowell that I inadvertently passed on to her at birth. I do not know if that cancer gene was passed on to my granddaughter. I do know that Doug Crowell is dead, and I am alive with Lucy and Audrey at the moment.

That's good enough for now.

AUTHOR'S NOTE

They say authors should write about what they know, and that's what I did in *Beyond the Headlines*. This latest TV journalist Clare Carlson mystery of mine is about the glamorous world of celebrities; about the ramifications on people even today from the traumas of the Vietnam War; and, of course, about the media.

I've had quite a bit of experience with all three.

* * *

As a longtime journalist at the *New York Post*, *New York Daily News*, *Star* magazine, and NBC, I covered celebrity news like Julia Roberts' romances, Elizabeth Taylor's divorces, Oprah's diets, Lindsay Lohan's and Britney Spears' epic meltdowns and Michael Jackson's scandals.

But the celebrity story that I drew upon the most to tell the tangled tale of Laurie Bateman in this book was the O.J. Simpson murder trial.

I spent two years at *Star Magazine* consumed by that story—first with the news that Nicole Brown Simpson and Ron Goldman had been murdered; then the bizarre white Bronco chase through the freeways of LA; O.J.'s arrest on a double murder charge; the circus of a trial with Judge Ito, Kati Kaelin, Johnny Cochran, and the whole other cast of characters; and finally O.J.'s stunning "acquittal" by the jury.

The Laurie Bateman case I write about here is a lot different, but I wanted to tell another story—albeit a fictional one this time—about a celebrity whose popularity sways public sentiment enough to take over a courtroom and beat a murder rap. In Laurie Bateman, I tried to create a character who was the ultimate Kardashian-like celebrity for our times: someone who is famous simply for being famous.

* * *

My firsthand experience with Vietnam, on the other hand, was not as a journalist but as a soldier in that long-ago conflict.

I was drafted and spent a year in the U.S. Army there before the Vietnam War began winding down in the early '70s, just like Charles Hollister and Bert Stovall in the book. And, believe it or not, I worked in an intelligence unit just like I put them into for *Beyond the Headlines*. But that's where the similarities end: I didn't kill anyone or steal anyone's multi-million-dollar idea for a microchip while I was there.

I did try to write a Vietnam novel about my experiences after I came back from the Army, but never was able to quite pull it off. Maybe some day. But, until then, this is the closest I've come to creating a fictional version of some of the things I went through in that war—and the impact it had on all of us who were there when we were very young.

*   *   *

But the biggest focus in *Beyond the Headlines*, just as in my previous Clare Carlson books, is on the media: I try to give readers an inside look at what a big-city newsroom—and the journalists who work in it—are really like when they're chasing after a sensational headline story.

Clare Carlson herself is modeled after many of the colorful characters I've worked with in that kind of newsroom. Men and women both who are totally obsessed with their jobs, with breaking the big story—and, as a result, their personal lives are often pretty much of a disaster.

Yes, Clare Carlson is definitely a flawed character.

But, despite all her faults, a lot of people still like Clare.

Hey, I like Clare.

And I like writing about her.

I hope you like her, too . . .

PUBLISHER'S NOTE

Dear Reader,

We hope that you have enjoyed *Beyond the Headlines* and suggest that you read R. G. Belsky's prior Clare Carlson Mystery novels; that is, if you haven't read them already.

The series starts with *Yesterday's News*. TV news director, Clare Carlson won a Pulitzer Prize more than a decade ago for her coverage of the heartbreaking disappearance of eleven-year-old Lucy Devlin. Now new evidence plunges Clare back into the sensational story—forcing her to confront her own tortuous past to untangle the truth about Lucy Devlin.

    This fast-paced page-turner introduces Clare Carlson, the indomitable reporter who won't give up—can't give up.

Clare returns in *Below the Fold* when her reporter's instinct propels her to dig deeper into the murder of a "nobody"—a homeless woman found on the streets of New York. Soon there are more murders, more victims: a female defense attorney, a scandal-ridden ex-congressmen; a decorated NYPD detective; and—most shocking of all—a wealthy media mogul who owns the TV station where Clare works. No way they can be connected—but Clare Carlson won't give up—can't give up—even when she knows she'll be the next victim.

The Last Scoop, the third in the Clare Carlson series, like the others, can be read in any order. The story begins when Martin Barlow, Clare's first editor, a beloved mentor who helped start her career as a journalist, approaches her for help in what he claims is a sensational story—the biggest in his career. Clare initially attributes his far-flung conspiracy allegations to the rantings of an old man, but when Martin is murdered during an apparent mugging, Clare digs deep into his secret files and uncovers the shocking last story he was working on—about a mass murderer no one knew was out there.

That wraps up the Clare Carlson Mystery Series to date. We are happy to announce that *It's News To Me* will follow in 2022. We hope you will read each book in the series and will look for more to come.

Oceanview Publishing